The Order of the Nine Seals

BOOK 2 OF THE GAVAN MADDOX CHRONICLES

ALEX POLAK

Published 2021 by Your Book Angel
Copyright © Alex Polak

The characters are all mine, any similarities with other fictional or real persons/places are coincidental.

Printed in the United States
Edited by Keidi Keating
Layout by Rochelle Mensidor

ISBN: 978-1-7356648-6-6

This one is for my Dad, I love you
And for my Mum, I miss you.

Note from the Author

This is a work of fiction, and no comparison is intended with any person, living or dead.

That being said, many people may find parallels with their lives and, ideally, some sense of hope or inspiration in my writing.

If you would like to talk to others about your and their enjoyment, look for my group on Facebook which I've called 'Dinas Affaraon – Followers of the Gavan Maddox Chronicles'. Come and join us, I'd love to hear from you. I once heard another author state that the worst thing a writer can do is not be in contact and listen to his or her readers, and I don't want to make that mistake.

Come and join the family, I'm always about and interacting with the group. The people there are supportive of each other, just like a true family, and we'd love to expand. You'll find out updates about the next release, I do giveaways of signed books with each new release, and I'm always happy to discuss my books.

Hope to see you there soon.

Introduction

Greetings, and welcome to Dinas Affaraon. For those of you who haven't met me before, or who simply forgot since you last heard from me (it was two minutes ago outside the shop, but anyway), my name is Gavan Maddox. I own a small shop dealing in crystals, incense, symbolic jewellery, and books. Everything from spell books that are really just diaries for eleven-year-old girls up to books that deal with genuine magick (not kept next to each other, don't worry).

I had arrived home last night after a trip to Tibet, where I was on a commission to locate the Veil of Isis. I'd been away for five days *here*. The Veil had transported me to another plane, which I referred to as Aaru, where I had actually *met* Isis, unlocked my magick, learned how to use it, spent just under a year there, then returned to find less than ten minutes had passed. Oh yeah, I brought a friend back with me, but you'll meet him in a bit.

The commission had been brought to me by a woman who was acting as liaison for some mysterious group. She hadn't told me anything about them, not even their name, except that they were interested in magickal abilities as well as more worldly concerns. I was disturbed on first meeting her to find out she was telepathic and reading my mind. I created a mental defence of erotic images, rapidly switching to images of torture when the first idea became too... *hard*... to maintain.

Now that I was back, I needed to work out what I was going to tell her about my trip. The Veil was no longer available to give to her, since

Isis had helped me infuse it into myself. It had apparently increased my magickal potential, although I hadn't been taught to access it during my training.

I also now had a new star ruby ring, which I had named Seren. The ruby was my heart-stone, allowing me to store vast amounts of energy for future use. I had managed to store *some* during my time in Aaru, but it was not even a millionth filled since it could apparently hold an almost unlimited amount.

Now I had to find a way to explain all this to my best friend, Summer, who also happened to be the assistant in my shop and was currently staring at me in shocked disbelief.

Chapter 1

"I'm sorry, you've been *where* with *who* for *how long* learning *WHAT* now?" Summer stood in the middle of the shop with her mouth open while I went to start the coffee. She normally did that while I opened up the shutters but, after the bombshell I had dropped on her, I was willing to cut her a little slack. However I wasn't prepared to wait for the coffee, as to my mind I had been caffeine deprived for almost a year.

"Surprise!" I offered lamely as I set the drip machine going to brew the first pot of Cafegeddon for the day.

"SURPRISE?" Summer yelled. "Try shock. You texted me last night to say you were home, didn't have what you went for but had, and I quote, 'picked up a thing or two', and you'd see me this morning. Then I find out that the thing or two you picked up was a *year's worth of education in using your newly unlocked friggin' magick!*"

"Hey, yell it louder; I don't think the deaf guy in the tailor's shop three streets over quite caught that." I grimaced, digging a finger symbolically into my ear. She looked around guiltily and lowered her voice, much to the relief of my eardrums.

"Sorry," she continued at a more normal conversational tone, "I was just a little shocked. I knew you'd gone to Tibet, but you didn't tell me what you were looking for, and as far as I knew your trip was unsuccessful. Humpf, so much for *that* theory!" She crossed her arms and stared at me like a mother catching her kid not just with his hand in

5

the cookie jar, but his cheeks bulging out with two cookies already and she's just put dinner on the table.

"Yeah, I guess we have a little catching up to do." I offered sheepishly, rubbing the back of my neck with my left hand, while looking at my right with its shiny new ring and leather wrist strap.

"Oh really, ya *think*?" Summer responded, sarcasm literally dripping from every word. "So where would you like to start?" Fortunately I knew what a softie she was at heart, especially for anything cute, so I knew *exactly* how to defuse her. Sorry bud, I thought at my bracelet, you definitely need to take one for the team.

"Let me start by introducing a new friend I made," I said and called Gauvain with my mind. With a soft whoosh of feathers, a familiar white hawk burst out of the talon on my wrist and landed on my shoulder. "Summer, this is Gauvain. Gauvain, Summer." Summer stood there with her mouth hanging open again. Man, this was gonna be a *very* long day.

"He's beautiful!" Summer whispered, and Gauvain shuffled and basked on hearing the adoration in her voice. I, meanwhile, mentally sniggered at him, remembering the nickname of Vain which I had bestowed on him for his tendency towards narcissism. "Can I... stroke him?" she asked timidly. Now I was the one in shock. I didn't know Summer had a timid bone in her body. Mind you, this morning had certainly been enough to throw anyone for a loop.

"Ask him," I replied kindly. "He can understand you." She looked at me in awe, then turned to Gauvain.

"May I?" she asked softly.

Absolutely, he replied directly into her mind, the same as he would with me. *In fact, I've a terrible itch just between my eyes, if you wouldn't mind... oops!* He trailed off as Summer fainted dead away.

I caught her by absorbing the kinetic energy of her fall, then lowered her carefully to the floor so she wouldn't hurt herself. I then gently infused her with the energy I had just absorbed to help wake her up (unlike when I woke up Heffernan in Tibet). She opened her eyes and looked at me, confused to find herself on the floor.

"Did I just hear what I thought I heard?" she asked, fixing me with a gimlet stare.

Indeed, as long as you thought you heard me conversing with you! Gauvain laughed, bobbing up and down on my shoulder like a demented parrot in excitement at the unfolding drama.

"Not really helping right now, buddy." I desperately tried not to laugh. It *was* kind of funny, especially as she had been so vocal only moments before and now was almost scared to talk.

Excuse me, but I believe you were the one who introduced us and informed her of my level of comprehension. I was merely being polite by engaging in discourse. Oh, and I do still have that itch, Gauvain replied. I reached up to his beak and scratched just above it. *Oh, that is a considerable improvement, thank you.* He sighed dramatically in relief. Summer stared up at him from the floor in disbelief.

"I know parrots can say 'Pretty Polly', but actually having a proper conversation? Where on Earth did you get a talking bird?" she asked.

"That's the point," I replied. "Like I said, I wasn't *on* Earth. I rescued him when he injured his wing, so he stuck with me. Then when my magick got unlocked, Isis healed his wing and linked us fully."

Indeed, he definitely obtained the better side of the arrangement, Gauvain joked. *His partner is certainly the more attractive one!*

"Oi!" I said. "Watch it *Vain*, or you'll be a feather duster by lunch!" We both laughed and this time Summer joined in, relaxing in the wake of our humour. I held out my hand and she grabbed it, using it to pull herself back up on to her feet.

"We've got about three quarters of an hour until we open. Let's grab the coffee and go into the office. We can sit down and I can catch you up," I told her. "I also need your help to work out what exactly I'm going to tell Angelica's group, seeing as I don't have the Veil to give them. Mind you, this was actually only a simple research commission. I suppose I *could* tell them the Veil never existed, and it was just an empty box which the monks used to bump up tourism. I do actually *have* said empty box here. My only concern is Angelica will probably be able to tell I've got magick now, so I was thinking I might tell her a watered down version of the truth. Something along the lines of I touched the Veil, it crumbled, it unlocked some weak magick, that's it." I pulled out the box I had brought back from Tibet with me.

"That reminds me," I continued, "did Angelica ever come back for her gloves?" I tried to act nonchalant, but Summer wasn't fooled for a second.

"Wow, you're *really* gonna try to pretend you aren't bothered? You definitely *were* taken with her, weren't you?" she teased me, and now I was the one feeling awkward. I blushed bright red and Gauvain flapped his wings, screeching with laughter.

Oh my stars and garters, he called. *You should feel the emotions I just experienced through our link! 'Taken with her' is not even close!* he chortled.

"Traitor!" I snarled semi-playfully at him out of the side of my mouth. Summer snort-laughed into her coffee cup and said nothing. After a few minutes to calm down and drink some more of her coffee, she looked over at me.

"So can you tell me what you learned, or is it all hush-hush, top secret, 'you could tell me but then you'd have to kill me' or some shit?" she asked.

"Actually, Isis never told me whether I could share or not," I replied thoughtfully. "I guess she thought it was my choice. Besides, most people wouldn't believe me anyway. Your average guy on the street thinks magick belongs in *Lord of the Rings* or *Harry Potter.* Just ask Frank. Hey, I can finally prove to him I'm not crazy for believing in magick. I can hopefully get rid of my schizo-typal personality disorder diagnosis."

"Well I'm better informed about magick," she retorted disdainfully, "and I've been asking you every morning about your attempts to unlock your magick for more than a decade, so don't you *dare* hold out on me now! But yeah, it would be great to lose that millstone around your neck at long last. Now stop trying to change the subject and spill it." She fixed me with her mom stare again. I swear, how the hell did she learn that when she has no kids? She eyed me beadily over the rim of her coffee cup.

"Uh, you do remember which one of us is the boss, right?" I joked lamely, knowing I was only delaying the inevitable. Once she got like this she was like a force of nature, so it was better to either get out of the way or simply go along for the ride.

"Oh right, play the boss card, that'll help!" She almost looked more annoyed at that than at my hesitancy to describe my new abilities.

"Remember last time you tried that three years ago? You tried to pull rank over inventory check duty, and…"

"And I ended up doing the whole thing by myself. Oh yeah, it's all flooding back to me in glorious 3D Technicolour and Dolby THX surround sound!" I finished. I had tried to order her to stay late one night to help me (I had been in a bad mood for some reason, I can't remember exactly why). She had responded by leaving early. She had then not come in for a week, leaving me to do the entire stock-take alone while trying to run the store. It had taken me four times longer than normal, as a result of which I had never tried to order her again (I never had to, she was a diamond who always went above and beyond, but that's beside the point).

"OK, OK!" I laughed, pretending to fend off her laser eyes by leaning away and raising my hands. "I would never dream of keeping this from you. I know you're not going to blab it around, and you know enough about some of the things we've dealt with to understand." I proceeded to give her a potted recap of what I had learned in Aaru. I demonstrated a couple of simple things at first like telekinesis, then finished by turning into a wolf again. That reminded me, I was definitely going to need a book on basic animal anatomy if I wanted to use other forms.

Through it all she sat there, her mouth getting wider and wider, absently stroking Gauvain who had walked over to her while we were talking. I would need to get a couple of decent perches for him, too.

After my demonstration I showed her Seren, the ring Master Harfi had made for me. I also showed her the wrist band I had fixed Gauvain's claw to, into which he could place his energy when it wasn't wise for him to be in full form. I finished by getting out the two pendants I had bought for her and Emily, her long-term girlfriend. They were Celtic shield knots in gold on golden chains, and Summer instantly forgave me when she saw them. I had placed shielding wards on both necklaces after the nightmares I had following my accidental *time viewing* during my training. I'd figured out how to place shield wards easily enough after analysing the rose quartz which Angelica had left for me.

"Right, let's open up, we're actually running a touch behind after all our chatting," I said.

"Well, whose fault is that Mr Secretive?" she replied as she got up to head out of the office. I laughed, then retrieved the recording of my meeting with Angelica. I set to work transcribing it, ready to send her a copy. I also set the box with the Tyet symbol on my desk, ready to show her when (if?) she came back.

Once I was done with the transcription, I decided to review the protection wards on the shop. I could now not only detect them, but I knew from how they felt to me and my previously mentioned experiments with the quartz that I could replicate and even enhance them. I added some protection against fire in light of my nightmare, then strengthened the energy of the existing runes and symbols. I also took the rose quartz off my necklace. It had been left for me by Angelica in one of her gloves to protect me on my quest. My own magick was now far stronger, so I thought I might use the crystal to add protection to the vault in the basement. Summer watched intently as I beefed up the magickal security. She occasionally expressed her amazement that I seemed so comfortable using magick already.

"Hey, remember that for me it was almost a year of studying. It took a fair while for me to pick it up," I wasn't ever planning on telling her I'd picked up some of this stuff faster than Isis herself. I'm not *that* stupid!

"Gods, I'd forgotten that," she replied, shaking her head in amazement. "It's gonna take me a while to get my head around all this."

"No worries, it was the same for me," I laughed. As I finished my enhancements, I had a better idea for the rose quartz. I retrieved it from my desk, using the wrapping wire that had held it to my Mjolnir pendant to fashion a flat hook at the back. I fixed it to the computer where it looked simply decorative, but I was hoping it would prevent any further magickal intrusions into our system. Summer nodded in approval, both at the aesthetics and the reasoning behind my actions.

"You never did answer my question," I said, surveying the shop to make sure I was happy with my upgrades. "Did Angelica come back or has she been in touch at all? I messaged her before I went to Tibet, but I haven't since I've been back. If she hasn't been in touch, I'd better let her know to come in so I can update her. They did give us a rather nice retainer after all." This time Summer was able to keep a straight face at my enquiry, though her eyes did betray her mirth somewhat.

"No, she's not been back since that first day," she replied.

"OK, can you give her a ring and ask her to come in? Then I can let her know what I found out, which will hopefully draw a line under everything," I replied, handing her the card with Angelica's mobile number on it.

"I'm just going to nip round to the pet shop to see if they've got some decent stands for Gauvain, to use in the shop and at my place," I told her. "I'm thinking two for the main shop, one for my office, and two or three for home. Good sized natural branch perches, fit for a large macaw, should be about right for him. You OK with that mate?" I looked at Gauvain, who was busy preening his wing on my shoulder and dropping bits of feather on my shirt. "I'll get the sort with a large metal tray under them too, *Vain*," I said pointedly, dusting off my clothes. He chuckled, then nodded to me and ruffled his wings to settle his feathers.

That sounds as though it would be sufficient. Ensure they have water dishes on them also, if you would be so kind.

"Good idea," I replied. "They'll probably need to order them if I'm getting half a dozen, but they might have one or two in stock to start us off with. You gonna stay here with Summer, or hop back into your claw? I can't exactly walk around town with you on my shoulder."

He looked at Summer, then flew over and landed on the back of the chair behind the counter.

I shall remain here. I can keep you informed if anything untoward occurs while you are away.

I nodded but laughed. "Just what do you think's going to happen, the Normandy invasion?" I asked him. He shuffled around and looked at me.

Most amusing Gavan. Go and fetch my perches, he sniffed imperiously. I laughed even louder and simply waved as I walked out.

Chapter 2

Fortunately, for the sake of my clothes and the shop furniture, the pet shop had one perch and stand large enough which also had two metal bowls for food and water. I knew Vain wouldn't eat seed from a bowl, but I could certainly tease him about it. I could always use the second bowl to put meat in at meal times.

The pleasant young man promised to order me the extras I needed if I left a ten percent deposit, which I did along with paying for the one they had in stock. He said their normal delivery was in three days, so my order should be there in time to catch that shipment.

I thanked him, then headed back to Dinas Affaraon with the stand. I still couldn't believe that the city in Aaru had the same name as my shop. Was it a coincidence, did they get the name out of my head, or was it something more? I shook my head and strode into the shop to be greeted by a flurry of feathers as Vain launched himself towards my shoulder.

"How fares the battle lines, commander?" I joked with him, and he chuckled.

Hilarious. Very well, you were right, nothing happened. He preened my hair as he often did to show affection. *Oh, Summer did make a phone call. I believe a certain woman named Angelica will be coming in tomorrow at two o'clock...* He eyed me sideways to see my reaction, and my smile and blush didn't disappoint.

The smile slipped from my face as my ever-present anxiety helpfully popped up, reminding me that there were risks to any version of the story that I gave her. If I lied and said I found nothing, even if I tried to close my mind, she'd feel there was something different about me which would raise questions. If I told her everything, her group would want to study me and probably want me to at least take them to Aaru so they could get magick.

I was still of the opinion that the safest way forward would be telling her part of the truth. Summer would need to be away from the shop, however, so that Angelica couldn't pick up more from her mind than I wanted her to know. I didn't *want* to lie, but I had to be cautious. I had no intention of leading hordes of people to Aaru to pester Isis and Danu for magickal abilities. Even if I did, there was no guarantee they'd be able to obtain magick.

I had been born with a gift I'd accidentally locked as a child. Isis had just unlocked it for me, then enhanced it further with the Veil. Not everyone on Earth was born with magick in their blood. To those without, it could no doubt be a source of significant resentment if they found out that magick was real.

The thing that worried me most was that Angelica was employed by this mysterious group, and they clearly had access to magick users since they used a psychic as their liaison. They might want to meet me if they heard I'd unlocked even a small amount of ability. If they found out *everything* I'd learned, the faecal matter would definitely hit the rapidly rotating object!

I also realised with Angelica having already been to the shop, she was aware of how the magickal defences had felt from her first visit. I had now gone and beefed everything up, so it was highly likely she would feel the difference. I didn't want to take anything down again, but I started considering if there was some way I could make it feel less potent temporarily.

I mused on the issue while I put Gauvain's stand together, making sure everything was well bolted together so it didn't fall apart when he landed or jumped off. I used magick for the final tightening since I didn't keep a full tool kit in the shop, then filled one of the bowls with cold water. I put the stand at the end of the counter so Vain could sit there and survey his domain. It would also enable him to be admired by any customers who came in, which he approved of immediately. As

I finished the stand, Summer came out of the stock room and walked over to me.

"Gav, I think there's a bulb out in there. The back corner is a bit dimmer than normal," she said, heading into the kitchen to wash her hands.

"OK," I replied absently, "I'll just get…" I trailed off as what she had said triggered an idea: a dimmer switch. Could I create some kind of magickal dimmer switch to turn down the power of the defences? It would only need to work once, as I doubted I'd want to regularly have *less* protection after I'd just put in the effort to increase their effectiveness.

I reached out for the defences and pulled some of the power from them into Seren, then released it back. I could feel the link between the defences and the stone during the reduction, so it might be noticeable to Angelica as well, which would make the effort a little pointless. I then thought about linking the defences to an actual, physical dimmer switch but had no idea how to do it. I would think on it during the day.

I went into the stock room and replaced the bulb on autopilot while I kept thinking about how to deal with Angelica's upcoming visit. I still hadn't worked out exactly what I was going to say about the results of my search either, so I had some planning to do. I went back into my office and emailed a copy of the meeting transcript to Angelica, printed out a copy for the file and one to give her, then took my copy of the printout along with the recording down to the vault.

As I came back upstairs, I remembered a book I had been looking at before the whole Veil quest had landed in my lap. I went into my office and found it amongst my genuine arcane volumes. One of the chapters dealt with something called apotropaic symbology. This was actually *anti* magick, all based around symbols that blocked magick. Since it was designed for people to protect themselves from those with abilities, it didn't require magick to make it work.

The benefit of being in a city centre was there was always a shop nearby that had what I needed for a particular project. I had a think about the best option for something organic, new, cheap and inconspicuous. I thought of a wooden pen holder to put on the counter, underneath which I could carve the symbols. I couldn't, however, think of a shop that would have a wooden pen holder. I had a sudden flash of inspiration.

"I'm just popping out, I'll be back in half an hour!" I shouted to Summer and Vain. "You two get acquainted while I'm away."

I ran out and jumped in the car, heading straight to Ikea. I went in and walked to the kitchen area. It didn't take me long to find a bamboo kitchen implement set in a wooden cylinder holder for all of five pounds. I paid for it and drove back to the shop with a smile on my face. When I got back, both Summer and Gauvain asked me why I'd left so abruptly. I explained my idea and Gauvain nodded in approval. Summer just shrugged her shoulders.

"If you say so. I have a feeling there's going to be quite a lot I don't understand about how you do things now." I put the set of implements in the kitchen and took the holder into my office. I got out a small X-Acto knife from my desk and opened the book again to the chapter I had been looking at before.

I started carving symbols, assessing the feel of the magickal wards after each one. I stopped when the dampening effect left a feeling similar to how the shop had been before my upgrades, then took the holder out to the counter and put some pens in it. Once Angelica had been and gone, I would carve more symbols on it then put it in the vault to make it a completely magickal null zone.

I had another idea and got some note paper, then drew a few of the same symbols on it to put in my shirt pocket when Angelica came. My idea was to try to mask my magickal signature from her. The paper could be burnt afterwards, or maybe stored in the safe for future use. I might even need to consider looking into the creation of a magickal tool kit to keep on hand. I might even get one of those new across the body bags to keep it in, as I didn't want my kit to end up looking like a man-purse.

I spent the rest of the day looking for some animal anatomical texts and basic chemistry books, to enable me to further my knowledge and options for transmogrification. I looked on eBay and various bookshop sites, finding a couple of decent books on each topic and ordering them to the shop. I tried discussing bird anatomy with Gauvain, but he only knew what I knew. He could tell me how to read wind patterns, or describe hunting techniques, but he knew no more about his anatomy than a man on the street could tell me about their own.

When six o'clock came around, Summer and I closed up the shop. Gauvain merged his energy into the claw on my bracelet, and we headed out. I told Summer to take the day off tomorrow, then waved as we went our separate ways. I decided to order a pizza for dinner, since the food in Aaru was great but every once in a while you just needed to give in to that craving for grease.

I stopped into a supermarket on the way to pick up some fresh beef for Gauvain and a couple of beers to go with my pizza, then drove home. With the car settled in the garage I headed up the stairs to my flat, Gauvain erupting from his claw as we went through the front door.

I cut up some of the meat for my friend and grabbed a fast food menu from the magnetic clip on my fridge. I telephoned through my order and flopped down on the sofa, reaching for the remote. I checked the guide and as usual there was nothing decent on, so I decided to watch a film. I had spent almost a year without any kind of electronic entertainment and I just wanted a night of normality. I needed to centre and ground myself before my meeting with Angelica tomorrow.

My conversation with Isis came to mind, and I again wondered what other beings existed in the world. Were *all* the gods and goddesses real in some form? I decided to try to get completely away from anything to do with the magickal world, so put on the DVD of *Hot Fuzz*. I could do with a good laugh. I opened a beer and started the film, pausing it when my dinner arrived at the front door. The cheesy, greasy goodness warmed my heart, truly making me feel at home for the first time since I'd returned from my inter-dimensional sojourn.

Vain finished his dinner and flew to my shoulder, picking an occasional piece of meat off my pizza between preening sessions, this time picking at the dry scales between his toes. I shook my head with a grimace.

"Dude, seriously," I complained, "do you have to do your feet while I'm eating?" He just ignored me and carried on with his self-beautification.

I finished my slice and opened a second beer, sighing with contentment for the sheer mundane simplicity of my evening after the weirdness of the last few months. I put on *Paul* once the first film ended, continuing the comedy duo theme of my watching.

Once I'd eaten and relaxed I swung my legs up onto the sofa, dozing off about half-way through the film as the relaxation finally unwound the knots. I woke up as the last credits were scrolling on the screen, so I got up and gathered the detritus of my meal.

I put the leftover pizza into the fridge, since cold pizza was the gods' own breakfast in my opinion, then headed to bed. Gauvain snuggled up to my chin as he usually did and we drifted off to sleep together.

Chapter 3

I woke up at my usual five o'clock, putting on a t-shirt, tracksuit bottoms and running shoes to head out for my morning run. I usually did about three miles on a work-day, completing the course twice for a total of six miles on my days off. Since it was early and I lived in a small village with plenty of farmland around, Gauvain flew overhead. His sharp eyes scanned for any early-morning rodents as he wheeled and soared, revelling in the simple joy of his natural gifts.

We got home and I went to take a shower. Vain sat on the rail of the shower curtain, watching me and telling me how different the countryside here looked compared to the purple grass of Aaru. He spread his wings out to catch the steam and preen his pinion feathers. I shaved and put on my nice aftershave as opposed to my standard daily choice, then dressed carefully. I chose a white shirt and a pair of black jeans, wanting to look casual but still slightly dressed up for when Angelica arrived.

Vain merged with my bracelet for the drive to the shop, and I grabbed a slice of pizza from the fridge to eat on the way. When I arrived, I unlocked the shutter over the door then started the coffee. Vain emerged from his claw and flew to the stand, and I finished with the shutters before turning on the computer. I idly wondered how Summer was spending her day off as I waited for the system to boot up, then considered that it might be time to upgrade. The computer was almost six years old, so that alone could be a security risk.

It felt good to do a few everyday things as I had a funny feeling that once Angelica arrived, her presence would herald even more magickal upheaval in my life than it had the first time. I spent the morning serving in the shop. I sold one girl a caduceus brooch which she said was a gift for her boyfriend who was at medical school. Another customer bought a spell book diary for his niece's twelfth birthday, then a couple came in and bought some incense and candles, along with an ornate dreamcatcher. From the way they were looking at each other, the scented items would be seeing service tonight!

I got a salad bowl from the sandwich shop over the road for lunch and looked at new computers online while I ate. Vain laughed at my rabbit food but after having pizza last night I wanted something a bit lighter. With my stomach already in knots due to my excitement and anxiety over my upcoming meeting, I also didn't think I could stomach more than a light meal. I put on a fresh pot of coffee in preparation for Angelica's arrival, then got my slip of paper with the apotropaic symbols out of my desk drawer and put it in my shirt pocket as planned. Now I just had to wait for two o'clock.

A few minutes before two, I heard the familiar tinkling of the bell above the door. I looked up from the computer to see Angelica smiling at me, looking completely different from her last visit. This time she was wearing faded blue jeans, a white shirt and silver kitten-heel pumps. Her hair was in a loose ponytail and she had sunglasses on top of her head which she had clearly just pushed up as I could see the slight redness on the bridge of her nose from the supports.

"Well, nice to see you again Mr Madd... Gavan, I'm sorry. So I understand from your assistant that you found something in Tibet?" She looked around the shop as she spoke, then looked back at me. "Where is... Sarah, was it?"

"Summer," I replied, knowing full well what game she was playing by getting Summer's name wrong, "and she's having the day off with her girlfriend since she took care of the shop alone while I was away."

"Girlfriend?" she asked in surprise. "She's gay?"

"Yup, she's one of the happiest people I know," I replied, deliberately misinterpreting her comment. "Oh, wait, you meant... Yes, she's into girls. Why, is that a problem?" I continued, determined to put her

THE ORDER OF THE NINE SEALS

on the back foot and voice any prejudice. It might help throw her off balance for our meeting. "I wouldn't worry, you're not her type." I winked at her.

"Erm, no, I don't have a problem with that. Err, I wasn't worried about…" She stopped as she saw me fighting back a grin. "Oh, you monster!" She started laughing. "I'm not against anyone doing what makes them happy, and I didn't think she *was* interested in me. I *did* see how protective she was of you last time I was here, so I just thought…"

I suddenly realised what she was driving at, why she had flirted with me last time, and why she had 'forgotten' Summer's name this time. Wait, did that mean she *wasn't* interested in me and had just been play-acting last time? I mentally shook myself to stop getting off topic here. Vain chose that moment to *skree* loudly and stretch his wings, which immediately drew Angelica's attention.

"Oh, he's beautiful!" she exclaimed. "He certainly wasn't here last time I came. Is he yours? Where did you get him?" I thought for a moment and decided that, as with the rest of my story, my best option would be to tell the truth, at least in limited form.

"I rescued him on my travels, and he stuck with me," I said. "He seems quite taken with me, so I bought the stand for him. He even stayed with me when I went for a run this morning."

"You're very lucky," she said. "A white hawk like that would be extremely valuable to a collector."

"He's not for sale!" I replied immediately as Gauvain joined in by screeching loudly. Our simultaneous outburst drew a calculating look from Angelica, so I hurried to change the subject. "Let's go into my office, shall we?" I said. "Just let me lock the door while there's no one in the front." I went and turned the deadbolt, flipping the sign around to Closed, then walked back to join her. "Would you like some coffee?" I asked. "I just put on a fresh pot."

"Your special blend?" she asked brightly. "Oh, yes please. Several of the group members have ordered the three coffees in your recipe, but they haven't been delivered yet." Her innocent comment reminded me once again of the time difference between Earth and Aaru. I got the pot, two mugs, milk and sugar, then we went into the office to talk.

"Before I forget, here's your copy of the transcript," I said, handing it over. "Also, your gloves that you 'forgot' last time." I continued pointedly, and she grinned as she took them.

"Oh yes, sorry about that," she said cheekily. "Did the pendant come in useful at all?"

"How did you know I'd need protection?" I asked. "Were you aware Heffernan was following you?"

"I suspected he was more interested than he let on, and he's not as talented at magick as he thinks he is," she replied. I almost agreed with her but caught myself just in time, instead smiling at her disparagement of my old thorn-in-the-side. "So, tell me what happened in Tibet," she continued, sitting forward eagerly.

"Before I do, I'd like to ask you something," I said carefully. "Some of what I tell you will end up being quite personal, as this trip took some unexpected twists. Are you duty-bound to reveal *everything* I tell you to this mysterious group you work for, or just generalities?" She looked at me curiously and I immediately felt her reach out with her mind towards me.

I was shocked at how weak she felt compared to the minds I was used to in Aaru. Rather than simply lock my own mind down, which would make me unaware if she was trying something, I simply extended a tiny portion of my mental energy towards her and held her there. It was almost like a handshake where one party doesn't let go. She could withdraw if she wanted but could advance no further without my permission.

Her eyebrows shot up as she encountered my mental energy and she sat back, assessing me shrewdly.

"Well *that's* new," she said after a moment. "You certainly *must* have learned some new things while you were away. Now I understand your caution." I tilted my head, raised my eyebrows, smiled and spread my hands open with my palms up in a kind of 'waddya want me to say' gesture, to which she smiled and nodded in understanding.

"To answer your question, the group will *definitely* want to know that you now have some magickal ability, how you got it, what happened, can others do the same to get it, and they may even want to meet you to assess you further. In fact I would say that's almost definite. Any private specifics from your mind that you share with me, or non-business related personal details, are none of their concern and would of course stay with me." She spoke quickly and breathlessly in her excitement, leaning forward in her chair again in her eagerness to hear everything.

"Well if we're going to be sharing personal details, how about sharing one with me. What's your real name?" I asked, determined to find out at least that before we went any further. She laughed and eyed me knowingly.

"Ah, well, there I have to confess something. As you know, I was reading your thoughts when I arrived last time, and I felt your attraction to me even before your erotic barrage of self-defence. I actually put my name into your head, as I had modelled my look on Anjelica Huston since my parents named me after her. My father had a crush on her when he was younger. They decided to change the spelling so they could shorten it to Angel." This admission, far from making me smile, actually set the hairs on the back of my neck tingling.

"Are you saying you were manipulating me as soon as you walked in?" I was getting more annoyed as I thought about it and was beginning to consider kicking her out, returning her advance and having no more to do with her or her group, consequences be damned! My anger clearly washed across our mental connection as she rushed to reassure me.

"No, not at all, I swear! I just gave you my name since you were ninety percent of the way there already! I never manipulated you, I promise!" As she spoke, she opened her mind and drew my connection forward to see her memories, which were exactly as she said. Man, she remembered my Kama Sutra defence better than I did, although for her it was only a few days ago, so that made sense. She actually liked it, although she blushed deeply when I witnessed her reaction. Her show of trust and honesty went a long way towards calming me down, but I wanted to make sure one thing was quite clear before we went on.

"OK, but please don't do anything like that again. As I said last time, if I want someone in my head I'll invite them," I said.

"Oh, I doubt I even could now. Even though I can feel you're being deliberately gentle, I can definitely tell you're much stronger than I am. I can't wait to hear the story." She smiled at me reassuringly, although I had to calm my heart which had started racing at her guileless comment on my strength. Clearly, my ability here was even more remarkable than my learning speed on Aaru. Just what had Isis done to me with her Veil to turn me into this... magickal titan? And why?

My mind flashed back to my final vision on Aaru of a city in flames, with an army of monsters arrayed before it. Was I intended to fight in some upcoming apocalyptic magickal war? If so, when and where? Which city was possibly going to burn? Would I be alone or part of some army, maybe even having to lead them? I started to get a headache and put my head in my hands.

"Are you OK?" Angelica asked me.

"Yeah, sorry, it's just my abilities are still a bit new. They sometimes take more out of me than I'm expecting," I temporised, coming up with an excuse that sounded plausible after I remembered my headaches from my early lessons.

"Oh, I remember when I was learning, I had headaches all the time," she replied sympathetically, unconsciously echoing my thoughts to an almost eerie degree. "Let's stop the mental connection and just talk." I welcomed the suggestion, as it would also distract me from the disturbing images currently running through my head. I downed my coffee and refilled my mug, then sat back in my chair to cross my legs, both in order to look unconcerned and to relieve certain pressures. I steepled my fingers, taking on the air of a story-teller with a particularly juicy episode to impart.

Chapter 4

I told her everything that had happened after she had left until I got to the cave in Tibet. I only omitted Yeshe and Gonpo's names, the exact location of Gonpo's hut and of the cave itself. I *did* include all of Ciarán's shenanigans, and she was glad her pendant had protected me the first time. Also that the thought of it had stopped him trying magick against me again, at least until he had lost his temper.

She applauded my intuitive leaps to work out where to start looking and then how to short-circuit the search to speed it up, but she was definitely annoyed that Heffernan had behaved the way he had in the cave. She fully supported the monk's action of shoving his own magick into his face, which still made me laugh every time I recalled it.

When it came to the Veil itself, I explained how there had been a prophecy that it was only meant for one person. I told her about the warning that if it had not been me, my memory would have been modified. She nodded and looked suitably impressed that I had been the one to get the box and open it.

I then simply explained there had been a fragment of caul inside, but as soon as I opened the box and it was exposed to the air it had started to crumble. I had touched it and received a flash of images from my childhood which unlocked the abilities I now had, but the Veil itself was gone.

I showed her the box which she was unable to open but which opened easily for me, and then showed her some weak telekinesis to go with my weak telepathy. Both were impressive to her, but virtually insignificant compared to my true level of ability. I didn't want her going back to the group and reporting on my *actual* range of abilities, level of magickal education and strength.

Fortunately, the apotropaic symbols seemed to be doing their job in keeping my energy signature suppressed. After I completed my tale, she too sat back in her chair with a look of awe on her face.

"I can't believe I was an instrument in a prophecy, sending you somewhere you were apparently destined to go!" she whispered.

I have to admit, that wasn't what I had expected her to say but seeing it from her point of view, it must have seemed a bit odd.

"Well how do you think *I* felt, knowing that apparently I've been expected for hundreds if not thousands of years? Especially since I've always prided myself on being early to my appointments!" I laughed at the ridiculousness of it all and she joined in.

"For sure no one else is going to be able to get abilities the same way," she said, clearly thinking about how the group would react.

"I'm sorry," I replied. "I didn't exactly plan it that way. I know your group gave me a significant advance. I felt physically sick once the Veil crumbled, knowing I was going to have to report back that there was nothing to hand over to you."

"Oh, don't worry. It's obvious from the simple fact that you're the only one who can open the box, even now that the Veil is gone, that it was meant for you." She smiled at me. "The group will be disappointed, but they can't exactly blame you."

"Of course, with the box being the only thing left, your group should have it," I said, trying to appear fair. They had certainly paid enough for it! "You'll just need to keep it open, otherwise you'll have the equivalent of a block of wood." She smiled impishly at me.

"Maybe I'll 'accidentally' close it, so I have to come back for you to open it. Wouldn't that just be *so* awful?" She put her hand over her heart in mock horror and I laughed on cue. Maybe she *was* interested. I was starting to get dizzy following the potential yes's and no's of her possible attraction.

"You just want more coffee," I joked to cover up the way my heart had leapt at the thought of her coming back.

"Well, it *is* very good coffee," she replied, picking up her cup. "Smooth, strong, almost intoxicating and addictive really." She stared straight at me over the rim off her mug as she spoke, and I smiled so wide it felt like my ears were being strained. "Well, I'm sure you'll be needing to get on with your afternoon as Summer is off," she continued, setting her empty cup down and standing. I rose as she did, reaching out to hand her the box as she reached for it. Our fingers tangled and we ended up simply holding hands and looking at each other for a moment.

"Erm, here, don't forget this!" I quickly handed her the box, then the lid. "Let me know if you need anything else," I continued as we walked out of the office. Vain roused himself and stretched his wings up above his head as we came through, clearly having taken a nap whilst we were talking. Angelica looked at him again, then we walked towards the door.

"Oh, I'm quite sure I'll be seeing you again Gavan," she murmured huskily. She smiled at me seductively and with that parting shot, slid her sunglasses back down from her head and walked away as I held the door open for her.

I certainly understand your infatuation with her now. Vain flew to my shoulder as I walked back into the shop after flipping the sign back around to read Open. *She certainly has admirable taste if she considers me to be beautiful and valuable.*

I laughed at him posing with his beak raised and eyes closed as if waiting for a photographer.

"If she knew you could talk, she'd have had you in a cage and carted off to that group of hers for study!" I teased him.

Humpf! he retorted, sinking into a sullen silence on my shoulder. I stroked him while I thought about what Angelica had said. I hoped it meant she wanted to come back to see me, but I was worried she meant her group would want to question me again. For now, I took my suppression sheet out of my shirt pocket and put it back in my desk.

I retrieved the kitchen implement holder off the counter, then put it back down again and walked into my office to grab my book. I took my X-Acto knife and the book back to the counter so I could carve while minding the store, and gradually covered the whole surface of the cylinder with the relevant symbols from the book.

I could feel the effect increasing as more and more symbols were carved, until eventually I couldn't even feel my link with Gauvain because of the suppression.

When it got to closing time, I locked the door and took the cylinder down to the vault. This succeeded in transforming it into a total magickal null zone as planned, so protecting it from magickal intrusion and destruction of the contents. Once that was done, I relocked the vault and shut the shop up for the night. I drove home and Gauvain popped out of his claw as soon as we were inside.

I have to say, travelling in that manner is really quite humiliating you know! he griped. I could see his point. As a bird of prey, he was one of the freest and wildest creatures in nature, either on Earth *or* Aaru. I decided to spend the evening doing some research on keeping a raptor as a pet, to try to remove the need for him to keep hiding. I found that here in the UK, as long as you had the relevant licence along with documentation to prove the bird was captive bred, you could own a bird of prey and even hunt with them.

I knew there was a large regional wildlife centre about an hour away and resolved to go that weekend, in order to talk to the head of raptor care. Hopefully, my new mental abilities would enable me to convince them to provide the appropriate documentation in return for a donation. I also learned about imprinting, whereby a baby bird identifies with (normally) its parent. This can happen with humans, and the bird then identifies with humans for life.

If treated correctly this can create a significantly potent bond, so having this as part of Gauvain's back story might help me explain our attachment. Apparently it also affected the bird, preventing them from learning many natural behaviours, which would also help explain his less than typical bird mannerisms.

I told Gauvain my plan, and he looked relieved that he might soon be able to travel more openly. I did remark how taking him around the local supermarket still might not be the greatest idea, and he laughed along with me at the imagined mayhem that could create. I worked out a few finer points for my discussion with the raptor keeper, then we headed to bed.

The next morning I went for my normal run. As I left the building, I saw a black SUV with dark tinted windows parked on the other side of the road. It was almost too Hollywood cliché for words, but one thing the movies got right was that it was impossible to see who was in the car unless I intended to walk right up and stare through the windscreen at them.

I shrugged and set off for my run, and as I went past the car the engine started. OK it *could* have been a coincidence, but they were starting to accumulate and my anxiety was already screaming that it was as separate as salt and water in the ocean. I reached out gently with my mind but felt no one else reaching back, so I increased the strength. I detected two minds in the car but although they weren't reaching out, they seemed to be locked down completely so I could read nothing from them. Coincidence number three.

I wondered whether this mysterious group Angelica worked for had heard her report and decided to gather some more information about me, possibly prior to a meeting and exploring my newly acquired abilities. It would make sense, given what she had told me about their interests in the magickal field.

When the car set off and followed me on my run, my suspicions were all but confirmed. I looked around as I ran and saw a rusty nail lying in the gutter ahead. I grabbed it with my mind and set it right in the path of the car behind me. I positioned it so that it hit the tread but angled out through the side wall. I wanted to properly blow the tyre rather than just giving them a slow puncture.

Since they were only doing about ten miles an hour, the driver simply stopped and got out to check it. I saw a nondescript medium-height medium-build twenty-something man with medium brown hair (clearly the most boringly innocuous member of staff they could find), but at least I was able to continue my run unaccompanied. If they wanted to talk to me, let them ask outright. If they wanted to find out more about me and my abilities, they could do the same.

I refused to be followed like some cheap spy movie. I was just glad Gauvain had left via the kitchen window and stayed away once I saw the car, so they hadn't seen him. I might have to call Angelica once I got to work to ask for an explanation. At least I could formalise my displeasure and tell her to ask the group to be more up-front about things.

I got home and showered, dressed and had breakfast, then we headed to the shop. I felt Summer arrive as I opened up the shutters. I was smiling at the memory of Angelica calling her Sarah out of a misplaced sense of jealousy over our suspected relationship.

"Morning Summer!" I called out as she approached. "Nice day yesterday? What did you two get up to? Did you go out, or stay home?" I turned as I spoke, waggling my eyebrows suggestively at her. She giggled at me and slapped my arm.

"Perv!" She giggled again. "Just because *you* have a one-track gutter for a mind, don't go tarring me with the same brush."

"A thousand apologies, fair maiden." I gave a sweeping bow for emphasis. "What high-brow intellectual delights did you two ladies partake in?"

"We stayed home and got sweaty!" She laughed uproariously and I joined in, enjoying the simple pleasure of laughing with a friend after yesterday's conversational minefield.

"Gods, it's amazing you two even have the strength to get up in the morning, the way you behave!" I teased her, but she just beamed at me.

"Hah, you're just jealous because your sex life is verging on monastic right now!" She gave as good as she got, which was why we always got on well together.

"Well, if you *will* set me up with philistines and troglodytes as dating material," I joked, remembering the last disastrous blind date she'd sent me on, "what do you expect?" She actually winced at that.

"Yeah, sorry again about that one," she said, "but you should have seen Emily's face when I told her. I thought she was gonna choke from laughing so hard! Oh, she told me to give you this..." She kissed my cheek and gave me a rib-cracking hug. "She loves her pendant, same as I do, and told me to thank you for her." I smiled at her usual exuberance.

"I'm glad you both like them. When I saw them, and saw they were a matched pair, I just knew they'd be perfect for you." I checked to make sure no one had come in yet, then leant over and whispered, "I enhanced them a little myself as well. Those protective knots should be *particularly* effective now." I widened my eyes at her as I said that last sentence, and she immediately understood.

"Thank you," she breathed, "I'll make sure Emily understands, and we'll never take them off!" I heaved a sigh of relief in the knowledge that at least they would have some protection in the future. I had no idea what might be coming, but I would defend those I cared about to my last breath.

"Oh, I meant to tell you," she continued as she shrugged out of her light jacket, "Frank rang while you were away. He's moved up your monthly meeting to this Friday. Something about having more patients now so wanting your session out of the way."

My stomach clenched at the idea of my community psychiatric nurse coming to see me, just as it always had, but then I stopped short. I had been diagnosed as a child because of my belief in magick. However, now I actually *had* magick!

Maybe I could prove that my belief wasn't crazy, perhaps even get discharged from follow-up completely as I had mentioned to Summer a couple of days ago. This could turn into my *last* appointment with Frank, and I was going to do my utmost to make sure that dream came true.

Chapter 5

I decided to send Angelica an email rather than ringing her. I'd find it much easier to be stern if I wasn't talking directly to her. I told her what had happened during my run, leaving out my little trick with the nail and making it sound like a lucky coincidence. I told her to tell her mysterious group they needed to either leave me alone, or be up-front and honest about what they wanted from me. I then rang the wildlife park and made an appointment with the head of bird keeping for Saturday.

The next few days passed almost normally, although we seemed to have a few more people coming in to browse than usual during the week. I made sure to keep my suppression sheet on me while we were open, as I was almost certain I was being evaluated by members of Angelica's group. I had sensed people reaching out towards me mentally, so I employed the same mental handshake I had used with her while keeping the energy I used to a minimum.

When Friday finally rolled around, I was eager to see Frank and prove after all these years I wasn't the nut-job that I had been labelled as when I young. Decades of resentment were bubbling away, so I would have to be careful not to overdo it. After all, it wasn't Frank's fault. He was just doing his job by checking up on me once a month, and to be honest he'd always been pretty decent about it. He had never belittled me, made sarcastic comments or challenged me in a confrontational manner about my belief in magick, unlike some of his predecessors (a couple of phone calls had soon shut that down and led to a change in who was assigned to me a few years ago).

I went for my morning run, thankfully without a shadow this time. I actually hadn't had one since the email I'd sent to Angelica, although I hadn't heard back from her directly. I completed it slightly faster than normal thanks to the adrenaline in my system.

The exercise helped burn some of it off and settle me down a little, ready for my meeting. I still wasn't completely sure how to go about demonstrating to Frank that magick was real, and I certainly had no idea what his reaction would be. I was determined to get at least one of my mental health labels dispelled today, however (there was no chance with the anxiety one, that's just who I am).

I showered and dressed, chatting with my feathered Narcissus as he performed his morning preen, then headed off to the shop. Frank was due at ten, and I wanted to make sure this went well. As a result, I was distracted and somewhat monosyllabic towards Summer as we opened up. She just looked on understandingly and got on with the usual set-up.

Frank wasn't a coffee drinker (which, as far as I'm concerned, made him far weirder than I could ever be) so I prepared the teapot with some Earl Grey, which was his favourite. Personally I prefer broken Pekoe Assam if I drink tea, but a nice Earl Grey isn't bad.

I set up my desk with a few items to use during my demonstration: a polished orb, a candle, and an onyx ashtray that had belonged to my grandfather with a leaf laid in it. Then I moved Vain's perch into the office so he could be with me for support, but he was under strict instructions not to speak to Frank unless I asked him to. This was going to be stressful enough for the poor guy without suddenly having a bird talking to him telepathically! I heard the bell over the door ring and I was so wound up, I could swear I heard the hinges squeak. I took a couple of deep breaths and headed out into the shop.

"Morning Frank!" I said brightly, desperately trying to downplay my excitement and failing miserably. I felt like a kid who had been practicing a talent the whole summer and couldn't wait to show off to his friends on the first day of school. "How've you been?" Frank looked at me quizzically which, combined with his short, rotund stature, and thinning hair, made him look like Danny DeVito in ninety percent of his films.

"OK, I think this is quite literally the first time ever that one of my patients has been this happy to see me," he said, looking suspiciously up at me. "Have you been taking drugs? Because that would really screw up your perfect record." My smile slipped away as I tried to figure out if he was serious, or if he had a previously underplayed sense of humour. Mind you our visits had always been as clinical and brief as I could make them in the past, the occasional cup of tea notwithstanding.

"Uh, n–no," I stammered, desperately trying to figure out how my good mood and excitement got derailed quite so swiftly. "I've just had a good few weeks recently." To my relief, his face cracked into a smile.

"Just kidding, I know you've never been into that sort of thing Gavan." He smiled again. "I'm glad things have been going well for you. Let's go and sit down and have a chat." I sighed in relief and smiled back.

"You had me going there for a minute!" I laughed. "I'll put the kettle on and we can go into the office." I went into the kitchen, my good mood and excitement rapidly returning. I heard Summer and Frank chatting quietly and smiled to myself at the thought of him trying to get any information from her that would cast me in a bad light. Once the kettle boiled, I filled the teapot and set it on the tray to carry through to the office. They both looked round as I appeared.

"I was just telling Frank how well business has been going," Summer said brightly. "I *may* have even let slip about a certain someone, and just how taken with her you are." She smiled evilly, knowing she'd just dropped me right in it, so I glared back at her.

"That's it, next inventory check I'm phoning in sick!" I said, pretending to get upset. "And your Christmas bonus just got halved!"

"You wouldn't dare!" she gasped in mock horror. I laughed my 'Dr Evil' chuckle and ushered Frank into the office, hearing her mutter under her breath as I closed the door.

"You know, she had nothing but good things to say about you," Frank hurried to reassure me, clearly concerned I might be genuinely annoyed with Summer for speaking out of turn despite my apparent humour. "In fact, I don't think I've ever heard her say anything bad about you." I laughed finally, and it was his turn to relax. "You know, after all these years, I really should be better at picking up on the subtext!" He laughed self-deprecatingly.

"Oh come on," I scoffed at his attempted modesty. "You're not telling me you really believed I was upset after I did my fake evil chuckle! I refuse to fall for that. With your experience, you could probably tell me my innermost thoughts just by reading my expression," I hyperbolised, but only slightly as I knew him to be a truly shrewd individual. His eyes twinkled cunningly, belying his seemingly bumbling affability and hinting at the sharp-minded intellect I knew resided behind his kindly smile.

"No getting round you, is there?" he chuckled. "Fine, let's sit down, have some tea and we can chat about how everything's been going." I walked around the desk, stroking Gauvain lightly as I passed him which drew Frank's attention to him for the first time. "Oh, is that a real bird? I thought it was stuffed because it wasn't moving. So you got a pet?"

A PET? seethed Gauvain in my mind, while outwardly seeming to remain perfectly calm. *I'll give him 'pet'! I'll...*

Hush, I thought back calmingly as I simply smiled at Frank and went to pour the tea. *He didn't mean anything by it. Don't forget he's got no idea magick is real yet, so he'd have no clue about familiars, other planes of existence or any of it.*

Huh, he groused, his thoughts calming slightly. *I had forgotten. You are quite correct. Having spent my formative months in Aaru, and then having conversed with Summer once we arrived here, I had momentarily overlooked the fact that the majority of Earth's populace are woefully unaware of these things.* I smiled at Frank as I sat down and nodded.

"Yes, I was tired of being alone," I said, remembering my disastrous date with Summer's friend, "so I decided to get a companion." I sipped my tea and looked at him expectantly. He also tried his tea and nodded approvingly – whether at the tea or my life choice was unclear – then set his mug down and looked at me with what I called his professional gaze.

"Something's changed," he said simply, astute as ever. "You're still anxious, that much was obvious from your response to my drugs joke. Sorry again about that, by the way. I never *really* suspected you. Still, you've got a new air of confidence I haven't seen on you before. You seem… centred, more comfortable in your own skin. It suits you, and I'm pleased to see it," he raised an eyebrow expectantly, and I set my cup down with a smile.

"Thanks. If you don't mind, I'd like to ask you something I never have before. I'm hoping it will be relevant to our discussion this morning." I saw his other eyebrow join the first in a race for his receding hairline at my mysterious comment, but he nodded his willingness to go along with me. "Just how much faith do you put in this whole schizo-typal personality disorder diagnosis? I've been thinking that my belief in magick is absolutely no different to a devoutly religious person's faith in their respective belief system.

"It strikes me that I'm suffering from the fact that magick doesn't have a large, structured religion built around it. Although if you think about it, the Egyptians worshipped Isis thousands of years before the emergence of Christianity.

"All that means is a belief in magick is just one that has fallen out of favour among the general population, having been a naturally established system of worship in the past." Frank started nodding before I was even halfway through my speech, giving me hope that I might be able to rid myself of the label without even revealing magick was real.

"I was wondering when you might adopt this approach, and you're absolutely right," he started out promisingly, but his next words made my hopes droop like a neglected fern. "Religious belief, especially when taken to the extreme of zealotry, has in the past often been labelled as madness. The problem you had as a child was you didn't just have faith, you held an absolute and unshakeable certainty in the existence of magick. It wasn't a reasoned analysis, it was a whole being attitude."

"But isn't that what religions teach is required?" I argued, getting into the philosophical discussion. "If you read any accepted religious text, that degree of certainty is held up as an example for all to follow." I was enjoying the exchange of views, but I was now absolutely certain I would have to prove the existence of magick if I ever wanted to be free of Frank's monthly visits. A psychiatric menopause if you will!

"To be honest, if it were up to me, I would never have saddled a child with this kind of label," he said ruefully. "I think children should be allowed to find their own level, as long as it's not harming them or others. Unfortunately now you're stuck with it, since there's no proof your ideas have any more substance than whichever deity someone else may choose to worship." Now it was my turn to have a twinkle in my eye, since Frank had unwittingly given me the opening I needed.

"So you're saying if I could prove to you beyond any shadow of a doubt that magick exists, then you'd report I no longer held any erroneous beliefs and I'd be discharged?" I asked, preparing to walk through the door he had just opened for me.

"Well... yes, I suppose so," he said good-naturedly, but I could already see the report taking shape: no lessening of abnormal ideation.

"I'm *so* glad you feel that way," I said smugly, preparing to hold him to his word. "I think it's time for a little show-and-tell."

Chapter 6

"Before we go any further," I continued, noting Frank's interested look at my somewhat cryptic comment, "there's something I want to check. Just how far does patient confidentiality extend? For example, are you duty-bound to report *everything* from our meetings, or can you limit what you tell the team and enter into my record? Can you just put in your opinions and conclusions?" Frank sat back in his chair, crossed his legs resting one ankle on the other knee and crossed his arms, dropping his chin onto his chest as he thought about my question and its implications, likely considering what exactly I meant in view of my previous comments.

"Interesting," was his only response for a good few minutes, during which time I finished my tea and refreshed our mugs. "I suppose it would depend on how whatever you were to show-and-tell me would impact your mental health and other follow-up needs."

"So if I were to prove to you I no longer have any beliefs in something that cannot be proved, you could sign me off without fully explaining *how* I convinced you?" I asked eagerly. This was the crucial point; I didn't want Frank committed to a rubber room for admitting to knowing magick was real. Nor did I need an entry into my official medical records that might lead all kinds of scientists to my door looking to examine me and test me six ways from Sunday.

"As long as I'm happy that any erroneous beliefs are gone, then that's enough for the record," Frank said cautiously. "Although the diagnosis will always be there, you would just be signed off from follow-up. But how can you prove that conclusively?" he continued, turning shrewd. "I know you're a smart guy. You're more than capable of telling me what you think I want to hear, while not believing a word of it yourself. So how can I be sure of the truth of what you're telling me?" I smiled at his astute assessment and prepared to throw the curve ball I had been winding up all morning.

"Quite simply," I replied, watching his eyes grow wide in surprise and confusion at my confidence. "I have absolutely no intention of trying to convince you that I have abandoned my beliefs, for two reasons: firstly, you're quite right that it's impossible for you to know I'm not lying and secondly, because I *haven't* changed my mind at all. My faith in magick is as strong as ever, if not stronger." Frank's forehead crinkled in his confusion, but I didn't give him a chance to interrupt with the questions I could see on his face. "Instead, I'm going to prove to you my thinking isn't misguided." His surprise was once again reflected in his expression. I really hoped this guy wasn't a poker player, because he'd lose his shirt every time he sat down.

"The only way to convince me of *that* would be to prove to my satisfaction that magick is real," he remarked, striking the heart of the issue. "This is going to be like proving the existence of a deity. In your case, Isis as the goddess of magick you just mentioned." My mind flitted to the possibility of taking him to Aaru and introducing him to Isis in person, but I rejected the idea just as quickly. She wasn't some performing monkey to be trotted out and shown off just to make my life easier. I would stick to my plan of showing him some of what I could do.

"So what would it take to convince you that magick *is* real?" I asked, interested to hear what he would consider as conclusive proof. He looked thoughtful as he mulled over just what he would accept as irrefutable evidence.

"I'd need to see something I couldn't explain any other way," he said bluntly.

"OK, like what?" I asked, prepared to show him almost anything to free myself of this monthly torture. "Do you want me to start small and work my way up?" For the first time, I saw a flicker of apprehension on Frank's face.

"Wait, are you saying that *you...*" he trailed off and I nodded slowly.

"That's one of the main reasons the last few weeks have been so *empowering* for me," I said, trying to calm him down while my own excitement was increasing. "I finally managed to unlock the potential I believed in as a child. So keep your eyes on that orb." I pointed to an amethyst ball I had placed on my desk earlier, specifically as it was non-metallic so magnets wouldn't be an excuse. I lifted it up with my mind and floated it over to him. He looked impressed but not convinced.

"Great, but stage magicians can make things float," he said pedantically. "Wires, magnets, no real magick. In fact, just a simple parlour trick." I passed him a steel paperclip.

"Put that up against it," I said. "You'll not feel any magnetic force, nor are there any wires." I waited while he checked it, looking a little more surprised. Then I made the orb perform one of the complex patterns from my early training with Alex and Liam in Aaru. I floated it back to the stand on my desk and set it down gently. He definitely looked impressed but not shocked, certainly not looking as though his world view had been turned on its head.

"OK, how about this?" I said, creating a small ball of fire in my hand. "Check all around that candle, make sure there are no wires." He did as I asked, and then I slowly floated the flame over to the candle and lit it. He nodded, but still didn't look convinced. "Now have a look at the leaf in the ashtray," I told him, and he picked it up and looked at it. "Are you satisfied it's a normal leaf?" He nodded and I gestured for him to place it back. I deliberately didn't touch it, to avoid any claim that I'd switched it using sleight of hand, then turned it into water. As the liquid sloshed back and forth, he looked up at me with the first sign of wonder I had seen on his face.

I then decided to step things up a bit, so next I picked him straight up out of his chair in the same way as I had the orb. I knew he wouldn't feel any wires or pulleys; it would be a simple sensation of weightlessness. He squawked as I lifted him, then flailed around inelegantly to try to gain control, but I simply sent him on one slow circuit of the office before setting him back down in his chair. Finally I entered his mind and spoke to him, allowing him to feel the power I now had but not harming him in any way, just making a point.

SO DOES THIS CONVINCE YOU? I asked in a powerful, grandiose voice from within his own head. *NOW DO YOU UNDERSTAND?* I withdrew and sat back in my chair, putting my own ankle on the other knee and raising an eyebrow as I let him come to terms with what he had just experienced. He reached for his tea with a shaking hand and took a long pull, then looked up at me and I was amazed to see tears in his eyes.

"I'm so sorry!" he whispered, almost too softly for me to catch. "What you went through as a child, the ignominy of a mental health diagnosis for simply knowing something others didn't believe! And what you just showed me... How are people so unaware that this exists?" He finished his tea and set his mug down, then completely dissolved into tears. I let him cry for a couple of minutes but when he didn't show any signs of stopping, I looked into his mind again, much as my friends in Aaru had checked on me when they were concerned.

His mind was in a complete turmoil of conflicting emotions and memories, all whirling around like a tornado. Rather than slowing down, his thoughts seemed to be gathering momentum and becoming more unstable as they did so. I was no psychiatrist, but I was fairly certain I was witnessing a total breakdown. The only advantage I had was that I knew exactly what had caused it, namely me. Or to be more precise, the irrefutable evidence that magick was real.

The only thing I could think of to do was to remove the memory of the conversation and revelations he had just experienced. I could then replace them with an alternate version. A psychic neuralyser, so to speak. Man, where were the *Men in Black* when you needed them? Hey if gods and goddesses were real, did that mean aliens were too? Maybe they actually *were* aliens, like in that old *Star Trek* episode. I mentally shook myself out of my unhelpful tangent and focused back on Frank.

The first thing I did was slow his thought processes down to help calm him. It worked, though came with the added side effect of putting him to sleep. Still, that was probably going to be helpful and I had already worked out how to use it in the new scenario I would create for him. I pinpointed the memory of where our conversation in the office had started, and I completely erased all memories from that point forward. His thoughts immediately settled and he entered what seemed to be a relaxed dream state. I created a tranquil beach scene for him and let his mind wander through the dreamscape while I went to work structuring a new memory for him.

I latched onto Summer's mention of Angelica, however unsubtle, and built from there. I wove an impression of a conversation, mostly one sided on my part, of describing Angie (I felt a rush of warmth at even thinking of the more familiar, diminutive version of her name which I preferred to her parents' choice of Angel).

I needed to explain my earlier comment of having had a good few weeks, so I also created the recollection of discussing the commission she had brought me. I built in the tale of my quest to Tibet and a description of the box I'd found, although I stopped short of any reference to it only opening for me or what was inside.

I continued on by adding a memory of a conversation about the existence of magick. I included how I had convinced him of my disappointment but resignation that my years of research had apparently proven to me that it *wasn't* actually real. As a result, he was happy to sign me off and discontinue the follow-up meetings every month. Finally, I gave him an image of me being called out into the shop by Summer to deal with a customer enquiry. While I was outside, he had dropped to sleep in his chair and started to dream. I slipped out of his mind and saw a soft smile on his face as he relaxed into his peaceful reverie.

I came around the desk and touched his shoulder as if I had just come back into the office. I was surprised not to feel a dip in my power after manipulating his mind so extensively, but I realised it had been for the right reasons. Much to my surprise, I actually felt a slight boost. Maybe karma understood the old adage of the end justifying the means.

"Wakey-wakey sleepyhead," I said softly, and he jerked slightly as he surfaced from his nap.

"Oh! I must have dozed off!" he said in surprise. "Sorry about that Gav, work's been manic recently. To be honest I'm really glad your research has finally shown you the light, and you've concluded magick doesn't in fact exist. I know it must be hard for you to come to terms with, but it'll be nice to be able to sign you off and have one less patient to see each month. I'll miss our chats and your Earl Grey, but I'm so proud that you're finally moving forward."

"Thanks Frank," I replied, feeling a little choked up at his genuine happiness for me and slightly guilty as it was the result of a lie. Still, better that than the prospect of him losing his sanity and everything he'd built in his life, simply because he was unable to handle what I'd shown him. "That means a lot to me. I think I might miss you too, but I definitely won't miss being monitored each month like a child!"

I let some of my years of irritation at the constant surveillance I had endured show through. I hoped that this would lend an air of authenticity to my performance. It must have worked, as he chuckled wryly and nodded.

"Oh, don't worry about napping. I often do it myself in here and I promise not to report you for sleeping on work time!" I winked at him and this time he laughed more easily.

"Well, I better get on with my day!" he said briskly, slapping his thighs and pushing himself upright from his chair. "Thanks for the tea, the chat and the forty winks. And with the best will in the world, I hope we never have to see each other under these circumstances ever again!" I laughed and shook his hand, walking out into the shop with him.

"Goodbye Summer. Keep an eye on him for me." He shook her hand as well, then headed to the door. He turned to look at us with his hand on the door handle. "Best of luck to the both of you. Gav, keep your nose clean and stay out of trouble!"

"Ah, go on with you!" I laughingly motioned him to leave, and he chuckled as he walked out of the shop for the very last time. Finally, I was free! I moved Gauvain's perch back out into the shop so he could be involved in the day and we all relaxed, getting on with the afternoon.

Chapter 7

On Saturday, I woke feeling lighter than I had in a while and set off to the wildlife park. I was eager to keep my appointment with the bird keeper. He turned out to be a middle-aged man with several scars on his hands from claws and one impressive chunk out of his left ear from what looked to have been a beak. I reached out to shake his hand, making a strong mental connection as I made the physical one. I immediately picked up his name, which was Dave, along with a brief overview of his extensive knowledge of birds of prey.

"Hey Dave, I see the ear still hasn't grown back in!" I greeted him jovially as if we had met before, impressing on him mentally that he vaguely remembered me.

"Oh, very funny!" He grinned at me. "So what can I do for you today?"

"I haven't received the paperwork for my hawk," I replied. "Did you send it out?" He looked at me both confused and slightly guilty, since obviously he hadn't sent any documentation out.

"To be completely honest, I'd forgotten all about your adoption. I'm so sorry," Dave said. "When did you adopt your hawk?"

"I was here for the hatching six months ago and he imprinted on me. Did you forget?" I pushed the memory towards his mind, and he smiled.

"Oh yeah, that was you?" I smiled and nodded. "Oh man, that was a hectic day. No *wonder* I forgot your paperwork! I'm so sorry. Have you been hassled about it?"

"Not yet, but I'd like to be ready when someone asks. You know what those governmental agencies are like." I looked at him knowingly, letting my natural anxiety help me show the right attitude and he nodded in response.

"Yeah, always better to be ready for those bastards. They even hassle me here, despite the reputation of this place and all the licenses being in order."

"Fucking bureaucrats, always up your ass for no reason!" I sympathised and he nodded at the sentiment. Nobody likes governmental oversight, so it was a pretty safe bet that adopting a sympathetic position would help.

"Let's go to the office and get your overdue documentation," he said kindly. I followed him to the centre's main complex, and we went into a room clearly devoted to everything feathered. He went straight to his filing cabinet and pulled out a folder labelled adoption forms, taking it to his desk and extracting a blank set.

"You fill in your details, and I'll fill in the ones for the centre," he said, handing me a pen. Between us we managed to get all the forms and licenses completed and stamped in under forty-five minutes, so I thanked him profusely. I then rang my bank and transferred five thousand pounds to the centre's charity account, earmarked for the raptor program.

He kept the yellow copy of the triplicate forms for the centre's records, the blue copy was to send to the relevant government bureaucracy, and the white copy was for me. Dave shook my hand one last time and wished me all the best, expressing his approval for Gauvain's name once I explained its meaning to him.

I left the park with a spring in my step, secure in the knowledge Gauvain's adoption and ownership was now fully documented and traceable (if not *entirely* above board but hey, he's from another friggin' *dimension*, what could I do?).

Gauvain would now be able to travel more openly with me and could even be seen flying with me on my morning runs. I decided to both scan the documents onto my phone, along with creating a laminated card with the relevant details to keep with me in my wallet. Better to be prepared in case some busybodies saw us together and decided to complain about me having him.

As I left the centre, I felt a sudden twinge in the back of my mind as my power took a slight dip. My manipulation of Dave's memories had come back to bite me, since it was more selfish than my actions with Frank. I felt my power levels recover as the donation to the centre balanced the karmic scales.

After all, the paperwork hadn't *hurt* anyone and it allowed my soulmate to act less like a feathered fugitive, whilst my donation would allow the centre to continue working to help endangered species. Clearly the same consideration of good deeds to keep improving my power level applied here, just as it had in Aaru. I also realised from the dip that using my power against someone for my own gain would have consequences as well.

As I analysed the fluctuations, it became apparent that they were less like a true reduction in my power itself and more like a restriction in my access to it. The power itself was mine, but the ability to use it was clearly dependant on my behaviour and karmic position. It made me wonder how those with less savoury stances kept going.

I headed to the shop to see how everything was going. Since I had finished earlier than expected, I intended to give Summer a hand. Gauvain came out of his claw on my wrist and stood on the passenger seat as I drove. He realised there was nothing for him to hold onto as he slid when we went around a corner, so went back into his claw with an irritated grumble.

Please arrange a means whereby I can travel in safety. I refuse to continue in this manner now that my presence is, at least to all intents and purposes, legal. I find it truly humiliating! I had to stop myself from laughing and sympathised with him instead.

"It might even be time to get a slightly bigger car. With your wingspan, this is a bit tight. I'll have a look online tonight."

Placated, he waited until we arrived at the shop. As I parked behind the building, I checked to see if anyone was watching and then he popped back out to land on my shoulder. I walked around to the front door and Summer waved as she saw me enter. She was showing a customer a couple of pendants, but the little girl with her turned around to look at me and squealed when she saw Gauvain.

"Pretty!" she yelled with the typical lack of volume control common to an excited five-to-six-year-old. Gauvain screeched at the sudden noise and flapped his wings in protest.

My poor ears! he complained across our link.

Mine too, bud, I thought back at him, while the girl's mother turned to her at the disturbance.

"Kaley! Not so loud! Inside voice, remember?" The little girl immediately looked up at her mother and calmed down.

"Sorry mamma. Can I go see the birdie?" she wheedled. Her mother turned further around to look at me and raised her eyebrows in surprise.

"Oh! He *is* lovely! Is he tame? Does he bite?" she asked cautiously.

"I've had him since he hatched," I said, "and raised him myself, so he's comfortable around people. As long as she's gentle, he'll be fine." I knelt down and she rushed over, stopping a few feet away then walking very carefully to get closer. She held her hand out hesitantly, and I said, "Just one finger on his head, nice and soft."

I held my arm out and Gauvain shuffled along it. I decided to brace my hand on my knee with my elbow pointed outward so he could sit on my upper arm. It's surprising just how heavy a full-grown hawk of his kind could be. There was no way I was going to try to hold him at arm's length for any appreciable period of time.

Kaley stroked his head, and Vain closed his eyes in bliss at the attention. She was utterly charmed and moved on to stroking his wings while her mother, reassured that she was safe, turned back and completed her purchase.

"I think I'll just take both," she told Summer, who beamed and rang up the sale. She put the pendants in little boxes with some cotton wool, which then went into a small paper bag with the shop's name on. We'd been environmentally friendly and plastic free long before it was trendy.

"Come on Kaley, time to go. Say thank you," she called to her daughter.

"Fank you!" Kaley said to me while giving Vain one last stroke. Then they walked out, the little girl craning her neck to keep looking at him for as long as possible.

"Nice timing, Gav," Summer said once they were gone, giving me a hand to stand up as my legs had cramped from kneeling. "I was getting more of a lookie-loo vibe from her before you came in. Her daughter had been whining about going home, then you walked in with Gauvin and totally distracted her so her mum relaxed and bought both pendants. Wanna permanent job?" she joked finally.

I laughed and replied, "Vain being here will certainly become a talking point. He'll probably bring in quite a lot of extra foot traffic, once word gets around. I think it might be a good idea to put up some signs on his perch, and the others when they get here. We can warn people not to feed him or touch him without talking to me. We'll also state that we're not responsible for bitten fingers if they disregard the warning," I continued, thinking of possible problems and trying to head them off before they happened.

Excellent suggestion, I certainly don't relish the thought of being poked and prodded all day, Gauvain chimed in, sending his thoughts to both of us.

"Man, that definitely takes some getting used to!" Summer smiled at Gauvain as she spoke, then looked at me. "That reminds me, the pet shop rang and the other perches are in."

"Oh, great," I replied. "If you stay here with Summer bud, I'll go get them. I might need to make a couple of trips with there being five." Gauvain flew to the perch by the counter and I walked round to the pet store. I paid the rest of the cost of my order, and the guy I had met before called a young man from the back with a box cart to help me move them.

With the flatbed trolley we managed to take all of the perches in one trip, although he barely said a word the whole way. He simply dumped the stands just inside the shop door and left, never even looking up to see Gauvain or Summer. Definitely not cut out for customer service, that one.

I put two of the stands together, using magick to fully tighten the bolts as before, then set one on the opposite side of the shop from the counter. The other one went into my office behind my desk, where I had moved the first stand temporarily the day before during Frank's visit.

Gauvain immediately criticised the second stand positioning, wanting it closer to the door. I argued that people might get concerned if he was too close, worrying he might escape. We compromised and moved the stand a little closer to the door, but not right next to it. I reinforced my point by warning him that he wouldn't want to be too close to the incense and candles, a point he agreed with after me standing next to the display with him on my shoulder for only a couple of minutes.

Summer looked on and laughed at our discussion, saying we sounded like the men off of *Queer Eye for the Straight Guy*. We quickly repositioned the stand and shut up after that. Several more customers came and went through the afternoon. Towards the end of the day when I had retreated to my office to review the week's books, Summer knocked on the door frame.

"Are you overly busy right now?" she asked, which was our usual code for 'I can make an excuse if you don't want to see anyone.'

"Nah, pretty much finished wrestling with the figures. It's been a fairly good week actually. What's up?" I replied, sitting back from the desk and stretching.

"There's someone here asking to see you," she answered coyly. "Shall I show them in?"

"Them?" I asked. "You said some*one*, not some people. That means it's a woman." Summer smiled brightly at me but gave nothing away. "Did she say what she wanted to discuss?" I continued, aware that I had no appointments. We never booked them at the weekend if we could avoid it, as that was our busiest time.

"No, she just asked if you were in. We've already had a chat but now apparently she wants you," she said suggestively. I heard a familiar throaty laugh out in the shop at the implications. I shot out of my chair, startling Gauvain on his new perch behind me.

"Angelica! Come in, come in!" Summer joined in the laughter, and Angelica peered around the door-frame.

"I couldn't help myself at Summer's choice of phrase, especially the way she said it!" she exclaimed, still laughing. I thought back to exactly what Summer had said, and immediately flushed at the connotations.

"Especially after her comment about the flat upstairs when you first visited!" I joked, at which both of them laughed even harder.

"I'd forgotten that!" spluttered Summer through her laughter. I certainly hadn't, especially after knowing that Angelica still thought about my XXX defence as I had dubbed it.

"Anyway, moving on before my face actually bursts into flames," I said, trying to redirect the conversation for the sake of my dignity and anxiety (along with my shorts). "What can I do for you today?"

"The head of the group that I work for wants to meet you," Angelica replied. The smile dropped from my face.

Here we go, I thought.

Chapter 8

"Did he or she say *why* they wanted to meet me?" I asked cautiously, my habitual nervous state setting my pulse racing and the sweat breaking out across my upper lip. "I thought I gave you a pretty comprehensive report when you were here last time." I motioned for her to come into the office and sit down, seating myself again as she did and trying to calm down. After all, I had expected something like this once they heard about my magickal awakening.

"Oh, you did, don't worry," she rushed to reassure me. "They were extremely impressed that you'd actually been destined to be sent after the Veil. Also, once they'd checked out the box, they closed it and then confirmed none of them could open it again. Once it was closed it even resisted being cut open, so there's no way anyone but you could have gotten as far as you did."

"So what's the problem?" I asked, already suspecting the answer and dreading it. "If they want the box open again, you could have brought it with you."

"Actually they said since the box is clearly meant for you, I'm returning it to its rightful owner," she said, getting the box out of her bag and placing it on the desk. "My boss wants to meet you to see if you'd be interested in working with us to further your magick. He wants to know what you can do already, then see if the group could help you enhance your abilities."

"So it's an assessment and recruiting drive," I stated, confirming exactly what I had been worried about. How could I get out of this without appearing rude, and without revealing I'd already studied and probably advanced way beyond anyone they had? "To be honest I'm happy where I am, and I love what I do. I'm not looking to get involved in something that takes me away from the shop."

I tried to think of an explanation that sounded polite but was still a no. I knew I'd eventually have to agree to at least one meeting, but that didn't mean I had to jump as soon as they snapped their fingers. I'd done what they paid me to do, they had no cause for complaint. Unless, of course, you counted the fact that *I'd* gotten the benefits they had wanted for themselves. OK, looking at it *that* way, maybe they had *some* right to be a bit pissed off.

"I understand, it truly is a lovely place." Angelica smiled at me to try to soften the blow. "Still, I think my boss wants to meet you at least once. How often does anyone get a chance to meet someone who has been chosen across centuries by a Goddess?" I could hear the capital G when she said goddess, so I knew that there was no way around that argument without appearing churlish.

"Did your boss tell you when to arrange this meeting for?" I asked, unconsciously feeling at my shirt pocket to make sure my suppression sheet was in place. She smiled at me and shook her head.

"He just said as soon as you could, but at your convenience obviously." I thought about saying that my convenience would be half-past never, but then reconsidered.

"Fine, as long as your boss knows that I'm coming in as a favour and consider myself to be under no obligation to accept his offer," I stated, picking up on her use of 'he' and sticking with the masculine pronoun. "We meet, we chat, I leave. Just because I got my abilities unlocked, doesn't mean I want to be affiliated with some mysterious group that seems to have its fingers in more pies than I've had hot dinners. He's interested in magick users, that's fine, but I don't have to be interested in him. I'm sure he's got stronger magick users than me anyway." (Yeah, right; he wishes!)

Angelica looked at me curiously. "I thought you would have welcomed the help. Magick takes a lot of study and practice to learn," she said. "I don't understand why you're being so defensive all of a sudden." How could I tell her the truth? She'd have to report back to the group, and they'd want me stuck in some magickal laboratory to study for the rest of my natural life. OK, I know how paranoid that sounded, but it's how I felt.

"I'll meet with him and hear him out, but I'm making no promises," I said. "I've always been a very private person, and I prefer studying on my own at my own pace. No offense." Her face cleared and she nodded.

"Of course, we're not wanting to force you into anything if you're not comfortable," she said placatingly. "You wouldn't be able to learn to use your abilities very well under those conditions anyway. You need peace and quiet and calm to be able to focus properly, at least until you become more accustomed to using your talents." My mind went back to my graduation exam in Thunder Cave and I smiled, nodding in apparent agreement.

"Fine," I said with a sigh, "as long as he realises that I'm probably going to say no to his offer but I'm not trying to be disrespectful or ungrateful, then set up the meeting. Maybe Wednesday morning, as that's usually a fairly quiet day for us and it's just a few days away so we can get it over and done with as soon as possible. Then we can all go back to our respective lives, me here in my shop and them doing whatever mysterious things they do."

Angelica smiled brightly at me. "Thank you Gavan, you don't know what that means to me." The smile slipped from her face and her eyes clouded over as she looked down for a moment and bit her lip. Then it was gone and she looked up again with her smile fixed back in place, although it appeared to be a little more brittle and forced than before. "I'll get it all set up. Nine in the morning?"

"Yes that's fine," I replied, "then I'll be able to get back and still get on with some work. Oh, what's the name of the man I'll be meeting?" She immediately looked away again, this time temporising.

"Um, I'm not sure which of the leaders it will be. There's one overall leader and then several department heads as it were, who lead the various sections within the group. I'm not sure which one will meet you, or even if there will be a few of them."

After her earlier comment regarding the leader's eagerness to meet someone from a prophecy, this new evasiveness definitely sounded fishy to me. Why was she reluctant to give me someone's name?

"Seriously? Can you at least tell me the *name* of the group, so maybe I can look up some background online before I meet whoever it is?" I asked, trying to see just how evasive she was going to be.

"Oh you won't find them online. The group is very close-knit and private so they don't publicise themselves," she hedged. "It's more influence than outright presence, plus they are more on the magickal side of the world than the mundane business world. They do have interests there as well though."

I thought to myself that was a remarkably interesting little snippet, yet actually evaded my question and still told me nothing she hadn't already explained in her first visit. She was definitely scared of revealing any information, which in turn was raising my hackles. I was now even more convinced that I wanted nothing to do with this mysterious cabal.

I would have to be polite but innocuous during my visit, and then have nothing more to do with them. It might even be best to sever any contact with Angelica, however attracted to her I might be. If I couldn't trust her and she was keeping things from me, it wasn't exactly a great way to start any kind of potential relationship!

"I'd better get going and leave you to finish up your paperwork," Angelica said, standing up. "Maybe I'll see you on Wednesday. I'll check that the time is OK with whomsoever will be attending, then text you the address once I know where they want to meet you." So I wouldn't even be able to Google the address to get any information. This was reaching towards MI6 level paranoia and secrecy. Who the hell was I meeting, James Bond?

"This has been... interesting," I said, walking around the desk to show her out. "I have to say, the cloak-and-dagger approach doesn't exactly engender a feeling of trust and openness. I guess I'll just have to wait to find out more on Wednesday."

She smiled apologetically, and I could tell she *wanted* to tell me more, but something was holding her back. Just what was it that this group had on her that made her so reticent? There was clearly a deeper backstory here, one that seemed to have a significant emotional impact on her. One more reason to steer clear, I guess.

She walked out of the shop and looked back at me sadly, then walked away down the street. Summer came up to me to ask what had happened.

"What did you say to her? She looked like she was going to cry as she was leaving, and she was laughing when she arrived! Just what have you done now, Gav?" She fixed me with an angry glare which I pretended to fend off by holding my hands up and crossing my index fingers to form a crucifix.

"She came to tell me that the head of her group wants to meet me," I explained. "Basically, they want me because I have magick now. They're planning to assess me and will probably ask me to work for them or at least with them, no doubt using my abilities to assist them in whatever ends they are aiming to achieve.

"I told her I had no interest in leaving the shop, but I finally agreed to meet her superior. Then she wouldn't tell me his name, the name of the group, or even the address I'll be going to until just before the meeting.

"There's definitely something off about all this. She clearly wanted to tell me, but there's something holding her back. I don't think she's as willing to help them as she seems. I've got a gut feeling she's being coerced somehow."

"Woah, just what the hell have you gotten caught up in Gav?" Summer asked, concerned.

"I don't rightly know, but it's definitely more than just some commission to find an artefact," I replied. "I finally agreed to a meeting simply to get them off my back, but I'm going to have to be incredibly careful. I'll take my suppression sheet to try to give the impression of being less powerful than I am, but with it being paper I can burn it if I get stuck so I can use everything I've got. I just hope this one meeting will be enough."

We finished off the day and locked up. Gauvain went back into his claw for the drive home, reminding me of my promise to look at bigger vehicles so he didn't have to keep doing this. I drove home thinking of what might happen at the meeting on Wednesday. I hoped a demonstration of my apparently weak abilities would be enough to convince them I had nothing new to offer them.

I made some pasta for dinner and cut up some meat for Gauvain, then we sat down together to have a look at some bigger SUV's. I didn't want anything too big, but there were some mid-range ones around fourteen or fifteen thousand new even with everything on them; you just needed to look at one of the less well-known manufacturers.

The name didn't matter to me, since I've never been a badge snob. With trade-in on my current vehicle I could certainly get a nice car without breaking the bank. I reminded myself I didn't have to worry quite so much any longer, but there was no point burning through my fee by being irresponsible. It was significant, but I'd missed out on the potential millions due to the way it had all worked out.

A bit more Googling showed me there was a garage only twenty minutes from me which was open on Sundays. I rang Summer to say I would be late in the morning, then shut the computer down to watch *Fantomworks* on TV while I looked through eBay for something to work with an idea I had.

The following morning I headed to the garage to find they actually had an ex-demo model, fully loaded, about to go on sale. I spoke to the sales assistant and we agreed on a trade-in price for my old car, then signed all the necessary paperwork to complete the title changes.

I paid for my new ride and drove off. My next stop was the home of a woman I had messaged last night as a result of my searching. I bought her old baby seat which had an Isofix system, then headed to the shop.

I took the baby seat into my office, ignoring Summer's look of shock, and removed the seat from the base. I went round to the pet shop again and bought a short, thick branch perch and took it back to my office where I fixed it to the baby seat base. Now I had something for Gauvain to hold onto while I drove. He flew over to it and gripped hard, bouncing up and down to check its stability.

Beautiful work, he said happily. *When you purchased the baby seat, I wondered what you were planning. I had visions of you wrapping me in a blanket and strapping me in, or at least attempting to anyway.* He laughed across our link and I joined in at the thought.

The next couple of days passed without incident, and I used the time to start looking through some of my magickal texts. I remembered

Danu's comments and disdain regarding spells, but I felt they might at least guide me in developing my abilities.

The first thing I tried to learn was a glamour. I thought it might be useful to be able to disguise either myself or Gauvain without actually changing our forms. That way we would still have all our normal abilities. The first few times I tried to make the pen on my desk look like a mushroom, it simply looked a bit hazy. I gradually improved, moving through the phase of creating what looked like a pale hologram, until I could finally cast an altered image real enough to fool even me.

Tuesday evening drew in without any communication from Angelica. Finally, as we were closing up at six, my phone beeped with a text alert. Nine AM was confirmed, and the name and address of a local hotel was included. They were apparently hiring the meeting room for the morning as a conveniently close location to me, rather than meeting wherever they were based. I drove home to get an early night, making sure to take my sheet of symbols with me ready for the morning.

Chapter 9

The following morning I got up bright and early as normal and went for my run. My stride was somewhat irregular, brought about by my distraction and concern over the impending meeting, and I narrowly avoided twisting my ankle on a curb stone as I neared home again.

I showered and shaved, then dressed in a shirt and tie, slacks and black shoes to look smart for my meeting. Gauvain and I had already agreed he would come along in his claw for moral support so he was with me but unseen. I was definitely nervous regarding what they might be able to tell about me despite my best efforts at concealment.

I'd been practicing locking my mind down as well as defending myself by deflecting, Gauvain assisting me as much as he could by attempting to get into my thoughts while I tried to block him out. I'd been storing as much energy as I was able since I had arrived home, both my own and elemental, into Seren but I had hoped I wouldn't have to draw on it so soon.

I knew it was still early but I decided to head to the hotel and maybe get some breakfast there, or at least some coffee since my roiling stomach might make food inadvisable. I headed down to the garage, got into my new car and put the hotel address into the satnav, heading out according to the irate-sounding woman's instructions. As I drove, I had a mental discussion with Gauvain about how we'd handle the ensuing events.

I knew that whomever I was meeting wouldn't be especially happy that I wasn't interested in joining their organisation, so we'd probably part on not particularly congenial terms. As a result I doubted I'd find out very much from them today, so I needed a way to augment any research I might do afterwards. Gauvain suggested he try to follow the person after they left, so he came out of his claw and landed on his perch in the passenger seat.

I put a glamour on him so that he looked like a magpie to attract less attention, along with a ward to protect him from magickal and physical harm. When we arrived, I put the car in the outside car park and Gauvain flew up to perch on the sign with the hotel's name above the front door.

I entered the lobby and asked at reception where the meeting room was, then made sure there was no one already waiting for me. I took the opportunity to hide a few apotropaic symbols under some tables and chairs to boost my sheet's effect. I then went and got myself some coffee in the restaurant. It wasn't great, so I got myself some toast to protect my already jumpy gut from the extra acid.

At eight forty-five I headed to the meeting room and saw there was still nobody there. I went in and sat down, deciding to spend a few minutes catching up on Facebook. I browsed down my news-feed, eventually realising with a start that it was already ten past nine and still no one had deigned to grace me with their presence.

I decided I would wait until half-past and if this mysterious overlord was still conspicuous by his absence I would leave, text Angelica that they hadn't turned up and inform her that I wasn't prepared to waste my time again.

I hated people who were late. I always thought it showed a sense of superiority over whoever you were meeting, that you felt your time was more valuable than theirs and that their time didn't matter.

It got to half-past and I stood up to leave. As I walked towards the door it opened and in walked two people – or was it three? My confusion came because the second body through the door actually had two heads. Both were human, both identical, but growing side by side up from one neck root that split to form a Y.

The heads had long brown hair, and the body underneath was definitely female. They must be conjoined twins with the only separation being their heads. I wondered briefly how they divided usage of the body between them.

The other individual looked nothing like I expected. He appeared to be in his early twenties with blond hair, blue eyes, and a tan. He was wearing a Bermuda shirt, shorts and sandals. This was a senior person in the group? He looked more like some Californian surfer.

"Sorry we're late Mr Maddox. Traffic was awful." The blond guy's voice, on the other hand, was exactly as I would have expected for a senior group member. A cultured, upper class English accent with cut-glass vowels and studied boredom. It sounded so incongruous coming from a 'surfer dude' that I did a double-take to check it was him speaking.

As they came into the room, they walked about five feet in and stopped dead. They looked around and then looked at each other. The surfer looked at me in a calculating manner before turning away.

"Actually, it's such a nice day, why don't we sit outside on the patio?" he said over his shoulder, already heading away. I cursed inwardly but couldn't object without a reason. Clearly they'd felt the suppression effect from the symbols I'd secreted around the room. Oh well, round one to them. Let the games begin.

We walked together out of the room and headed towards the hotel patio, which was in the centre of the complex and surrounded on three sides by the wings and front of the building. As we went past the reception desk, the surfer asked the staff to have some coffee sent out to us.

I looked at the twins and saw that their heads looked blurry. Clearly they were using some kind of glamour to prevent people staring at them all the time, which proved they were magick users. As we walked I felt them probing at my mind, so I deflected them away gently.

"I'm sure Angelica would have already told you that I don't like people attempting to meddle with my thoughts. Please don't try," I remarked calmly, while hiding my inner nervousness. Surfer-dude looked at me and nodded.

"She did indeed Gavin. You don't mind if I call you Gavin, do you?" he asked arrogantly, clearly feeling superior. Now usually I would correct people on the pronunciation of my name. However the disparity between his appearance, voice and behaviour already gave me the creeps, so I saw no reason to give him any help.

Also, one thing that just about every magickal book I had ever read agreed upon was that true names had power. By using the wrong name, it would limit any sway he could have over me.

When we got to the patio surfer-dude picked a seat with his back directly to the sun, clearly expecting me to sit opposite him and therefore have the sun in my eyes. I moved around the table and sat to his left, so he would have to strain his neck to keep looking at me. He nodded and moved to the seat opposite me instead. One all.

"So, we've established that you have magick users and I don't like them reaching into my mind without permission," I started off, positioning myself firmly to begin the power dance. "Secondly, I can defend my mind if I have to. So what more do you want to know? Also, seeing as you're already putting us on a first-name basis, what should I call you?" The beach bunny smiled at my little display of defiance.

"My name is Atma Mumm –" he began imperiously, but I reacted before he could say any more.

"At your mum's?" I interrupted, wanting to throw him off balance. "What, did you forget to pick it up when you left this morning?" The twins made a strangled noise as they tried to stop themselves laughing.

"I said *Atma Mumm!*" he snarled, then caught himself and calmed down. "You may call me Atma."

"That sounds Middle-Eastern, but your appearance is more Beach Boys than baba ghannouj," I responded. Despite himself, Atma smiled but then turned to stare at the twins as they snort-laughed for a second time.

"And what should I call you two ladies?" I asked politely.

"Oh, he's asking our names," said the one on the left.

"And he's calling us ladies," replied the one on the right.

"So should we tell him?"

"Well, I don't know, what do you think?"

"Should we ask permission first?"

"They are *our* names after all."

"That's true, and not many people talk directly to us."

"No they don't."

"So we're agreed?"

"Yes, let's tell him."

My head was switching back and forth like a Wimbledon tennis final as they had this strange conversation between them as if Atma and I weren't even there. Then they turned to me and spoke together.

"We are Gabriella and Isabella," they harmonised. I was almost as creeped out by their little performance as I was by the weird dichotomy between Atma's appearance and voice. I repressed my visceral reaction and smiled at them.

"It's lovely to meet such a unique pair." I nodded at them. They smiled back at me and Atma scowled in response. I looked at the magickal auras around the twins, noting a significant overlap and exchange between them.

There was also a solid flow between them and Atma. His aura was strange, fractured, almost as if it were shot through with other energy. It added to the sensation of wrongness that I felt from him.

"Fine, now we're all introduced so let's get down to brass tacks," he said, clearly irritated. "If not for us, you would still be some mundane little shopkeeper scraping a living selling incense to hippies." I sat back in my chair at the sudden change in his attitude. "You owe us. We gave you a quarter of a million pounds and helped you get your magick unlocked. We want more in return than a simple thanks."

I smiled and reached into my jacket, pulling out a copy of the transcript from the meeting with Angelica. I had brought it along for exactly this reason, with a couple of pertinent passages highlighted. I passed it across to him without a word, then sat back while he flipped through it. He got to the highlighted portions and threw the pages onto the table.

"And that's why I record all business conversations," I said casually. "That way no one can dispute anything. The agreement was that you paid me a quarter of a million pounds to look into the *possibility* that the Veil was a genuine physical item.

"I did that and more, and I didn't even charge you for the box. Mind you, since you kindly returned it due to the fact that neither you nor your underlings can open it, we'll call that one even shall we?" My stomach somersaulted as I waited for him to explode in temper, but I maintained my outwardly relaxed façade.

He stared at me, clearly angry with my preparedness and refusal to be intimidated. The twins, in contrast, smiled at me from behind their boss, looking almost impressed.

"Ooh he's a feisty one, isn't he?" said the one on the left.

"Yes he is, very feisty," replied her sister.

"I don't think the boss is happy with him."

"No, not happy at all."

"He seems quite adept for someone so new to his magick doesn't he?"

"Yes, very, especially if he can fend us both off at the same time."

"Shall we try again?"

"I don't know, something seems to be blocking us before we even get to him."

"That's true, I wonder how he's doing that?"

"It doesn't feel like him doing it; it's something impersonal."

"Yes, like the feeling in the meeting room."

I smiled at them in recognition of their sensitivity, while Atma looked from them to me. I felt a weak mental probing from him but it wasn't even as strong as Angelica's ability, so I diverted it with a mere touch. I wondered if his use of an incorrect name for me had weakened his ability to connect to me or given me some kind of protection from him.

I shifted my smile to him and shrugged my shoulders, then looked back at the twins and winked which made them smile and giggle. Atma scowled at them and I felt his mental energy flick out at them like a slap, making them physically flinch in unison. After feeling that, I was once again aware of a residual connection between them as I had seen earlier. It was almost like some kind of a leash or tether. I looked back at Atma and scowled myself.

"That was uncalled for," I said angrily. "I winked at them which made them laugh, it had nothing to do with you. Even my limited ability felt the irritation in that energy burst. Having experienced how you treat your subordinates, I'm now even more certain I want nothing to do with you or your not so merry band. I was always taught to judge a person by how they treat those under them, in which case you leave a hell of a lot to be desired. This meeting is over."

I stood up, at which point Atma also got out of his chair, shoving it back with his knees as he did so which caused it to rock and almost fall over. He turned and stomped away, not even waiting for the twins. When they moved to follow him off the patio, I quickly stepped around the table to hold the door open for them. As they went through, they looked at me in surprise bordering on shock at being treated with any sort of kindness. I went through after them and took their hand, raising it to my lips to brush their knuckles.

"It was a pleasure to make the acquaintance of such a unique pair. I hope we meet again," I said to them, allowing the mental connection that the physical had initiated. It was weak and fleeting but proved to them I had no ill feeling towards them. They smiled at me with genuine joy which lit up their eyes.

"Gemini, get over here!" Atma snarled as I released their hand, allowing our brief connection to fade. The joy disappeared from their faces as they whispered to each other, clearly forgetting I was there and could hear them.

"That's all he ever calls us."

"Yes, he treats us like his trained dogs."

"Yes, it's like we're not even human."

"It's so insulting."

"One day..." Their voices faded as they walked towards him and away from me. As they reached Atma, he turned to me and called back.

"You'll regret your actions today," he swore. "The Order of the Nine Seals does not forgive, nor do we forget!" They all walked out together and I was left standing in the lobby with my mouth open, watching the door close behind them. I suddenly recalled Danu's cryptic comment as I was leaving Aaru, stressing how even too much *order* could be detrimental. Had she been trying to warn me?

Chapter 10

I closed my mouth and thought back over Atma's last words to me. Nine seals? Last time I checked the Book of Revelations (admittedly quite a while ago), there were only seven seals opened at the end of days, but there were nine circles in Hell. Was this some group looking to end the world and drag it to Hell? Was *that* the ultimate battle I was supposed to fight? If so, I was *WAAAAY* out of my league!

I quickly sent a mental image of Atma and the twins to Gauvain, and he let me know he had spotted them and was hot on their tail. As long as they stayed in the city I knew he'd be able to keep up. The speed limit and sheer volume of traffic, along with the various signals and junctions, would prevent them from getting too far ahead of him.

And who the hell (pun intended) was Atma Mumm (and what was he doing with her? That joke wasn't going away any time soon)? He clearly had power, I had felt it when he mentally slapped the twins and reached out towards me, but he had left the main mental attempt to them. Did that mean they were stronger than him? Then why were they subservient to him? There was too much going on here that I didn't understand.

Gauvain let me know they had gotten into another ubiquitous black SUV and set off into the city. They were keeping to the speed limit and obeying all the traffic laws, clearly trying to avoid drawing attention to themselves, but were making lots of random loops and backtracks. Whenever they turned down side streets or dead ends (which he could see by flying above the buildings) he would simply perch on a streetlight until they resumed course or set off in a new direction. Then he would trail them again, disappearing amongst the city's crow and magpie population.

While Vain was playing tracker, I returned to the car and headed back to the shop to see what I could turn up now that I at least had a couple of names to work with. When I arrived, Summer asked how it had gone so I gave her a brief recap. She was fascinated by my description of the twins, and laughed at my play on Atma's name.

Once she was caught up, I headed into my office to see what I could turn up about Mr Mumm (was that the sequel to *Mr Nanny*? I should really start writing some of these down) and his elusive Order, putting my suppression sheet away in the safe before I sat down. When I tried to search for the Order, all that returned was 'Did you mean seven seals?' or *Dante's Inferno* and the nine circles of Hell, exactly as I had already thought earlier. No wonder Angelica had said I wouldn't find anything online. She was absolutely right.

Searching for Atma's name, on the other hand, confirmed the sensation of creepiness that he exuded. Atma, according to the internet, meant soul. Mumm was an ancient Egyptian word that meant eat, so his name basically meant Soul Eater. Bearing in mind his control over the twins, I wondered whether he'd chosen that name as a sort of personal joke. It would also explain why his mannerisms, attitude and voice didn't match up with his appearance. That wasn't actually his body!

The realisation hit me like a thunderbolt, sitting me back in my chair and sending a chill down my spine. What had happened to the poor boy whose body was now being used by that unholy bastard, and who or what was Atma really?

As I pondered, Gauvain contacted me to let me know he'd finally lost track of the car. They'd driven around for a while until they apparently felt safe that they weren't being followed, then drove out of the city. They joined the main road heading north, at which point they'd increased to the posted seventy miles per hour. There was no way poor Vain could keep up with those speeds, but at least we had a clue in which direction they'd gone. Now it might be a case of trying to track them magickally.

He was headed back to the shop, and in the meantime I decided to ring Angelica to see if she could tell me any more about the Order or Atma himself. I pulled up her contact details on my phone and hit call, only to hear the dreaded three tones followed by "The number you have dialled is no longer in service." Goosebumps ran down my arms. Why had her phone been disconnected all of a sudden? Then again, maybe she was done with me now that I had met her boss and all her earlier flirting really *had* just been an act.

My mind started racing down various lines, and then suddenly came to a screeching halt. Atma had called me Gavin. He would surely have been briefed by Angelica on everything he would need to know prior to our meeting. He would no doubt have blamed her for any incorrect information, whether it was her fault for telling him wrong or his own fault for misunderstanding what she told him. He was clearly the sort who took his frustrations out on those beneath him, something I'd already witnessed first-hand in his treatment of the twins. I suddenly feared for Angelica's safety, especially in view of the visions I'd had in Aaru.

A few minutes later I felt Gauvain nearing the shop, so I went outside. I saw a magpie flying towards me and removed the glamour, watching as he suddenly grew into the familiar form of the white hawk I knew. I reached up to him and he landed on my wrist, then jumped to my shoulder. He had already picked up on my distress over Angelica, so he rubbed his head against my cheek to try to comfort me. I knew intellectually that I had decided I couldn't trust her due to her evasiveness, but I couldn't simply turn off my emotions.

I went back into the shop and told Summer what had happened, then went out to the car to try to pick up Atma's route starting from the junction where Gauvain had lost them. I had no idea if this would work, but I was out of other ideas as to how to find them. Without Angelica as a point of contact, I had no other simple way to track down the Order.

Vain hopped onto his perch and started preening his wings as I started the engine, and I set off towards the last place he had seen them. When I reached the highway on-ramp, I turned onto the northbound carriageway and set the cruise control. Since it was an adaptive system, it kept a minimum distance from the car in front which allowed me to focus on reaching out with my magick.

I felt for the energy signatures of the twins and Atma, but no matter how strongly I reached out, I found precisely nothing, nix, nada, bupkes, dry-hump, squirt, diddly-squat, zip, zero, zilch, a big fat goose egg. I drove for a few junctions, then gave it up as a bad job and headed back to the shop.

I parked the car and walked in with Gauvain on my shoulder, giving Summer a dejected shake of my head to indicate my failure. I went straight into my office, Vain jumping off my shoulder to fly to his perch and start preening as usual. I sat down at my desk, put my elbows on the surface and my head in my hands.

My brain felt like cotton wool, and all I could think of was what that bastard might be doing to Angelica out of frustration for his failure to recruit me at our meeting. Gauvain tried to sympathise with me by pointing out that I was unlikely to be the first person to fall on the wrong side of dealings with Mumm, or even the Order as whole.

I stared at the leather writing surface of the desk, picking out tiny imperfections in the grain and a few imprints of past writing pressed into the material as I tried to come up with another way to track down Atma and the Order.

An organisation of that kind must have been around for many years. They must have been corrupting or co-opting anyone they thought they could use, either at the time or in the future, Gauvain said sympathetically. *If they have been perfecting their skills in those arenas for that long, they will have developed significant levels of ability at it and developed many kinds of contingency plans for when things don't go their way. Through no fault of your own, you are totally new to operating in these circles so you cannot expect to be as capable as them.*

As he said that, a dimly flickering lightbulb illuminated the weak reflection of a half-formed idea into the depths of my mind. If they had been collecting magick users for that long, they must have pissed off a great many people in the process. Some of them might be contactable and willing to work with me. I needed to try getting in touch with some of the other people in the magickal artefact game whom I'd dealt with before. Maybe some of any of them had previously had dealings with the Order, or at least knew of someone who had. I wasn't out of the game just yet.

I pulled my computer towards me and fired it up, opening up my contacts and going into the business subdirectory. I searched for anyone in my local area, coming up with four names of people I had dealt with before. I had no idea if they were magick users, only that they had helped me track down artefacts or texts in the past.

Three of them had helped me multiple times, so I worked my way through those first. Unfortunately none of them had ever heard of any Order of the Nine Seals or Atma Mumm. I thanked each one for their time and moved on down the list. After striking out for the third time I was forced to look at the fourth name, but I was definitely not happy about it.

Seirina Crow was a woman with whom I had had dealings only once. A client had asked me if I could locate a particular text and after asking around, she had been the only one capable of pointing me in the right direction. The text had turned out to be a particularly dark grimoire, so I had never turned it over to the requesting party. It was currently locked in the vault along with several other pieces and texts I had deemed too dark or hazardous to pass on over the years. That was another reason I'd had the idea to put the apotropaic utensil holder in there with them.

I had never felt comfortable about her and the fact that she had known where to find such an unpleasant item, which was why I'd never contacted her after that one time. The only reason I'd kept her details was because sometimes you needed to know people on the darker side of the line to find what you needed. It was looking like this was going to be another one of those times.

I poured some coffee from the pot to brace myself for what I knew I needed to do, drinking half of the mug straight down to get the caffeine hit. The slight scorch of my throat also served to centre my mind, and I put the mug down as I seated myself once again. I took a couple of deep breaths and then reached for the phone, checking the number on my computer before I started to dial.

Chapter 11

"*Uill tha sin na iongnadh*, Gavan Maddox!" The rolling Scottish accent flowed through the speaker as she picked up my call.

"Oh you know I don't understand that gibberish, Seirina!" I had to laugh. I had learned the first time we had spoken that she liked to pepper her speech with Scots Gaelic phrases at various times, and I never had any clue what they meant.

Her accent made her hard enough to understand when she got worked up as it broadened significantly, and she used more colloquialisms. When she went full Gaelic, I had no chance. Another reason I had not dealt with her after our one business interaction: After talking to her several times over the few days we had been in contact, I had had a migraine for about three days! Now she laughed on the other end of the line.

"Och aye, I forgawt," she said. "I was just expressin' me surprise at hearin' from ye. It's been a fair wee while, so it has."

"I know," I replied, "but after what that text you helped me to locate turned out to be, and the fact that you knew where to find it, I wasn't all that comfortable with the circles you seemed to travel in. I try to stick to the lighter side of the street, while you seem to revel in the shadows. Am I wrong?" My blunt honesty seemed to surprise her, as she hesitated before answering me.

"No many fawks wuild come righ' out an' say tha' tae a lassie," she said eventually, her accent actually lessening as she turned less playful, "but it's always guid tae ken where ye stand. So, wha' can ah do fer ye this tayme?" I took a deep breath and leapt in with both feet.

"Have you ever heard of the Order of the Nine Seals?" I asked her, now holding my breath in anticipation. She didn't disappoint, actually hissing loud enough to be heard over the speakerphone.

"Dinna tawk ta me aboot them *gòrach pìosan de cac*!" Her accent flew off the chart as she descended back into Gaelic, but I could tell from her tone that whatever she had said was definitely not complimentary.

"OK, I'll take that as a 'yes, you've heard of them' combined with a 'no, you don't like them' then, shall I?" I responded glibly, which at least broke the tension by making her laugh.

"Guid guess, ya wazzock!" she replied. "So what's yer interest in them fanny flaps? An' why do ye think I'd be helpin' ye, after ye've bin insultin' me just noo?" I winced inwardly, accepting her slight rebuke and admitting to myself I hadn't exactly been very gentlemanly, nor even subtle.

"Well for one thing, I have no love for them so once I track them down, it's not going to be to buy them dinner," I said, thinking fast to come up with good reasons for her to join forces with me. "For another, this isn't about me. I'm concerned about someone who seems to have disappeared at the hands of the Order, and I'm trying to track them down so I can help her."

"Oho, so it's a her is it noo?" I could hear the sudden smile in her voice and wasn't sure whether that boded well or poorly for me. "Fine. Come roond tae me hoose. Ye'll hae tae ring tha bell tae ge' in the gates, an' we'll tawk." She gave me her address and hung up, so I scribbled it on a piece of paper then disconnected the speakerphone.

"Well, buddy, at least we have a chance at a lead," I said to Gauvain, turning to look at him. "I'm not sure what, when or how much, but I have a feeling this information is going to cost me in the end. I just hope to hell it's worth it." He looked at me and said nothing, but I felt his love and support flow through our link, letting me know he was with me no matter what.

I headed out through the shop with Vain on my shoulder, stopping so he could be admired by a customer and then letting Summer know where I was going (just in case Seirina decided to play any silly games and try to stop me from leaving her house later. I doubted it, but better safe than sorry). We went out to the car and I put the address into the satnav. I couldn't believe how much I'd come to depend on the modern gadgetry in this car in just the few short days since I'd had it. This car was almost magickal itself compared to my old one. Gauvain caught the thought and chuckled.

From my knowledge of your memories, I believe the appropriate phrase to use in this situation would be welcome to the twenty-first century you troglodyte! he thought at me, making me laugh and easing some of the tension I was feeling. I set off but decided to come up with a strategy for when we arrived.

"I don't know if Seirina is a magick user or not, so when we arrive I'll reach out and see what I can feel. If she is, which seems likely given her knowledge of the Order, you may as well come in with me in full form. If not, she'd be no real threat to me now so you can stay outside and keep watch." Gauvain nodded, then added his own thought.

If she is a magick user, what are you going to tell her about your abilities? he asked astutely, reminding me I hadn't had my powers the first time I had dealt with her.

"Good point," I replied, thinking quickly. "She'll definitely be able to tell I'm a magick user now, so I'll simply tell her I'm still figuring things out and learning what I can do. It's true to a certain degree, after all. She just doesn't need to know how much I've *already* got figured out." Gauvain chuckled again.

You're learning, he said simply, winking at me. It was little comments like this that made me sure Isis had gifted him with knowledge of his own, outside of what he had gleaned from my memories. I'd have to ask him some time but for right now, we had places to go and people to see.

We drove for about twenty-five minutes, ending up in a nice upscale suburban neighbourhood. Almost all of the properties were set back from the road with walls at the front, most having gates across their driveways. I found the correct one and pressed the button on the intercom on the gate-post. The voice that crackled out was pure Yorkshire, so clearly Seirina had at least one person with her. Either family or, more likely, a member of staff of some kind.

"Gavan Maddox to see Miss Crow. I believe she's expecting me," I said politely, and the gate began to swing open immediately in response. I drove slowly up the drive and parked by the front door. I had been reaching out with my magick since pulling up to the gate, and as I got closer to the house I could definitely feel something although I wasn't sure what. It was like no type of magick I had encountered before, but there was no mistaking the fact that it was magick never-the-less.

It felt heavy, cold and almost slimy against my awareness, making me want to shudder and take a long hot shower. Even if I had never dealt with Seirina before, this feeling would have put my hackles up. I focused my eyes into the magickal spectrum as I had learned in Aaru and saw a greyish haze surrounding the house, confirming my feeling.

I got out of the car and Gauvain joined me, sitting on my left shoulder as usual. I was going to have to find a way of fixing some padding to the shoulders of my clothes to protect against his claws. He did his best, but he did have to hold on. Then again, I supposed I could always protect them magickally. I needed to get out of the idea that everything had to be done the mundane way.

I shook my head and brought myself back to the here and now, walking up to the front door and ringing the bell. I drew my awareness in slightly, but kept it active, so I felt the approach of someone behind the door. Whoever they were they were certainly no magick user although the presence was different from anything I had previously felt. It must have been the owner of the voice on the intercom, although she herself was clearly something other than simply human, if my senses were accurate.

The door opened and a matronly woman stood there, immediately making me think housekeeper as opposed to anything else.

"Come in Mr Maddox, Ms Crow is waiting for you in the study," the broad Yorkshire accent was the same as over the intercom and I noted the Ms instead of Miss or Mrs, so clearly Seirina was staking claim to her independence. More power to her, I certainly had no problem with strong women.

I followed the housekeeper down the hall to the study, admiring the antique Welsh dresser laden with ornamental painted plates that we passed on the way. The intensity of the cold, slimy sensation increased as we went, clearly emanating from the door ahead. She knocked on the door, then opened it to announce me.

"Mr Maddox to see you, Ms Crow," she intoned politely.

"Thank ye, Mrs Wilson," came the familiar lilt, and I was shown in.

Seirina rose from behind her desk and came around it. As she came towards me, I glanced around the room. It was comfortable and welcoming and I noticed a large glass and wood tank occupying the wall behind her, something akin to a terrarium. Did she have a lizard familiar? I was sure I'd find out soon enough.

I could tell the feeling of magick was definitely coming from her as I could see streamers of energy rising to join the haze I had noticed outside. It was clear if I looked for it but disappeared when I refocused away from her aura. She seemed completely unaware of any power from me and I felt no psychic probing from her, so clearly she specialised in other fields. She did look very curiously at Gauvain, who eyed her just as suspiciously. I, meanwhile, was looking at Seirina in surprise.

While she had the fiery red hair of her Celtic ancestry, her skin was not the ultra-fair, freckled appearance one might expect. Instead she had a smooth, even tan. It was almost Mediterranean but a shade or two lighter. Her eyes were also not the expected green and were even mismatched, the right one being amber and the left one ice blue. She was dressed totally opposite to what I had expected, too.

No flowing gown, no pendants. Instead she was wearing a simple (but expensive looking) summer dress with an abstract semi-floral print. She was also quite short, probably only five foot two or three, but the magickal aura radiating off of her like heat from a bonfire was warning enough not to underestimate her. She looked me up and down as if assessing a horse for sale (although she stopped short of inspecting my teeth).

"Welcome tae me hawme, Gavan," she said cordially, holding out her hand. I reached out to shake it, and as my skin touched hers I felt her reaching through the physical link. I firmly but gently blocked her attempt and her eyes flew to meet mine with a new level of respect and fresh assessment.

"A pleasure to finally meet you in person," I replied, letting go of her fingers with a smile.

"Och, ye say that noo yer reet afore me, bu' awnly minutes agaw ye was awmost sayin' ah was a demon," she looked sternly at me and the smile slipped from my face.

"Uh, no, that wasn't what I..." I rushed to try to repair my earlier misstep and stumbled in the face of her frosty disapproval. She glowered at me as my words dried up and then she turned, heading back around her desk to sit down.

"So wha' the hell did ye do tae get mixed up wi' them arsebadgers in the Order?" She gestured for me to take one of the chairs in front of her desk.

"Much the same as with our previous dealing, I was commissioned to find something for them," I replied, sitting down. "It didn't work out the way they wanted, and now they're all bent out of shape about it. They also, by extension, seem to be pissed at the woman who was their liaison with me since she seems to have disappeared and her phone number has been disconnected. She did nothing wrong, but the head of the Order met with me and called me Gavin instead of Gavan. It seemed to make him unable to form a psychic link to me, which pissed him off even more, and he's probably blaming her for his mistake."

"Aye, that'd be reet," she said thoughtfully, her chill demeanour dissipating somewhat in her growing interest. "No havin' yer reet kennin' is like no' havin' any knowledge of ye at aw'. A reet kennin' gies ye poower o'er a pairson, tha's wha' he must hae wanted o'er ye. He cuid nae get it wi'oot yer kennin'." Gauvain and I looked at each other at the end of her little exposition and burst out laughing.

"I'm sorry," I gasped, "I honestly mean no disrespect, and I suspect you're absolutely right. It's just your accent got thicker as you got more thoughtful until you finally sounded like Billy Connelly crossed with Mel Gibson portraying William Wallace. Any second I was expecting you to stand up and yell FREEDOOOOOMM!" She looked at us both and gave a half smile and a gentle nod.

"Yeah, well, most people like the idea of the wee Highland lassie when they come asking for what I can provide. It appeals to their sense of the macabre. The image of primitive folk casting curses and spells," she said smoothly, raising one eyebrow at me and tilting her head, hinting at the multiple layers of intricacy in her carefully woven persona.

My laughter dried up and I stared at her with my mouth open as she spoke. Her accent was almost undetectable now: it was all an act! I suddenly realised I had no idea what about her was real and what was façade.

Fuck it, I thought. I need to know just what the hell I'm dealing with, and the longer I piss about the longer that asshole has to work on Angelica. I reached out with my mind, easily connecting with her thoughts as I ignored my discomfort at intruding on her privacy and my distaste for the feel of her magick.

She felt me enter her consciousness, as evidenced by the way her eyes locked to mine and widened significantly. There was nothing she could do to stop me, however, and I looked through her memories to find out just who she really was and what she was really about. I heard a rustling from the tank behind her, no doubt the tank's occupant was becoming agitated at the displeasure its partner was experiencing.

As I understood, I withdrew so fast she actually bounced back in her chair. She was no mere dabbler and charm spinner. She was an enchantress, a necromancer, and she was over three hundred and fifty years old!

Chapter 12

She was looking at me with as much fear and distrust as I felt for her right at that moment. Clearly she had felt my strength and ability when I touched her mind and she had no clue what I was capable of, the same as I had very little knowledge of her arts. I knew they *existed*, but that was about it. From what I had seen in her mind, while she was certainly powerful and knowledgeable within her own fields, she could no more do what I could than she could fly to the moon by flapping her arms.

I wiped the cold sheen of sweat off my forehead with my handkerchief and swallowed dryly, while Gauvain screeched and flapped his wings at my sudden movement and disquiet. I winced as I suddenly felt a reduction in my power access, much as when I had left the wildlife park, as my assault on Seirina's mind came back to karmically bite me in the ass. I took a deep breath, then sat back in the chair. I could still hear a rustling from behind her which ceased when she simply raised one hand above her shoulder, clearly signalling whatever it was to calm down.

"I'm sorry, I shouldn't have done that. My anxiety over my friend made me forget my manners, for which I apologise." I shifted in my chair feeling as awkward and disgusted with myself as if I'd just peeked in on her when she was in the shower.

To my surprise her face softened, and she actually smiled at me. I was unsure how to respond, given her earlier attitude and knowing what she was. Given her dual nature, I doubted I would ever be truly comfortable or relaxed around her.

"I understand, I felt your concern for her come across your connection. Your worry is making your control slip a little," she said kindly. "As an enchantress, I'm well aware of what love can make people do." My eyes flew open and I put my hands up in front of me, making Gauvain finally give up on my shoulder and glide to the back of the chair next to me.

"Woah, woah, woah! Nobody said anything about the L word!" I now felt uncomfortable for a wholly different reason. "We've only met three times over about a week and a half, all to do with work. Yes, I find her attractive, but I'm concerned for her as a person. Her boss is pissed off and is a nasty piece of work; secondly she's been the one in contact with me, so he'll blame the failure on her; lastly, her phone's been disconnected. I never said ANYTHING about *love*."

My words ran together and I almost tripped over my own tongue as I rushed to set her straight. I could hear Vain laughing in my head, but I ignored him. Seirina on the other hand just crossed her arms and pursed her lips.

"It's always the same, a hooked fish only starts to struggle after it's too late." I glowered at her silently, which made her shake her head like an exasperated teacher. She fixed me with a look I could only describe as old-fashioned, sighing deeply at my continued denials.

"OK, so I *may* possibly be developing some feelings for her…" Her eyes just rolled up to the ceiling and she shook her head. "Hey, gimme a break here, I'm trying –"

"Very," she interrupted dryly, making me smile as it was one of my favourite responses as well. I gave her a similarly old-fashioned look in reply.

"Hardy ha. Anyway, now you understand my motives and reasons, how about sharing some of yours? Why are you so against this Order? Have you dealt with them before?"

"You might say that." She winced and rubbed at her left shoulder, appearing lost in thought and memory for a moment. There was a knock at the door followed by it opening, and Mrs Wilson brought in a tray with a teapot, cups, milk, sugar and even a plate of biscuits, placing it on the desk. She nodded to Seirina who smiled in thanks and then Mrs Wilson walked out, quietly closing the door behind her.

I looked suspiciously at the tray, reaching out to feel if there was anything magickal about it. Seirina saw what I was doing, shook her head, sighed and then poured two cups before adding milk to one and taking a sip.

"This is *precisely* why I keep my abilities a secret. I haven't put any zombifying juju beans into the tea. I didn't *choose* to be a necromancer; it's the power I was born with. That and the enchantress abilities kicked in when I hit puberty, and I managed to ensnare all four brothers in one family before I even knew. That got *seriously* messy, ending up getting my parents and me driven from our second village. The first was after I managed to somehow resurrect a mouse skeleton at age twelve and an old biddy in the village saw me playing with it.

"After that, my parents found a local wise woman. That's what we called them back then in the Highlands, or the less charitable called her a *bana-bhuidseach* which means witch. Anyway, she taught me to control my abilities. It took years of training, and that training is what brought me to the attention of the Order."

As she talked I relaxed and absently reached for the other cup of tea, adding milk and taking a piece of shortbread. I crossed my legs, putting my ankle on my knee, and Vain hopped over to sit on my raised leg. I stroked his feathers, soothing us both as Seirina continued her tale.

"Necromancers aren't inherently evil, despite what most people think. The arts we have are certainly darker than most, and definitely more open to abuse, but like any magick it all depends on the intention of the wielder. The Order doesn't have any true necromancers. They've got a couple of enchantresses who they use as honey-traps for unwary businessmen or politicians, and they have a couple of people who have *studied* necromancy but they can't do much. *Born* necromancers like me are really rare, and the few I knew of have all been hunted down for some of the shit they've pulled.

"The Order wants as many magick users of different types as they can get, as well as different kinds of mystical and legendary creatures and beings: vampires, weres and the like. From what I can tell, they've been collecting followers and building their ranks for almost two hundred years. When they found out about me they tried to recruit me, first with promises of protection and help. Well I was already over a hundred and fifty, so that was like a child offering to protect his uncle. They then eventually threatened me and mine if I didn't go along with them. I refused and they took my husband, the only mundane man who ever accepted me for who and what I was without any enchanting tricks." I looked at her stunned, now understanding her hatred of the Order and everyone in it.

"When did they take him?" I asked sympathetically. "Maybe we can save him when I go after Angelica." She started shaking her head even before I had finished speaking.

"That was over a hundred and fifty years ago and besides, there's nothing to rescue."

"What do you mean?" I asked and she looked at me sorrowfully.

"Their leader, the one you met with, what do you know about him?" she asked. I thought back to my encounter with him (had it really only been this morning?) then my subsequent Googling.

"He has some psychic ability, but it's weak. That may have been the whole wrong name thing I mentioned earlier. He also has some kind of hold over the twins who were with him. He looks young but speaks old, and I don't think that was even his body. I looked up his name, Atma Mumm, and found out it translates to 'soul eater', which I'm guessing is his idea of a joke." She looked at me, apparently impressed that I had found out or deduced so much so fast.

"Not bad, kid, that's more than I found out in my first two years of dealings with them. Only one thing: his name is no joke. I don't know exactly what he is; I've never been able to find out. He changes bodies every few months or years, depending how tired he gets of them or how damaged they become. He seems to burn them up if he stays in them too long, so he's clearly a being of significant power. Then when he moves to a new body, he actually consumes the soul that's already there. I've also seen him consume a soul without taking over the body. That's how I know my husband is gone, and why I hate him so much. One of the bodies he's taken and used up, one of the souls he so casually ate, was my love. The sick bastard made me watch as it happened."

She turned away as the tears ran down her face, so I stood up, dislodging Gauvain who flew back to the other chair, then I walked around the desk. I knelt next to her and offered her my handkerchief, then took her hand.

"I am *so* sorry. I can't imagine what you went through, but I can promise you this: Once I've rescued Angelica, you and I are going to find every other magick user or creature that the Order has coerced, bereaved, blackmailed, stolen from, or even just mildly inconvenienced. Then we're going to destroy that bunch of arse-reaming cockwombles once and for all. I'll even save their illustrious head twatface just for you." She looked at me and her face hardened, her tears disappearing like snowflakes under a blowtorch.

"Done. You help me destroy the Order and I'm yours for life." I fell onto my butt as I scooted away from her.

"Umm, that's very flattering, but..." She actually laughed darkly at my sudden discomfort.

"I didn't mean like *that*, you fool. Although you don't know what you're missing. After all, I *am* an enchantress..." She allowed her power to blaze briefly in her eyes, touching for a moment something within me that made me understand that if she wanted to, she could have me grovelling at her feet with no will of my own. As quickly as it appeared it vanished, and I found my trousers uncomfortably tight through no desire of my own. "I just meant that if you ever need *anything*, I'll be there." I wiped my brow in a not altogether exaggerated motion.

"Phew, *that* was a close one!" I laughed nervously, desperately trying to find my equilibrium after her shocking display. I walked back to my chair and sat down, trying to surreptitiously find a comfortable position in my aroused state. She looked at me knowingly, not fooled for a moment.

"Speaking of life, I do have a question," I continued, trying to change the subject to safer ground. She looked expectantly at me and nodded to give me permission. "How are you as old as you are but looking like you're in your early thirties? Is it part of being a necromancer? Part of your enchantress abilities?" She looked surprised but smiled at my compliment regarding her apparent youthful appearance.

"Did your parents never teach you about this?" she asked in amazement.

"Um, my parents had no magick," I replied guilelessly. I saw the first sign of shock I had observed on her face since I had entered her mind so rudely.

"You're a First?" she asked me in surprise. My quizzical look told her I had no idea what she was talking about, so she continued to explain. "Sorry, a First means the first member of a family to have magick. It's not uncommon, as there's always got to be a First somewhere along the line, quite obviously. It is, however, unheard of as far as I'm aware for a First to be as strong as you." I smiled and thanked her but waited to see what else she had to tell me.

"In answer to your question, almost all magick users have significantly extended lifespans. As humans we're not immortal, but there have been mages who have lived over fifteen hundred years." I sat back in my chair at her comment, completely stunned.

"You said as humans. Does that mean you're aware of races that *are* immortal?" I asked, starting to feel a creeping sense of unease. I remembered Isis' cryptic smile in response to my death and taxes quip about nothing being certain, and I knew she herself was well over four thousand years old.

"There are certainly races with individuals that have been around for millennia, often creeping into legends as gods or other beings, but I honestly don't know about true immortality." Seirina told me thoughtfully. "Every being or race I've ever heard of can be killed eventually *somehow*, so I don't think any being is truly immortal to the point of being unkillable. The so-called gods and demons (which are pretty much the same, just varying in their actions) most certainly have vastly extended lifespans compared to us."

Oh, crap! Now I knew what Isis had been smiling about. My lifespan was apparently already extended because of my having magick, and then she helped me to infuse myself with the power of her Veil. I had a funny feeling that fifteen hundred was now going to be barely middle-aged for me, if I survived that long!

"Now I have a question," Seirina said, looking at me curiously. "If you're a First, how the hell did you get so powerful? Who taught you?

And why did you even need my help to track down that grimoire a couple of years ago?"

I had thought this might come up, especially after Gauvain's astute comment earlier. I trusted Seirina more now than before, but I still wasn't prepared to tell her *everything*. We had only just met, after all, and I was still significantly off balance around her. I told her the same story I had told Angelica and by extension, the Order. She expressed her amazement that I had become so used to my magick after just a couple of weeks, but I could tell she thought there was more to the story. She wasn't wrong, but that would have to wait until we knew each other a little better and trusted each other quite a bit more than we did right now.

"OK, now that we've exchanged potted origin stories, how about we get this superhero team-up moving?" I said, holding myself back from an Avengers joke. "Where can I find those motherfuckers?"

Chapter 13

"From what I saw when they took me to their offices, plus overhearing conversations while I was there, they're based in the Yorkshire Dales," she said, looking a lot more serious all of a sudden. "An ancient fortress called Bolton Castle."

"Seriously?" I replied in surprise, recalling a trip I had made a few years ago during the summer. "That's a national monument. They have educational trips for schoolkids, they do falconry experiences in the grounds, they have weddings on a regular basis, and they even have a Magickal Mayhem event to invite kids to the Bolton Castle School of Magick and Design to make their own witch or wizard hat and mix potions; it's all fake of course. But how the hell could an organisation like the Order remain hidden in such a well-travelled monument?"

"There're always some restricted areas in a place like that, so they have a few offices in those places, but then they've got more space underground. It's apparently like an entire hidden building," she told me, seeming to be lost in her memories as she spoke. "They've got meeting rooms and offices, recreational areas, even prisoner holding cells and interrogation rooms. The only thing I could never learn was how to get down there. I know there has to be some kind of secret staircase inside, but you'd have to go through their offices to find that. They probably also have access from somewhere in the grounds, but I could never find it."

I couldn't believe it. I'd even been to Bolton Castle when I was a kid one holiday, memories of which had prompted my return trip. One thing I did remember, which popped into my mind now, was they had several areas in the gardens that were used for different activities. The entrance could be in any one of them, or even one of the outbuildings. This wasn't going to be easy.

"Have you done any research on the castle itself?" I asked absently. I was thinking over the potential difficulties and pitfalls of assaulting not just an Order stronghold but one that was in an actual friggin' castle, and a National Trust monument open to the public to boot! That meant there would be significant numbers of innocent mundanes around, a large percentage of whom would be children.

"What do you mean?" she asked me, appearing a little confused. "I've been out there and looked around dozens of times and listened to the tour guides." I smiled and shook my head.

"That's the one weakness of having had magick all your life," I winked at her impudently. "You forget about the simple mundane way of doing things. Have you Googled it?" Seirina looked at me as if I was nuts.

"I'm not an idiot, but what could Google tell me that I didn't already live through?" I'd forgotten for a moment just how old she was.

"You're not *that* old," I said, doing a quick search on my phone. "The castle was built in 1378. Even you weren't around back then!" She actually looked surprised at the information I'd unearthed.

"Oh! I didn't realise it was quite as old as that," she replied. I scanned down some information from a couple of sites on my phone, including the official Bolton Castle site.

"Mary Queen of Scots was held there for quite a while, and an abbot hid there during Henry VIII's dissolution of the monasteries."

"OK, well that's fascinating history, but what use is that to us?" Seirina asked with some asperity. "We're not writing a paper on the history of the place, we're trying to figure out where those bastards are hiding."

"And that's the point," I replied patiently. "If they had people hiding there, there are likely to be priest holes and secret tunnels. I also noticed they hold a ghost hunting event. What do you think the chances are that there are actual ghosts there that an experienced necromancer such as yourself didn't detect, as opposed to various people or creatures moving about and using magick that mundane minds translate into ghosts?" Seirina stared at me with her mouth slightly open in surprise.

"Oh my gods, I never even considered that! How the hell did I miss something so obvious?" she continued, now clearly irritated with herself. I smiled in sympathy, understanding now *why* she was so motivated.

"Hey, it's just being used to using different resources," I told her. "Up until recently I had no magickal options, so I made do with the mundane way of doing things and I got pretty decent at it. Now I have to sometimes remind myself there's a magickal solution to a problem rather than struggling with a mundane issue, and the reverse can also be true. If you only look at a problem magickally, you can miss a perfectly sensible and simple mundane solution. I'm hoping *that* is going to be something the Order and its members have overlooked as well, since most if not all of them will have had their magick all their lives." Her face took on an arrested look as she considered what I had said and as she thought about its implications.

"They'll have made sure none of the mundane visitors to the castle are able to just stumble into somewhere they don't want them going," Seirina said thoughtfully, "so the entrances will probably require some kind of magick to get in…"

"What about any of their members who can't use magick?" I said, trying to think of all the possibilities. "Can all non-human species use magick? You said they have all sorts of creatures among their ranks, plus some human-derived species like weres and vampires. Does having any degree of the supernatural in their make-up mean they can actually *use* magick, or are they just powered by it but unable to truly wield it?" She looked at me in amazement at my completely unfamiliar way of analysing things.

"You're thinking about magickal problems using mundane terms," she remarked in surprise. "I've never known anyone else do that before. The magickal world doesn't have scientists to analyse everything. Those of us aware of it just accept it the way it is. If someone's a vampire, then they're a vampire, we don't study them to figure out what makes them tick." I smiled, thinking back to Danu's reaction to my use of science when I learned magickal techniques.

"Yeah, I've heard that said before," I said without thinking. Seirina looked curiously at me at my statement, but let it slide. I cursed inwardly for my slip. I'd have to watch myself: I was getting used to being around her and my caution was starting to relax, which could lead to future indiscretions if I wasn't careful. That was all the more likely with her being an enchantress, as she was hardwired to get men to like and trust her even without being aware of it.

"So anyway, can they all use magick?" I asked, trying to divert her attention back to the matter in hand.

"Actually no, many of them are completely helpless in the magickal arena," she replied. "They have enhanced abilities like strength and speed just as the legends say, but that doesn't give them magick."

"In that case, the Order will have to make their headquarters accessible to those without magick. Maybe if they have enhanced strength, that would be their way in," I theorised. "It would still have to be something a standard mundane couldn't manage."

"I'm afraid any more than that, you'll have to discover when you're there," Seirina said pragmatically. "We can theorise all day, but you'd need to actually be there to try to discover the entrance. You might even need to watch them for a while to try to work out exactly how they come and go."

"Gauvain might be able to help with that," I said, reaching out to stroke him. "With them having falconry displays, he'll fit right in." Seirina looked at me like I was insane.

"He's very pretty, but how can a bird help?" she scoffed.

You call yourself a magick user? Gauvain said in disgust, projecting to both of us. *Have you never heard of a familiar before?* Seirina looked shocked.

"Of course," she said indignantly, "but finding a familiar takes a large amount of luck, trial and error, followed by a period of learning together to become used to each other. If you've only had your magick for two weeks, there's no *way* you could have developed a bond. There's something you're not telling me." Gauvain and I looked at each other awkwardly, and he shuffled on the back of the chair.

Oops. My sincere apologies Gavan, I forgot myself, he said. I rolled my eyes, but the cat was already out of the bag, so I just had to make the best of it. I turned to Seirina and took a deep breath.

"You're right, I haven't told you everything, but we don't have time to get into it all right now. Also no disrespect, but you haven't told me the details of your training so why would you expect me to share all my intimate details with you?" She looked between the two of us a few times before shaking her head and smiling.

"You're one of the most unusual individuals I think I've ever met," she pronounced, stabbing the surface of her desk with her index finger in time to her last two words. "You were born with magick but locked it as a child so it never flowered naturally when it should have in your early teens. Then you get it unlocked by some artefact you were apparently destined to find and learned to use your magick faster than anyone I've ever even heard of." I shrugged and grinned.

"One day, *if* we develop enough trust, I'll tell you more. For now, you know all you need to." I smiled at her and she shook her head, rolling her eyes again at my mistrust despite her help thus far.

"Fine, but I'm going to hold you to that," she stated firmly, holding up a warning finger.

"So what now?" I asked, eager to get on with actually trying to save Angelica before Atma decided to eat her soul. "Can we get going and head up to Bolton Castle? The sooner we get there, the sooner we can figure out how to get in and start trying to rescue my friend." Seirina smiled but shook her head.

"If I came with you, your cover would be blown before you even got out of your car. Don't forget, they tried to recruit me and then I was watching them for years. They'd spot me in seconds." Gauvain lifted his head and looked at me.

Gavan, if she does not accompany us, you will have free reign to use your abilities. Why not utilise your shape-shifting to sneak in? he suggested. *Or obtain an image of the inside from someone's mind and teleport in? It enables us to consider more options if there is just the two of us.* I nodded thoughtfully, and Seirina looked relieved. I realised she hadn't heard Gauvain's suggestions, so I continued on as if responding to her last comment.

"You're right, probably best if you stay here," I agreed with her. "You might want to start reaching out to the magickal community to see who has issues with the Order. Start building a list of people and creatures who might be interested in joining us. I might be able to get away with a sneak rescue this time, but I seriously doubt we'll be able to take the whole Order down the same way. That's going to take numbers."

She nodded sharply, then turned to open a cabinet behind her. To my surprise she got out an old-fashioned rolodex, stuffed full of contact cards. I had to stop myself from bursting out laughing but my face betrayed me, and she narrowed her eyes at me.

"Yes, I'm still using pencil and paper, shut up," she said and I lost the fight, bursting out laughing. "It never crashes, can't be hacked, and doesn't need to be plugged in to be useful," she continued.

"Hey, I'm a big fan of things that can get the job done without needing batteries," I replied, winking suggestively at her. Her eyes flared briefly with the same power I had seen earlier and she dropped back into her broad Scottish accent.

"Aye, ye gotta prefair it when ye dinnae need artificial help!" I raised my eyebrows in surprise at this first evidence of humour. I smiled, then stood up and beckoned Gauvain who flew up onto my shoulder. Seirina stood up to walk us out, already seeming to be focused on her task.

"I'll start tentatively sounding a few likely people out. You just make sure you make it back in one piece." When we reached the front door, she reached up to lay her hand on my shoulder.

"Good luck," she said, then turned to walk back to her office. Mrs Wilson opened the door and ushered me out, closing the door behind me. I took a deep breath and squared my shoulders, then headed to the car to start my trip north.

Chapter 14

Once again I thanked the gods for satnav. With Bolton Castle being a tourist attraction, it was listed under points of interest so I just set off according to the angry woman's instructions. (Seriously, why do satnavs always sound like you've just slept with their best friend?) According to the computer it was about a two-hour drive, so I used the hands-free system to call the shop and update Summer on what was going on. I didn't give her any specifics, just in case, but simply said I had a lead and was following it so might not be in for a couple of days.

Since most of the drive was on main roads, I could leave the cruise control to handle the speed which allowed me to let part of my mind think about how to deal with things when I arrived. Gauvain's suggestion of using some of my magickal abilities was a good one, but how? Any magick user would know in seconds if I started rooting around in their heads for images clear enough to teleport. I seriously doubted people would just ignore a frickin' enormous wolf strolling around, and I couldn't just start ripping up great chunks of the landscape using telekinesis.

I thought a bit more and started idly wondering about invisibility. Pretty much every guy has fantasised at some point when they're growing up about becoming invisible and sneaking into the girls' changing room or creeping into a bank vault. (I thought about both. Hey, if I did the first I'd need the second for bail money!) I knew there were various spells purported to create invisibility, and I started thinking about how they might work, once again remembering Danu's advice on understanding the method and what was being achieved rather than just blindly using a spell.

There were scientific methods of creating the illusion such as small cameras on one side of an object and display plates on the other, like they did on the flying ships in *Avengers*. Then there were science fiction methods such as the cloaking devices in *Star Trek*. Plenty of fictional characters had also had various magickal invisibility techniques, like Harry Potter with his cloak. They say write what you know, so maybe one or more of these writers had actually had some first-hand experience.

I needed to work out the least energy-intense way of creating invisibility, otherwise I wouldn't be able to maintain it for long and the energy surge would be felt by every magick user within ten miles.

I needed a bathroom break after Seirina's tea, so I pulled off at a motorway service station and decided to take a few minutes to try various techniques. After a few attempts, I was able to magically bend the light around myself, creating an effect similar to the eponymous alien in *Predator* but more efficient. If I moved too fast it became obvious, so no running, but at a simple walking pace it was really quite effective. Gauvain made me laugh by telling me to stay away from the La Perla boutique once I had it mastered, then I got back in the car and set off again.

Now that I had a plan, I enjoyed the drive and used the time to absorb some of the energy from the wind by opening all the windows. I removed the kinetic energy of the incoming air, so we still didn't get blown about. The energy was poured into Seren, making the image of the wings glow like a beacon to me, but it was still not even close to one percent full. If I ever managed to fill that thing, I mused idly, I'd probably be able to shift the moon single-handedly. That would give a whole different meaning to mooning someone!

As we drove into the Yorkshire Dales, the countryside changed to rolling fields and hills. I had forgotten just how nice the Dales were. One of the perils of living nearby was that you started taking such things for granted. Other than the colour of the grass it reminded me a little of Aaru, and I absent-mindedly wondered how my friends were doing.

I knew they would have returned to their normal formless existence, but I still thought of them as the physical beings I had spent so much time with. I hoped Roman and Poppy were happy together and mused over how reproduction might happen for formless beings. Would they merge energies in some way? The mind boggled. I decided I'd happily stick with the good old human method on that one!

That thought led me inexorably back to Angelica, which wiped the smile from my face and kicked my nerves into high gear along with a healthy dose of stomach snakes as I considered what Atma might be doing to her in his displeasure. I gripped the steering wheel tighter and put my foot down just a little harder in my desire to get there as soon as I could, locking the cruise control into the higher speed.

I arrived at the car-park for the castle, beating the satnav trip time by twelve minutes, and found a space near the back under some trees. Gauvain hopped to the windowsill on his side of the car, then flew off to get an overview of the grounds. I stayed in the car to begin with, closed my eyes and reached out to him to merge and see through his eyes like we'd practiced in Aaru. Our regular use of this was making it easier and easier, the walls between our minds less formidable as the days went by. If we kept going at this rate, we might ultimately achieve a state where we were thinking completely in sync and even merging our identities.

We saw the church on the same side of the road as the car-park, with the castle looming on the opposite side. The courtyard in the centre was largely in shadow as it was getting later in the day now, but my thought was that the late hour would mean most tourists would be leaving and heading home. That should hopefully mean any people still around would be either staff or members of the Order.

The gardens were divided up into different sections, one clearly set up as a maze. The area next to it was a flat, open expanse that the castle's website had said was used for falconry displays. The other side of the maze looked to be set up as a vegetable garden, and there were some ornamental garden areas as well. Nothing in the grounds screamed secret entrance, so Gauvain perched on the corner of the south west tower to keep a watch over the grounds.

Meanwhile I locked the car and strolled along the road to the church to have a look since, with it being an active parish church, it would be open much later than the castle. I slipped into a pew at the back and sat down, bowing my head as if in prayer and reaching out with my magickal senses.

I immediately became aware of two individuals, one in the choir stall and one in the pews at the front. Neither one reached out to me psychically but from their energy signatures I could feel they were both more than human. Not having been around any of the classical monster types, I had no idea what they were other than one thing. Their presence was a blaring siren that I was in the right place.

A slick of perspiration broke out on my forehead, and I hoped the smell from the hanging censer would help hide my scent from the watchers, whatever they might be. I was really going to have to work on my anxiety, since pumping out my sweat around creatures with enhanced senses of smell could definitely become a problem.

I spent only a little longer in simulated prayer, then walked over to light a votive candle in the rack, deciding to ask for protection for Angelica as I did so. I'd found out that many (if not all) of the gods were real, and I could use all the help I could get, so why not?

Then I walked out of the building without so much as looking at either of the sentries, trying to appear to be just an innocent tourist who'd stopped in to pray before heading home. As soon as I was out, I headed back to the car and called Gauvain to me. I took the precaution of memorising the area where I was parked as a useful landing zone for teleportation.

He joined me at the car and we got in, deciding to find a place to get some food and plan our next move. I found a drive-thru Burger King since I couldn't exactly take Gauvain into a village pub, so I got him some chicken nuggets while I decided on a burger, fries and a milkshake. We found a quiet lay-by on a hill and watched the sunset as we ate, considering how to proceed.

Gauvain agreed that he was far too visible to come along in full form, so he would merge with the claw on my wrist. He would therefore be with me if needed but would remain otherwise undetected. I would use my new invisibility to sneak into the church and keep watch to see if I could spot anyone using a secret entrance of some kind.

I had a sudden thought and Googled the church on my phone, but I could find no record of an underground crypt or any catacombs that would have been a perfect entry point to any secret tunnels. Oh well, back to plan A.

I decided to leave the car in the lay-by so it wouldn't be found near the castle by the Order, but I waited until the sun had fully set before heading back. There was always the risk that the setting sun would increase supernatural presences around the grounds, but I hoped the darkness would cut both ways by enhancing the effectiveness of my invisibility.

Gauvain descended into the claw on my wrist and I visualised the shadowed end of the parking area that I had committed to memory. I teleported and immediately bent the light around myself, finding that in the darkness it was indeed even more effective. I grinned invisibly, and whispered "cloaking device active, captain" to myself. Gauvain laughed in my head at my nerdiness.

I walked the length of the car park on the grass verge to avoid my footsteps crunching in the gravel, making my way to the front door of the church. It was closed and there was no way I could just open it and walk in. Invisible or not, I'd be noticed straight away. My only option was to wait until someone came out and sneak in before the door closed. I reached out gently with my mind and felt someone moving towards the side of the building.

I crept around the corner in time to see a figure step outside. I was too far away to sneak in, but I saw the flare of a lighter as whoever it was lit up a cigarette. Thank heavens for bad habits! I stayed nearby and waited for him to finish so I could tailgate him inside. I had no choice but to remain downwind in case he had an enhanced sense of smell as I had considered earlier, but I used magick to keep the smoke away from my face otherwise I'd have ended up coughing and thereby revealed my presence. I picked up a small stone in preparation and waited for my chance.

He took one last drag and ground the butt out under his toe, then turned and pulled the door open. I threw the pebble into the bushes behind him and as he turned towards the sudden noise, I slipped past him into the church. I kept moving forward to prevent the watcher bumping into me as he came back in, then moved to the side once the short entrance hall met the main body of the church.

I crept around the edge but found no signs of a tunnel or stairs heading down. I knew there had to be an entrance somewhere, but damned if I could find it. I found a secluded corner near the confessional and settled down to wait.

It had already been a long and exciting day, and I found my head nodding onto my chest. I pinched the skin inside my wrist to wake myself up, and asked Gauvain to talk to me to help me stay alert. Since Isis had linked us, he already had access to all my memories of sci-fi shows and books, but he had his own opinions of what he had seen in my recollections.

We started discussing some of the shows I had watched back in the eighties and nineties, revelling in and laughing at the cheesiness of some of the depictions. Some of the shows had dealt with magick and we mocked the blatant, over the top 'Hollyweirdness' of the imagery they used. We also enjoyed the simple act of sharing our thoughts, reinforcing our link and reaffirming our bond.

I was beginning to think nothing was going to happen tonight and I'd have to come back tomorrow, but at around half past one there came a knock at the side door in a complex pattern. This was clearly a pre-arranged code since the smoker, who had been out a few more times since I snuck in, went to the door and opened it.

Three individuals walked in. One man, one woman, and one seven-foot, green-skinned troll-looking motherfucker that I had no idea what gender it was. The smoker and the other watcher led them towards the altar, and I stood up to creep along behind them. This was it!

Chapter 15

As soon as I got within ten feet of the new arrivals, I stopped worrying about anyone picking up my scent. That troll-thing exuded enough musk to keep twenty perfume companies running for a decade. I reinstated the filter in front of my face to prevent me from gagging, since the splattering of regurgitated fast food hitting the stone floor just might be a bit of a giveaway that someone was here.

The two watchers went to either end of the stone altar and crouched down. They tilted it towards the back of the church and slid their fingers underneath. They then heaved it up which resulted in the grinding sound of stone on stone. They lifted the huge block of masonry slightly, then moved it back towards the stained glass window at the end of the church, revealing a gaping hole underneath with stairs inside leading underground.

The new arrivals nodded at the two watchers and headed towards the stairs. The watchers were panting from the effort and their eyes had gone red. I looked at their open mouths and saw fangs, clearly having popped due to the strain of moving such a huge lump of rock. No wonder no one had ever discovered the entrance to the Order's tunnels. Without supernatural strength it was impossible, and even then it took two and was *still* a struggle!

After a second to catch their lack of breath the two vampires, since that's what they clearly were, crouched at the ends of the altar in preparation to replace it. I darted forward and onto the staircase, mentally crossing my fingers and hoping the other three had moved on far enough that I wouldn't simply go barrelling into them on the way down.

The light from above was cut off with a grinding and a thump as the altar was replaced, but suddenly bulbs flared to life along the walls. Replacing the altar must have completed a circuit, pressed a switch or pressure plate, activating the lights. The walls were rough, unfinished stone and the steps were so old, the procession of feet over the years had worn them to a curve in the centre. Based on the degree of traffic that seemed to have passed through, these tunnels may have started out as an escape route dug during the time of the Tudors. However, I'd bet they had a different mode of access back then and not two vampire doormen!

I was expecting the tunnels to continue in this vein, with dirt walls and floors along with chambers hacked out to resemble caves. Instead, as we rounded the corner at the bottom of the stairs, I found myself staring down what appeared to be the corridor of an office building that could have been in central London. Someone had clearly been watching *Resident Evil* at some point and copied the idea of an underground base, although this was real.

They had obviously used magick to create their complex undetected, and expanded it as needed. This must have taken decades to create and probably overloaded the abilities of dozens of magick users in the process. No wonder Atma Mumm had gone through so many bodies. Channelling this kind of power through a vessel that wasn't used to it would burn it out like running a Smart car on high performance rocket fuel.

I could tell by the feel of the lights as we passed that they were powered by magick, so there would be no draw from the national grid to betray their location. I just didn't want to know where they sent the contents of the toilets when they were flushed! There were no windows, real or magickal, so they hadn't copied the film that closely. What they did have were plenty of paintings of countryside landscapes and beach scenes to lighten the walls.

I suddenly realised that while I had been standing with my mouth open like some Cub Scout on his first visit to a whore house, the three I had been following had disappeared into the maze of corridors and offices. Still, I was inside. Now I just had to figure out where they might be keeping Angelica.

Since the place clearly used magick to function, once I found her I could try to translocate us both out. At least unless they had some way of blocking that particular ability. I'd cross that bridge when I came to it, but for now the problem would be finding her in the first place.

I thought about trying to follow the musk from the big green stink machine I had tailed in here, but they must have included some kind of magickal air filtration/conditioning system in here. It obviously filtered the carbon dioxide out and replenished the oxygen, but it apparently also filtered out the various body odours of the different creatures that the Order had working down here.

For once, I was actually thankful for their foresight, as it did at least keep me breathing without gagging. It would also keep some of the more nasally sensitive among them from detecting my far more pleasant after-shave while I wandered around trying to find my way. I made sure my invisibility cloak was still in place and stuck close to the walls, trying to keep out of the way of anyone or any*thing* I might encounter.

Fortunately, unlike a real office block, the halls here were not a bustling hive of executives and mail carts. At least not at this ungodly hour of the night, although seeing a werewolf stick its head out of a door and yell, "Who let that foul smelling green fucker back in here?" before ducking back in and slamming the door will forever be ranked as one of the more surreal experiences of my life. That includes the purple grass of Aaru.

I found some elevators which appeared to be surrounded by a green haze of magick when I looked at them with my altered vision (I really needed to come up with a cool name for that, like spidey sense but better). I wasn't sure if that was simply powering them or also acting as some kind of arcane ID check, so I decided to forgo the convenience and stick with the stairs.

I knew they had to have them somewhere for those creatures that either couldn't operate the elevators or wouldn't fit. I just needed to find them. I had no idea if the corridors were so deserted due to the late hour or if they would be like this all the time, but I couldn't afford to waste time catching forty winks. I used some of the energy I had been saving in Seren to wake me up (better than two Pro Plus, a Red Bull and eight shots of espresso), and set off to look for the way down to the next floor.

The door to the stairs was on the opposite side of the hall from the bank of lifts, just a little further down. I looked up and down the hall to make sure no one was watching, then crept through into the stairwell. The stairs were certainly big enough to take creatures even larger than the troll I had seen, I just had to hope I didn't run into one.

I looked over the railing and saw what looked like four floors, including the one I was standing on. Unfortunately there was no building directory to point me towards any particular area. I had a brief moment of amusement as I imagined some of the department titles that would have been on that: The Full Moon, werewolf puppy grooming parlour; Grinders, weapon, fang and tusk sharpening service; Doc's magickal fuck-up reversal (St Mungo's Hospital eat your heart out). Finally I set off down the stairs.

On the very next floor I almost blew my cover right away, since the hall just beyond the door was filled with some kind of mist and I nearly walked straight out into it. I don't care how invisible you *think* you are, a big person-shaped hole in a cloud is a dead freakin' giveaway. Anyone who's watched films knows that. I quickly let the door close, although keeping it open a crack to hear laughter from the floor and the voice of someone clearly too pleased with their own ingenuity.

"I told you that fog bank would keep the weird bastards away! Stupid monsters. Some hate the smell, and the rest don't like the cold and wet. Now we can get on with our research in peace. Where did you put the Codex?"

"It's on the table in front of you, underneath Solomon's Key and your fried chicken which is about to drip grease and mayonnaise on the cover," came a second voice that sounded thin, high and nasal. The sort of whiny voice that immediately made you want to punch the speaker, since they were clearly someone who spent their entire day with their nose firmly glued up their boss' backside. "You make a mess again and I'm reporting you, you fat fucker!"

"Ah, you're just jealous 'cos you can't get anyone to make a food run for you," the deeper first voice spoke again. "Not my fault they're repulsed by you. Maybe next time don't test out a curse before you've figured out the reversal. Now you're stuck with green and purple warts all over your head. You look like walking gangrene, and you're starting to smell like it too."

I had to stifle a laugh at the image the description conjured up in my head, and I quickly looked around to check I was still alone in the stairwell.

"Fuck off, you dick," came the whiny voice again. "Just because you can't do more than research and pass information on to the *real* magick users…"

I let the door close the rest of the way and moved on down. I doubted Angelica would be in amongst the research team, since she was usually a liaison as she had told me previously. Also, if she were being punished, then she would more likely be somewhere Atma could take his time and not disturb the other work he wanted done.

Clearly the night shift of magick users were about as much use as a bunch of frat boys with too much time on their hands, and about as focused. From what I had just heard they weren't exactly brimming with power, so I started to feel a little more secure. Maybe the Order was more show than go?

No wonder they were so eager to find out more about me and my abilities, then recruit me if they could. Based on how easily I had defended myself against their members thus far, my training was on a whole different level to anyone else they had.

I hoped that meant I would be able to find Angelica and get out with her without too many issues, but I remembered the age old saying about the best laid plans. Also the one about for want of a nail, and I hadn't exactly planned this like the D-day assault. Powerful or not, all it would take would be something unforeseen and I'd be up that famously malodourous creek again. I made it down to the next floor without incident, but once I was out of the stairwell I had two close calls in just a few seconds.

First I walked into the back of the troll I had followed down the stairs in the church, but fortunately it seemed to be as dumb as it was big and stinky so it didn't even turn around. I went back around the corner I had just come past and immediately had to flatten myself against the wall as two werewolves walked past me.

They stopped and sniffed, either smelling my cologne or the troll sweat I had just been doused in, but to my relief the troll came around the corner at that point and shoved them both out of its way.

"Hey, watch it!" yelled one of the wolves as he bounced off the wall just next to me. The troll simply grunted and kept going, while the other wolf snarled at its retreating back.

"Bloody thing's too dumb to even say excuse me!" she groused, clearly female if the prodigious breasts were anything to go by. She went over and stroked the ruffled fur of the other wolf. These two were obviously mates, or were at least heading that way if their behaviour was any indication, and the female went on, "And did you smell it? Phew, its stink came round the corner before *it* did! Smells like someone tried spraying some after-shave or something on it, but that's about as much use as a fart in a hurricane on that thing!"

My blood went cold at how close they had been to detecting me and I continued holding my breath while they walked away, griping to each other about the apparent shortcomings of some of the other creatures in the Order.

Once their voices faded, I let my breath out slowly and wiped the sweat off my invisible brow with my unseen handkerchief. That was a little too close! I crept around the rest of the floor but other than a couple of larger open areas, which looked like they could be used either as meeting rooms or ritualistic spaces, this floor looked to be almost identical to the top floor. Clearly magickal office designers went to the same school of lack of imagination as the non-magickal ones!

I found my way back to the stairs and crept down the final flight. Why was it always the basement? Given the fact that Atma would probably have the best and plushest of the above-ground offices in the castle, why couldn't he keep his interrogation room and holding cells on the top floor? This guy was such a cliché!

He was clearly stuck in the past of dungeons under castles. Just check out his choice of location for a start! I just hoped that didn't extend to a full-blown torture chamber. While I wouldn't mind getting the kinks out of my neck and back after a long day of tension, I wasn't sure the rack would be a pleasant way to achieve it, nor that the operator would stop there. Iron Maiden had never been my favourite band and I doubted the spikes would help that, plus I had never been a fan of BDSM so it was unlikely that a more serious application of various restraints and pain would be in any way appealing or enjoyable.

I had a funny feeling the charming and endearing Mr Mumm, on the other hand, would greatly appreciate the skill of a long, drawn-out education session. At least as long as he was the one doing the teaching. I definitely needed to make a point of skipping *that* class!

Chapter 16

When I reached the bottom of the stairs, there was nothing to indicate this floor was in any way different from the three above it. Could Seirina have been wrong? Did the Order have another centre where they carried out their interrogations? Some kind of magickal black site for their top secret schemes, prisoner detention and torture? Then again, maybe I should stop being so over-dramatic and not try to make things more difficult than they had to be.

Or, worse still, had Seirina played me for a fool and sent me here to get captured? Was she actually working for the Order? Her grief over her husband had seemed genuine, but she *was* an enchantress. Had I been sucked in too easily in my concern over Angelica?

Then again, was I just looking for the second gunman on the grassy knoll and vastly overthinking this? This was basically the Order's Area 51. I doubted they wanted or needed to split their focus to Area 52 as well. I had either watched too many spy films or not enough.

I didn't know whether I was over-thinking, under-analysing, or missing the obvious point completely. What if Angelica just wasn't interested and had disconnected her phone herself to stop me from bothering her? Man, that would suck on an epic scale. Not least because I would likely give away my true level of ability when I escaped.

Well, this introspective second-guessing was getting me absolutely nowhere. I needed to just get the hell on with this and then get out, either with Angelica or without her. At least I'd know where I stood after this, and I could either stop mooning after someone who couldn't care less or start thinking of where to take her on a date.

I wouldn't have to even worry about drinking and driving now. Although was it safe to tipple and teleport? Get tanked and translocate? Get pissed and portal? Drink and disapparate? Get sozzled and shift? *Not helping!*

I cautiously opened the door, creeping through once I saw the hall was deserted. The layout seemed to be slightly different from the floors above, since the hall dead-ended to the right after about ten feet. I followed it to the left, peering around the corner when I got there before remembering I still had my cloaking spell active. Too much overthinking, dick-head!

I stepped quietly but openly around the bend to see something new. A second dead end to the hall, this time caused not by a wall but by what appeared to be a door better suited to the vault at Fort Knox. Sitting in front of it was someone in a hooded cloak reading something on an e-reader, who must have been there to open the door for those who couldn't for themselves.

There was no keypad, no combination lock dial, not even any palm reader or retinal scanner. Just a big ol' lump of metal with hinges at one side. The corridor was still large enough for three trolls to walk side-by-side, so that should tell you how big a door we were talking about.

I took a wild guess that magick just might be involved in opening it, which meant the person in the cloak had to have at least some degree of skill. That made me consider what I would need to do in order to get past him. I doubted very much whether he'd just open the door if I asked nicely. My only chance would be to hit hard and fast, leaving no chance of retaliation.

I crept around behind the seated and hooded figure, then summoned a ball of concentrated electricity, much like Ciarán had done in Tibet only more powerful. I slammed it onto the top of the hood. The figure dropped the tablet and crumpled to the floor, the hood slipping back from its head to reveal the fresh young face of a blonde girl barely in her twenties.

I'd just tazed a girl. I felt like a complete shit but then consoled myself with the thought that if this *was* a detention centre of some kind, she knew and was helping. Plus, she'd chosen to work for the Order in the first place.

Then I worried that maybe she had been coerced into being here, which would make her a victim. I screwed the lid down on my self-flagellation and potential guilt, deciding to view her as one of the bad guys so I could just get on with my quest.

Yeah, I didn't even buy it from myself and I still felt crappy but it had needed to be done. I tried one of the doors further down the hall and found it led to an empty office, so I used strips torn off the bottom of her robe to tie her hands and feet and gag her. I didn't want her raising any alarms if at all possible.

I was surprised not to feel a dip in my power access when I zapped her, but then I considered my reason for doing it: I was here on a rescue mission. I was fighting against an organisation lead by an individual of proven evil intent and action, so karmically I was on the right side even if the girl *was* here under duress.

I stood in front of the door and reached out with my magick. I couldn't detect any lock keeping it closed; it must just be sheer mass. I pulled telekinetically at the side opposite the hinges, and the massive hunk of metal started to swing open. It moved all of about three inches before I heard a soft *snick* and alarms started screaming.

As the door swung wider I saw a small wire that had been attached to the bottom of the door, pulled free by the motion of opening it. No magick to detect, just plain old-fashioned circuitry. Something the person *trained* to open the door would know about and know how to deactivate.

Just how impressed with my own magick had I become that I hadn't considered something so simple? Too late now, but my own pride had just bent me over and given me a prostate exam with no lube. I hoped it hadn't just got me killed.

As the alarm blared out, familiar symbols flared to life along the walls and my invisibility faded. I wasn't fully visible again, so the apotropaic dampening effect wasn't complete, but it was enough to block a weaker magick user or dampen a stronger one. I looked like a blurry image seen underwater, so I released it completely rather than waste energy holding it in place any longer.

The doors along the hall started swinging open, so I turned to deal with the threat by flinging up a shield in front of me and preparing more taser balls. As I did so, the door continued to move so I stepped down the hall slightly to avoid getting squashed against the wall as it swung open. What I hadn't anticipated, but probably should have, was that the vault/prison wasn't unguarded.

The creature that grabbed me from behind was definitely strong based on the power in the arms that wrapped around me, pinning my arms to my sides. It was also definitely female if the boobs squished against my back were any indication. I heard a hissing near my ear, and only one name came to mind so I slammed my eyes tightly closed. The alarm shut off and I heard the voice I had been dreading.

"Stheno, don't kill him! I want to question him and discover how he found us and accessed these levels. Then we'll uncover everything he tried to hide from me when I met him." Atma's gloating voice floated out of the vault behind me, where he must have been interrogating some poor prisoner.

My heart fluttered at the thought that his presence might indicate Angelica *was* a prisoner and was here, then I registered the name he had used. Since it wasn't Medusa, it must be one of her sisters which I confirmed by looking down and seeing chicken feet rather than a snake body. The next thing I felt was a burning sting on my neck as one of her snake-hair heads bit me, at which point I passed out in seconds.

★

I woke up and immediately wished I hadn't. My head was pounding. My neck, where I had been bitten, burned and itched. The rest of my neck felt like I'd slept with a crappy hotel pillow for about three weeks. As I tried to lift my hand to rub at it, I found to my chagrin that my arms were firmly secured behind my back.

As I became more aware of my body again, my shoulders communicated their displeasure at being wrenched back in that position and I groaned as the pain flared down my arms. My back cracked about four times as I sat up, blinking to clear the sleep from my eyes, at which point I noticed that my left leg was numb from me laying on my hip on a hard floor for who knew how long.

My ears felt curiously muffled, as if my head was wrapped in cotton wool, and I finally understood that old literary reference 'the silence was deafening'. I reached out to share the joke with Gauvain and felt… nothing! I couldn't hear him!

I could feel the bracelet still on my wrist, so clearly the protective wards I had copied from Master Harfi had stopped anyone removing it. I could also still feel Seren on my finger, but I couldn't feel anything from either of them. The only thing I *did* feel was a rush of fear as I fervently hoped this would not be a permanent loss. Then I calmed myself by reasoning that Atma wouldn't have destroyed the very thing he wanted to exploit.

I reached for my magick to break the ties holding my hands, but again felt nothing. I finally recognised the sensation from when I had carved the symbols into the wooden utensil holder back in the shop. Something was suppressing my power, and the rush of relief I felt at understanding that my magick *hadn't* been taken away again was immense. I struggled to my feet and started shaking my leg to try to bring it back to life, using the activity to look around and take stock of exactly where I was.

The floor was bare concrete and completely seamless, so had either been poured as a single slab or more likely created magickally. The wall was the same, and there were bars like a jail cell on the other three sides. The bars looked rough, so I went over to see if I could use that to work through my bindings. Close-up, however, I could now see that what I had initially thought of as roughness was actually thousands of symbols carved into every inch of the metal.

I saw a few shapes I recognised from the book I had used containing the chapter on apotropaic symbols. There were warding runes to protect against breakage, and some symbols were similar to the feedback symbols in my shop so I could tell that using force on the bars would end up hurting like hell.

There were plenty of carvings I didn't recognise too, but it was patently clear to me I wouldn't be simply popping out any time soon. Gauvain was similarly trapped in his claw as he needed magick to get in and out of it, and I couldn't even talk to him to reassure him.

I was rolling my shoulders as I walked to get the blood flowing into my arms again. There was nothing I could do, however, about the snake-venom hangover currently drilling violently through my skull with all the alacrity of a roadwork crew at seven in the morning outside your window on your day off.

There appeared to be about half a dozen cells here but none of the others were currently occupied, so it looked like Angelica was either not in trouble at all or was being held elsewhere. *Great! Fucking marvellous! So I went through all this, including getting captured, for nothing. Genius-level planning and execution, you wanker!*

I continued berating myself for a while, my self insults becoming increasingly creative and colourful as I went. My insecurities helpfully chimed in with the "I told you so" chorus regarding Angelica's lack of interest.

My shoulders and leg soon eased and felt almost normal again, although my neck cramp stubbornly refused to go. My hangover also seemed to improve by getting my heart rate and blood pressure up the more pissed at myself I got, so I wallowed in my irritation and started recalling some of my past frustrations.

One thing I had always been good at was nursing a grudge. I still remembered the name and face of the boy who pushed me down a slope next to the school tennis court when I was five, breaking my wrist. I even remembered how to get to his house. Not the street address but the actual physical location! It was one of my greatest weaknesses: I just couldn't let things go.

It could cut both ways when it came to caring about people, as my current situation exemplified, but it could eat me up when I thought about things from my past. It was the reason I had never had a good relationship with my father.

He had run his own business and had travelled extensively in Europe and Japan for work, working long hours even when he was at home, so I had hardly seen him for months at a time. Then whenever I had handed him my report cards from school he had only ever focused on the negatives, often calling me lazy or stupid rather than encouraging me. I could get ninety-five percent on a test, and he'd focus on the five percent I had missed. We hadn't spoken since I had left home at twenty, having completed my degree in business management. Again, driven by his wishes.

To be fair, looking back with the benefit of a more mature understanding, he *had* shown he cared in other ways. Taking us camping during the holidays, teaching me to fish and play golf (mostly because he enjoyed them, but at least he had included me), building radio-controlled monster trucks with me, basically doing what he could when he could.

Even his long working hours and business trips had only been his way of providing the best he could for the family. The problem was, I remembered what I viewed at the time as harshness better than I remembered the good things. Even now when I knew it was just his way of pushing me to do better, however ham-fisted and awkward, I still resented him for it.

Even worse, when I combined that with my pride, I couldn't simply forgive him and start afresh. No matter how many times I thought of picking up the phone and calling him. However, thinking back over those things definitely got my adrenaline up which seemed to blow away the last of my headache and leave me spoiling for a fight.

I also recalled something I'd seen somewhere about escaping from plastic wrist restraints, which was what these felt like. I wasn't sure if they were simple zip-ties or more professional cuffs, but they certainly bit into my skin like plastic. They didn't feel like rope, nor did they clink like metal cuffs.

The video clip I had seen said they could be broken by slamming your wrists against your backside as hard as you could repeatedly, and the strain should snap them. Since I had no better options at the moment, I decided I might as well give it a try.

After several minutes, all I had managed was to give myself sore wrists from rubbing against the cuffs and a throbbing in my lower back and upper buttocks from repeated impact. Clearly they had been reinforced by magick as well, and I called myself a variety of fresh new creative insults for not anticipating the obvious.

Then I heard someone coming down the hall.

Chapter 17

"Where you want dis?" a deep gravelly voice asked as the footsteps came nearer. I considered lying back down and pretending to still be unconscious, but then I thought the gorgon would be well aware of how long her venom lasted from her millennia of experience. I decided I may as well watch to see who was about and what they were doing. Information is power, and I was seriously lacking in both right now.

"Any cell will do, there's no concern over magick suppression with *this* one," came the haughty response. That one was definitely female, and I had a bad feeling who would be coming around the corner so I closed my eyes.

The legends regarding Medusa were easy, everyone knew them. Her sisters, Stheno and Euryale, were less clear. They were gorgons, but their ability to turn men to stone was disputed. Some said yes, some said no. Some said they had snake bodies like their famous sibling, some said chicken feet.

At least I knew the answer to that one now. I sarcastically considered informing Wikipedia if I ever made it out of here. They were thought to be immortal, but was that just because no Greek hero had tried to cut their heads off like Perseus had done to Medusa? I heard them come around the corner, then a disgusted snort from one of them.

"Bah, you don't have to worry! I have to try to turn you into stone, not like Medusa who had no choice. The boss has said he wants you alive for questioning, so you're safe for now."

I opened my eyes just a crack and peeped out to see a monster with snakes in her hair walking with a troll. The troll was carrying someone, but I could only see a pair of sneakers as the gorgon was in the way.

She was looking straight at me and while she was certainly hideous, I didn't petrify in the literal sense although I was certainly frozen in place for a moment. Her look, and the knowledge that this was a monster that had been around since the time of the Greek gods, certainly instilled a healthy sense of awe and caution.

She and the troll walked between the cells, stopping at the first one they came to on their right. The gorgon pulled a key from a bright yellow bum-bag (what the Americans call a fanny-pack, a term which always struck me as funny and made me think of a tampon rather than a bag) which looked hugely incongruous. She was wearing a loose kaftan to give her chicken legs freedom of movement, but since it had no pockets she used the bag.

The troll carried the unconscious body inside, bent down and unceremoniously dumped it on the floor. The troll stood up and walked out, then Stheno locked the cell. She sneered at me as she walked away, and I got my first clear look at the body on the floor. It was dressed in jeans and a black top, the delicacy of the limbs making me think it must be a woman.

She groaned and rolled over, pushing herself to her knees and retching. She straightened up and I saw black hair tumble over her shoulders, making my blood run cold. I gasped and she must have heard, because her shoulders tightened and she turned towards me. She parted the cascade of her hair and looked at me, revealing the familiar eyes I had both hoped to see and dreaded finding in here.

"Angelica!" I breathed, and she sobbed when she heard the raw emotion in my voice. I knew in that moment Seirina had been right, and my protestations had been the last desperate arguments of a condemned man. I was in love, or at least significant infatuation.

On reflection, I don't think we knew each other well enough to truly call it love but I was definitely well on the way and keen to see how far it would go. As soon as I admitted it to myself, I felt a release deep inside my chest. I buried the knowledge deep, fully cognisant of how it would be one of the easiest and most potent things the Order could use to torture me and force me to do what they wanted.

"Gavan?" she asked, sounding as though she hardly dared believe her own eyes. "Is it really you? What the hell are you doing here? How did you get in?" One look at her face and I knew my suspicions of her had been unfounded.

She had a black eye, a puffy cut lower lip and a bruise on her other cheek. Someone had beaten her, but carefully and systematically. I had a fleeting suspicion of how this could simply have been done with magick to further ingratiate her to me, but I squashed it down.

I knew I tended to trust too fast as Summer had warned me about that many times over the years, plus I'd spent almost a year in Aaru idealising Angelica in my mind, but it was difficult to ignore what I saw right in front of me.

"I came looking for you. I had my meeting with your boss which pretty much defined not going well. Then when I tried to ring you to warn you, your phone had been disconnected. I contacted some people I'd worked with before and eventually found someone who'd previously had dealings with the Order and knew roughly where they were based. Then I came here and managed to sneak in." I decided, as I had done before, to deal only in generalities so as not to give away any more information than needed. Who knew who might be listening right now?

"Wait, when was the meeting?" she asked, suddenly panicked for some reason I couldn't understand. "How long have I been in there?" I wasn't sure where she was talking about but decided that wasn't really the essential point just then.

"I don't know when he actually brought you in here, but the meeting was yesterday morning, unless that gorgon bitch knocked me out for more than just a few hours."

"That's impossible!" she whispered, looking panicked. "He's been questioning me for months in that damned room! This is the first time I've been brought out!" Her voice broke with the emotion of the situation and I stared at her, stunned.

A room where time passed faster than everywhere else? I had known beings from a place like that. A place where those who hurt others were watched and shunned and could conceivably end up cast out. A place that had sometimes been called Heaven where the occupants were powerful beings, some of whom had come to Earth in the past and been worshiped as gods.

Was Atma Mumm from Aaru? Had he been one of those few who had completed the figurative brick pile? Was he a cast-out god? Was he a fucking *DEMON*?

Maybe that explained how he was able to consume souls. He had relished consuming life energy and had refined that technique to take the power from souls. If so, why was he occupying bodies? Had Isis and the city council done something to him when they cast him out? If that was the case, he was going to be even more pissed at me if he ever found out where I'd got my power!

"I thought you worked for him. What the hell has he had to question you about for so long?" I asked, already afraid of the answer.

"You," she replied simply. "Everything I knew about you, including all the research I did on you before I first came to see you. All I learned from your mind that first time, and the sum total of what I knew about your abilities since you returned from your trip. You have no idea of the power of his mind! I'm so sorry, I couldn't stop him. He knows the lot, including the mental images you sent me and how they made me feel!" She blushed, then sobbed at what was essentially mental rape that she had had to endure.

"It's not your fault," I tried to reassure her, both embarrassed and indignantly furious on her behalf at what she had been forced to experience. "I'm sorry I ever used those images to try to block you out of my mind. I thought you would view me as some kind of pervert and stop looking into my head. I never expected you to actually enjoy them!"

I felt myself flushing and my breathing deepened as I remembered some of the scenarios I had imagined, and my body reacted involuntarily. My hands weren't even free to adjust things to a more comfortable position. I decided to try to get more information about where we were and who Atma was to take my mind off things.

"So is this the Order's only headquarters, or do they have other locations?" I asked. "I'm guessing this is where Atma, at least, has his office?"

"This is the main headquarters, but they do have some other locations up and down the UK, along with one in America," Angelica replied, sounding relieved to change the subject. "There are four in total in the UK, all under historic castles in the same way as this one. I'm not sure exactly where the American site is. They don't have anything old enough over there to make it obvious, but I know the Order always looks for sites like that for camouflage. It must be some kind of tourist attraction like a museum or something. As far as I know the American site is a fairly recent acquisition, only a couple of years ago. I *have* heard that the American site is very popular with the more monstrous members of the Order as they can apparently move more openly, but again I'm not sure why."

"We don't need to worry about that right now, we need to be more concerned with getting out of here." I didn't have the energy or spare head-space to be considering other locations at the moment, but I filed the knowledge away for future reference if we ever made it out of here. "What can you tell me about this place? How many members are based here? What sort of monsters are we dealing with? I've seen some werewolves and a couple of trolls, the gorgon, and a couple of vampires. There are definitely human magick users, Atma himself and his twin assistants. What else?"

"I didn't even know they *had* a gorgon until Atma threw me in here," she replied. "He got back from your meeting in a storming rage, came and got me then dragged me down here. He left me alone for about an hour, then that bitch Stheno came in and took me to another area. That's where they questioned me about you, just questions at first and then under torture.

"Atma would have people hurt me, keep me awake and starve me, then when I was too weak and exhausted to resist he would invade my mind to dig through and find out everything I knew in regard to you. He delighted in drawing things out and being as brutal as possible, going over and over the same details to be sure he knew absolutely everything I knew. I had thought I was in that room for months, as I said, but now you tell me it's only been about twenty-four hours!"

"I'm so sorry you went through that because of me," I said, feeling guilty but pushing the emotion away. I couldn't afford to wallow in my guilt right now, I needed to focus. "So what do you know about Atma himself? I've already learned he's a soul eater and he possesses some of the bodies he consumes the souls from, but I still don't know what he actually is. Do you know any more than that? He wasn't even as strong as the twins when I met him, so I was surprised to hear you talk about his mental powers."

"That was one of the reasons he was so angry when he got back," Angelica replied with a deep breath. "He was fuming that he wasn't able to take the knowledge of the Veil from your mind. He's been obsessed with it and the legends surrounding it for ages, and I found out he's been trying to track it down for decades in the belief he'd be able to use it as a gateway to get somewhere. He thought I lied to him about you, which was why he couldn't attack your mind the way he wanted. He got even angrier when he found out it was his own mistake at not listening to me and reading my notes carefully enough, then blamed *me* for not being clearer!"

She got more and more worked up as she spoke, finally crossing her arms and letting out an angry exhalation as she finished. At least getting angry had put some colour back in her cheeks.

"But how was he able to invade your mind so easily?" I asked. "I know you're not as strong as me now, but you're no slouch. He seemed like some ineffectual surfer boy when I met him."

"Surfer?" she asked, seeming confused. "Oh! He's changed bodies again! He took over the body of one of the Order's vampires. I recognised the face from meeting him previously. Atma must have decided to try a vampire body to see if it would enhance his mental powers and last longer than a human body. Also, because I worked for him directly, he had a pre-existing link to me. He does that with everyone who has any direct contact with him."

"I'm guessing he's severed that link now?" I asked, thinking of a possible means of attack (if I got out of this damn magick dampening field). "Or have you still got a back door into his mind?"

"Come now, do you truly have such a poor opinion of me? Do you actually believe I'm *that* foolish and naïve?" came a new voice.

I turned to see a pale, black-haired man framed in the doorway through which the troll had carried Angelica. He was dressed in black with a red cravat at his throat, which combined with his noticeable pallor reminded me of Michael Sheen as Aro, the leader of the Volturi from the *Twilight* movies. I wondered sarcastically to myself if he twinkled in the sunlight now or just fried. A spasm ran across his face, as if he was struggling for a moment, but it passed as quickly as it came.

"You'll not have the opportunity to find out anyway, *Gavan*," he continued, stressing the correct pronunciation of my name. "It's your turn to share your secrets with me, just as your little friend already has been forced to. Stheno, get him out of there and take him to The Room."

Chapter 18

The gorgon left his side and came down the corridor between the cells, bobbling her way over to the door of my little prison. Her walking motion was odd thanks to those chicken legs of hers, and I had to resist laughing. She *was* Medusa's sister, after all, and I didn't fancy being even partially turned to stone. I may have used the term rock hard when referring to various parts of my anatomy, but it *was* just a figure of speech after all!

She drew a single key that looked to be inscribed with its own array of symbols out of her bag and unlocked the door. As the lock clunked open, the symbols on the bars flared briefly and I felt my magick well up inside me. The restraints around my wrists suddenly tingled, and I felt a barrier between my magick and me. Although I could tell it was there now, I still couldn't quite reach it.

I *could*, however, now feel Gauvain's presence again and hear him muttering angrily to himself. I quickly reached out and reassured him, feeling his relief at being reunited with me. I advised him to stay quiet and sent a recap of what had been happening to him in a burst of thoughts. I then shut down our communication so Atma wouldn't pick up on it.

Stheno grabbed my arm and yanked me out of the cell, frogmarching (or should that be chicken-strutting I quipped sarcastically to myself, since goose-stepping would require webbed feet) me in front of her down the hall towards Atma. He turned and led the way out of the cells and down the hall beyond, stopping at a door on the right. It was surrounded by various runes and sigils that were unfamiliar to me, but which were all glowing.

He opened the door and the symbols went dark, then he led the way into a room that looked to have been set up almost like an operating theatre. The glaring difference was the table in the centre. The surface was almost upright and had restraints at the wrist and ankle points. Stheno pushed me through the door, following me in and then closing it behind us.

As the door closed I felt a moment of disorientation, almost as if I had had a few too many drinks. It passed quickly and I was shoved towards the table. I saw a door at the other end of the room as I managed to see past the upright surface, and it appeared to lead to a simple bathroom.

I wasn't sure if that was for water-based torture or my use if they left me in here for an extended period, but I wasn't particularly keen to find out either way. Atma stood next to the table and made a sweeping gesture, as if presenting it to me. I gave him a withering look and he simply laughed darkly, crossing his arms in satisfaction.

"Strap him down and let's get started," he ordered eagerly. Stheno grabbed my arm, spun me around and pushed me back against the surface. She held me in place with one hand in the centre of my chest.

"You'll have to take these cuffs off if you want to get me where you want me big boy," I said in a sarcastically camp manner, at the same time readying myself to fight as soon as my magick was available to me.

"Just how new at this do you think we are?" Atma asked snidely, dashing my hopes of an escape attempt. He made a short jerky upward nod to Stheno, who reached behind me with some kind of implement and the cuffs split apart but stayed on my wrists.

She grabbed my left wrist and strapped it to the table, surprising me with just how strong she was. Clearly the gorgons were more of a threat than just their gaze. She seized my right arm and strapped that down too, then did my ankles. As the last restraint clicked shut, I felt them being reinforced by magick. Only once I was secured did Stheno remove the separated cuffs from my wrists.

I felt my magick finally rush through me in a comforting wave, but without time to study and probe at the table restraints I still wasn't going anywhere. I doubted they'd leave me alone that long, but Atma clearly wanted to be able to test my abilities fully which must be why they were available to me again. He stepped around to the front of the table where I could see him, and I saw another brief spasm pass across his face. Was he still adjusting to his new body? If so, maybe that would limit his mental abilities. Angelica had said he was powerful but she had no idea of my true power now, so maybe I had a chance.

He scowled and motioned for Stheno to leave, so she bowed abruptly and left. The dizziness came twice in quick succession, once when she opened the door and then a second time when she closed it. Clearly, if this was the same room in which Angelica had been questioned, the time distortion effect was deactivated and reactivated by opening and closing the door. It made sense, otherwise they'd need some kind of elaborate temporal adjustment chamber to get in and out of the field.

"I guess you decided to go for a new image, huh?" I asked conversationally, deciding to try to stall for time and give myself a chance to get centred and come up with some kind of defence strategy. So far nothing was springing to mind. "What, did you get tired of the surfer boy look? Get fed up of having to show ID to buy a beer? Or did the idea of taking even more from people appeal to you? Their blood as well as their souls?"

"So you found out something about me, did you?" he asked pointedly, appearing impressed despite himself. "And just who have you been speaking with to *get* that information? I'll be interested to find that out along with all your other secrets, since whoever it is clearly needs to be silenced!"

"Oh, come on!" I sneered disdainfully. "You call yourself a name that means soul eater and you expect no one to figure it out? You clearly have an over-inflated opinion of your own intelligence, along with a vast under-estimation of mine. It took me all of five minutes on Google to get a translation of your name, you bonehead, and that was just the beginning."

I buried Seirina's name deep down, covering it with an imagined scenario of research on the internet for unusual occurrences, then narrowing down on Bolton Castle as the most likely location for the Order. The shocked look on his face confirmed my suspicions. He really did think he was smarter than any mere human, and was stunned to find out he was wrong.

"Bah, so you made a couple of lucky guesses!" he growled. "That doesn't mean you're on *my* level, you impertinent primate!" His response confirmed exactly what I suspected: He wasn't human, and the distain he had for us definitely pointed me towards him being from Aaru. The time distortion thing was another clue, and his obsession with finding the Veil of Isis to use as a gateway to get somewhere was the final giveaway.

Maybe I could use that knowledge to wind him up, stop him thinking so clearly and give me an edge to use against him. Any advantage was better than my current starting point of square boned, so I'd take whatever I could get.

"If we're so inferior, and you already *have* magick, why were you so obsessed with finding the Veil you sent me after?" I took on a lightly taunting tone just to piss him off and get him more worked up than he already was. "Are your powers so limited that you need to look for a boost from any source you can identify, including ones that aren't even proven to exist?"

"Fuck you, you ignorant talentless ape!" he snarled, slamming his hands onto the table either side of my head. I grinned and batted my eyes at him knowing it would infuriate him even more. The more off-balance I could keep him, the better it was for me.

"Hey, say it, don't spray it!" I taunted him again as flecks of saliva hit my cheek, and he pushed away from the table in disgust. "If I'm so inferior, how come you're the one who needed *my* inferior primate help to find the Veil? I'm not the one who can only survive in someone else's body either, you fucking parasite! You're nothing more than a jumped up STD. You're just herpes or the clap with consciousness."

I kept winding him up tighter and tighter, and he responded like a four-year-old on their first day of school. I was half expecting him to stamp his foot and burst into tears at how hard I was pushing him. He'd clearly never learnt how to deal with this sort of defiance, probably because none of his underlings dared speak to him with this level of disrespect. Another spasm passed over his face and he immediately calmed down, eerily fast, then smiled to show his new fangs.

"Nicely done, asshole," he said, suddenly sounding totally different. This new voice was deeper, smoother and with some kind of Eastern European accent. "You pissed him off so much, he even lost his grip on me!" Another spasm passed over his face and then Atma's voice came back.

"You shut up and stay down where you belong!" he said, sounding strained. "And as for you Maddox, I'll give you credit for your research skill and for taking a totally unexpected approach that was clearly much more effective than I had anticipated. However if you try anything like that again, I'll take your soul and then drain every memory from your mind before feeding your worthless corpse to the most disgusting monster I can think of."

I kept quiet, trying desperately to analyse what I had just seen and heard. 'Lost his grip on me'? 'You stay down where you belong'? My brain raced down various pathways. I was aware of vampires being much stronger than normal humans, which must be why Atma decided to take over one.

However they had no soul for him to consume, as that was apparently lost when they were turned according to the literature. I'd never met one before so I couldn't be certain, but most legends had their basis in fact which seemed to fit with what I'd just seen.

The apparent loss of the soul meant the personality and memories of the person were now independent of that controlling conscience, which was also largely why most vampires tended towards selfishness and evil. It wasn't inherent, however, and could be fought if the person who was turned had been of sufficient strength of character and morality.

That independent consciousness or entity must have been immune to Atma's soul-eating ability and must now be fighting him, which was why he was struggling to stay in control. Losing his temper at my goading must have made his dominance slip enough that the resident had managed to surface for a moment. Now *that* was information I could use, if only I could figure out how!

"We'll see how funny you think you are after a few weeks of starvation and pain!" he snarled at me. He walked over to the wall and flipped a switch on a console there, causing electrical shocks to start shooting through me at intervals. They were strong enough to hurt but not enough to knock me out or cause lasting damage. They were also random enough that I couldn't anticipate or prepare for them. He then walked in front of me, sneered and headed to the door.

He looked back with a smug, satisfied smile and walked out, causing the same two waves of dizziness as the door opened and closed.

I reached for Gauvain and he launched out of his claw joyously. I sent him the image of the switch I had seen Atma throw before he left and he flew over to it, swiping it with his claw and thus cancelling the electrical jolts much to my relief as I relaxed.

"Ugh, that's better, cheers G," I said in thanks. He flew over and landed on the top edge of the table and shook himself, then started preening again making me grin inwardly.

Well just think yourself fortunate you have not been cramped in a fingernail for the last umpteen hours! he griped. I rolled my eyes at his dramatic tone.

"Oh no, I've just been electrocuted, locked up, bitten by a gorgon's snake hair, chucked on the floor…" I wasn't exactly in the best of moods myself just then. "I don't even know what you're whining about! You're from Aaru; your natural state is formlessness!"

Actually, I didn't even exist until your arrival caused them to give everything form, he said, much to my surprise. *Even then, I didn't have this level of awareness until Isis joined us, so to me being fully formed and flying is the norm.*

I suddenly understood why he disliked travelling in his claw so much. I wouldn't appreciate being forced to turn into energy and confined into a tiny relic either. For one who was used to the freedom of soaring through the skies in total control and dominance over everything he saw, it must be even more restrictive.

"I'm sorry, I didn't know," I sent my genuine regret and sympathy across our link, and he ducked his head and shuffled along the top of the table.

Well, the claw was something I agreed with and to be honest, being in there is not painful or unpleasant. I would simply rather be out and about, he replied, blinking at me. I smiled at him, understanding completely from my current vantage point of being strapped down. At least now that the pain had been thankfully terminated.

Now to see about getting off this damned table!

Chapter 19

Now that I could concentrate, without Atma in my face or electro shock therapy singeing my short and curlies, I could feel the magick reinforcing the restraints. It was relatively uncomplicated, simply holding them closed and strengthening the structure.

I set about absorbing the power one restraint at a time, first to restore my own energy levels and then putting some energy back into Seren. The wings deep in its depths flared slightly as the energy was sucked into the seemingly limitless reservoir of the stone. Since it was filtered through me, Seren could absorb it with no problem.

Once the magick was removed, it was a simple matter to undo the catches with my mind and I was then able to step down and stretch. I went into the bathroom and saw it was a simple setup with a toilet, sink and shower. I splashed my face with cold water and then sat down on the closed lid of the toilet to think.

Since there was a time distortion in here, for all I knew Atma might have only just turned around from the door and still be right outside. That meant bursting out immediately might be singularly counterproductive. At the same time, I didn't feel like just sitting here playing with myself for several weeks while I waited for him to walk away. But how the hell was I supposed to figure out when it was safe to leave? I was aware my friends in Aaru had the ability to vary the degree of time discrepancy, so I had to assume Atma may possess the same capability.

I thought about trying to teleport out but as soon as I tried to *move* out of the room, it was like running into a brick wall. There was something stopping me from leaving. Maybe the time distortion acted like a separate dimension? Perhaps a portal would work better.

I focused on getting back to the car and concentrated on tearing through the curtain like Danu had taught me, but it was like stabbing the wall with a rubber knife. I couldn't get penetration. I laughed at myself as I heard my own description, since sometimes those childish jokes were all you had to keep yourself smiling. I decided to use the facilities while I was in there, then went out into the main room to see Vain preening again.

"Geez, dude, do you ever do anything else?" I laughed at him. "I swear, G, you're going to preen yourself bald! I know you're a very handsome bird, but you need to familiarise yourself with the legend of Narcissus. Bad things happen when you're too wrapped up in your own looks." He looked over at me and cocked his head.

I am not in love with my own reflection, thank you very much! he snapped. *I have to take care of my feathers so I can fly, and my talons so I can hunt. My life depends on taking proper care of myself, so I would appreciate you dropping that stupid and insulting Vain nickname! I don't object to G, but Vain is inaccurate and –*

"Not *completely* true?" I interrupted with a knowing smirk.

Oh, boil your head! he responded, laughing. *Very well, I admit that I take pride in my appearance. But don't forget that you do as well! You shave, use cologne, take care in how you dress… Observe the way you got ready when you knew Angelica was going to be attending the shop!* He said her name in a teasing sing-song voice and I flushed first, then laughed.

"Fair enough, G," I said, stressing the less derogatory nickname. "Just don't preen yourself into oblivion, OK?"

Very well, I shall endeavour to restrict my preening somewhat, he replied, fluffing himself up and then shaking to settle everything back into position. I turned and walked over to the console with the switch that had controlled the electric shocks, looking to see what else might be controlled from here.

There were several switches but none of them were labelled, so I had no clue what any of them did. I could always just start pushing buttons and flipping toggles, but with my luck right now I'd probably set off the alarms. I'd probably even trigger the self-destruct combined with knocking myself out until the bomb detonated. Man, I watched too many TV shows.

The only one we knew for certain was the electric shock switch. Could I use that somehow? Maybe cobble together some kind of gizmo that ran off the electrical surges? Possibly fry the door, or at least shock Atma when he came back in.

I looked around but unlike every single Bond film, *MacGyver* or *A-Team* episode, there were no handy coils of loose wire. No forgotten box of dynamite or metal-cutting laser, not even a decent Swiss army knife lying about. You just couldn't get quality bad guys or hideouts these days. It was just plain rude, as far as I was concerned. How was a guy supposed to escape these days?

I widened my magickal awareness as much as I could, but I ran into the same limitation at the periphery of the room. I examined all the switches, but the only thing I learned was they were connected to various electrical relays with no idea of what was triggered by them. I tried following the wires but they seemed to loop outside the limiting field before they came back in, so I couldn't trace switch to effect in that way either.

One thing I *did* feel was power spots in a couple of different places high up near the ceiling. I tracked them down and located a couple of pinhole cameras. I guess Atma must have left me alone to see what I was capable of, see what he could learn without making any effort himself. Sometimes mundane methods were enough and the simplest solution got the job done.

As soon as I became aware of the cameras, I flipped them the bird (not Gauvain) and went into the bathroom. G came with me, staying in full form as he had already been seen so there was no longer any point in hiding. I thought about trying to use the electrical surges from the table to charge up Seren, but they were too random and brief to be reliable.

I got some toilet paper and wetted it, making a couple of wadded pellets, then went out into the main room and stuck one over each camera using telekinesis. A telekinetic spit-ball, if you will. At least I'd be able to move around without having my every move spied on.

I looked at the table and saw some simple controls to raise and lower it, so I dropped it down until the surface was level. With nothing better to do, I climbed on and lay down to take a nap, Gauvain standing on my chest to keep watch.

★

I woke up after about an hour according to my feathered lookout, then went into the bathroom to get a drink of water from the tap. I cupped my hand for Gauvain to drink out of and used a little of the energy in Seren to refresh us both.

I went back out into the main room and did some push-ups and sit-ups, then jogged around the room a few times to work out all the kinks from being poisoned, bound and zapped.

I had no idea how long it might take Atma to get back down here once he saw the cameras were covered, so I decided to just keep limber, awake and wait. I practiced a little telekinesis and different energy forms – fire, electricity, plasma, sound, light. Then I started trying to analyse the steel of the table to learn its energy signature ready for transmutation usage in the future. Even with all that, several hours locked in a room still gets boring. There was very little for Gauvain and me to catch up on due to our link, so we very quickly ended up sitting together in silence.

Finally I felt the familiar wave of dizziness as the door opened once again. Atma walked in, closely followed by his pet gorgon who closed the door as soon as they were inside. The dizziness didn't wash over me this time and I looked up around the room in surprise, then back at Atma with one eyebrow raised.

"No time distortion this time?" I asked in surprise. "Has your *clock* gone *flaccid*?" I snarked, causing Stheno to slap her hands over her mouth and snort. This time even Atma laughed, easily getting the joke and refusing to get annoyed.

"Actually, I just felt you weren't worth getting turned on for this time," he responded. His well-timed response wiped the smile off my face but caused Stheno to burst out laughing. Atma smiled along with her, clearly feeling superior at his one-upmanship of my attempt to rile him, and I shrugged in acknowledgement of his riposte.

"OK, that one was nicely *timed*," I said. "Maybe if you're struggling, you could try winding it by hand." Stheno completely lost it at that one, and tears were now running down her face with the laughter. "So, what can I do for Atma the ass and his giggling gorgon?"

That last snide comment finally managed to wipe the smile off of his face. It even enabled Stheno to get her hysterics under control, probably fully aware that my insult would have annoyed her boss.

"Since you clearly have far more magickal ability than you showed Angelica, it's time to find out just what secrets you are attempting to conceal," he narrowed his eyes at me as he spoke and motioned Stheno towards me, but I jumped down off of the table as she approached.

"Oh, I don't think so Chicken Little," I said to her, and her face tightened in annoyance as she glanced down at her feet. "I think I'll pass on the electro-bondage this time." She kept walking towards me and her eyes developed a glow that immediately raised the hairs on the back of my neck. I instinctively threw my hand out towards her and formed a ball of electricity as I did so.

The energy hit her squarely in the chest and threw her back across the room. She landed hard and ended up sliding inelegantly into the wall next to the door with a thud.

Atma actually smiled at my reaction, nodding slightly to himself as if I had just confirmed something he already suspected. I didn't care, I was just glad I hadn't been turned to stone. Of course it might have been a ruse to see if I *could* defend myself, in which case I'd just shown even more of my hand.

"So, you have a familiar who can reside in the bracelet at your wrist, you can counter the magick in the restraints, you can open those restraints with your mind and you can use energy bursts. I already know of your psychic power from our first meeting, so overall your abilities and education are far more advanced than you let on."

Atma smiled at me as he spoke, almost salivating in his eagerness. I wasn't sure if he wanted to get me under his control, eat my soul and take my body, kill me outright or just try to take my power somehow. None of the options sounded particularly appealing to me, however. I could only hope my power was up to defending myself against him.

I felt him reach out to me mentally and it felt familiar while at the same time feeling totally alien. Familiar in the sense that his consciousness felt much like some of those I had encountered in Aaru, confirming his origins. Alien in the sense that the way he used his mind felt twisted and warped, almost like someone using a looped and gnarled tree root instead of a straight rod to do a job. The prodding was there, but it went through more twists and turns than necessary to deliver it.

It reminded me of when I had tried to harvest kinetic energy from my own kata practice. I had used energy stores to activate my muscles to move my body in order to collect kinetic energy to put into Seren. The result had been some energy stored, but it had taken longer and wasted far more time and effort than simply pouring my own power directly into my heart-stone.

His probing got the job done but involved more steps and required more energy than was strictly needed. He had clearly been given more teaching by someone or something else once he had been thrown out by Isis and her fellow council members. That person had obviously never received the complete training themselves, which was why they had been unable to teach him to be more effective.

I set my mind against him and rebuffed his probe relatively easily, although he was certainly stronger now than he had been in his surfer body. I would have said he was actually stronger than what I had felt from the twins now, so I could understand their subservience. He didn't, however, compare with the level of power Isis and Danu had exhibited. He wasn't even close to being in their league.

As he tested my defences, he redoubled his efforts and I felt him try to send a probe deeper into my being. This attempt was like someone had attached the hose to a vacuum cleaner, switched it on and thrown the end forward. I suddenly understood he was now trying to leech either my power or my soul, neither of which was something I was going to tolerate.

I deflected his attack and *shoved* back at him, allowing my anger at him and my disgust at his methods to strengthen my power. I saw him stagger slightly as my counterattack reached him, and the vampiric nature of his host shone through as his eyes went red and his fangs erupted in his anger.

He stood up straight and then did something I should have expected, but simply hadn't paused to consider that he might try. He leapt toward me, wrapped his left arm around my shoulders and grabbed my chin with his right hand, turning my head to my left.

I shuddered and a chill washed over me as I felt his fangs slice into my neck.

Chapter 20

His physical strength, thanks to his now being in a more supernatural body, far exceeded mine. The intimate physical connection linked our minds more closely than he could ever have managed any other way since it allowed him to slip past my defences, helped in no small measure by my surprise and revulsion.

The room seemed to fall away as he dove into my memories, carrying me along with him almost as a spectator in my own head. I was so shocked I never even thought of throwing him off me with magick, and then we were so closely entwined I wouldn't have known where to push to get him out of my memories. I could feel Gauvain trying to reach for me but Atma simply gripped tighter on my mind and forged ahead.

He saw my arrival in Aaru and my trek to the city. He grunted out loud through his mouthful of my flesh and blood in victory as he recognised the feel of the place through my recollections. He saw my arrival in Dinas Affaraon, witnessed my first day there, and watched as I went to my meeting with Isis.

His grip tightened on me and I felt his anger as he recognised her. I could feel his own memories spilling into my mind as he lost some of his control in his rage, but I was too confused to analyse them at that moment. I was aware enough to realise their importance however, so set a part of my mind to keep track of them for future reference and analysis.

He witnessed my magickal awakening, then I sensed his focus as I got out the Veil and offered it to Isis. His fury as I began to absorb it was almost overwhelming, but then as it entered me he tried to chase it through the magickal pathways of my mind.

He encountered what I can only describe as a valve or flow regulator, which seemed to limit how much power I could access from the Veil. It had no doubt been placed there as a safety system by Isis, probably to prevent me using the Veil as a crutch during my education. After a while I wouldn't have needed to use it anyway, so the restriction must have sat there unrequired and forgotten.

He ripped it away and tried to reach for the Veil, no doubt wanting to absorb its power into himself to then be able to use it to get to Aaru. Fortunately for me the Veil, or at least Isis via the Veil, had other ideas.

A massive blast of energy threw Atma out of my mind and back into his own body with such force that his fangs came out of my neck and he flew across the room to slam into the door. He dropped to the floor and crumpled into a heap as he landed. He stared up at me in a mixture of terror and rage, impotent in the face of Isis' power by proxy.

I could feel him straining to keep himself in the vampire body he had taken, the leech himself using this opportunity to fight back while the parasitic invader was weakened. I, on the other hand, was too woozy from what had just occurred to take any kind of advantage.

Instead I simply stood with my hand clasped to the wound in my neck, hanging onto the steel table to maintain my balance. G shrieked at Atma's actions and flew to my shoulder to glower protectively at him. Atma scrambled to his feet and wrenched the door open, shouting instructions to the troll waiting outside in the hallway.

"Take him back to his cell and lock him in! Leave the gorgon where she is until she wakes up." He stormed off down the hall and didn't look back. The troll came in and grabbed my arm, dragging me out of the time suite and back down the hall to the cells. He dislodged Gauvain as he did, but he paid no attention to (or maybe he was too stupid to notice) the fluttering around his head.

G flew after us, landing on my other shoulder again as we went through the door to the cells. The foetid freak stopped as soon as we were through the door, saw Angelica in the cell on the right, then turned to open the door on the left and shoved me in. He slammed the door and simply shuffled around and left.

At least the moronic malodourous mountainous monster hadn't put me back into the magick-suppressing cell, but right now my mind was too scrambled to even think about opening the lock. I still had Atma's memories swirling around in my head as well, and I wanted to try to sort through them whilst they were still fresh to see if I could pick up any useful information.

I went over to the wall and sat down with my knees up so Gauvain could perch on one. I rested my head back against the wall and closed my eyes, focusing inward to try to watch the movie reel of recollections spool through my mind's eye.

I saw flashes of his childhood, different to my memories of Conor from when I was there since he had been formless as a native Aaruan. Then came the onset of his magick and the commencement of his education.

The lessons in drawing energy from others, the discovery of the rush he felt when taking their energy and eventually even their life. His satisfaction at completing the formless equivalent of the brick pile challenge with ease, and his fury at being told he would receive no further training.

He had experimented by himself after that, drawing energy from everyone around him until finally killing two children. His tribunal held by the council with Isis at its head, and his eventual expulsion. I heard Isis' voice, clearly emblazoned on his mind ever since, as she banned him from returning:

"For your crimes, Elrulin, you are cast out and forbidden form even on the physical planes, never to return." I felt the burn as her power scorched him in such a manner that he would be unable to take physical form on his own. She then joined her power with the other council members to blast him across the dimensional barrier to Earth.

My eyes flew open and I gripped tight to the most important fact I had found in the memories I had seen: Atma's true name. Elrulin. Just like he had tried to do against me, the use of his true name could definitely help me build an assault and defence against him.

"Are you OK, Gavan?" Angelica called softly across from her cell. "You were only in there for about half an hour out here. How long was it in there? What did they do to you?" As I turned towards her she gasped. "Your neck! Did they send a vampire in to feed on you?" I smiled and shook my head, making her gasp as she understood exactly who had bitten me.

"Not exactly," I replied, confirming her suspicions. "They strapped me to that table and left me alone to see what I would do. I only found the cameras after I got off the table. Once I stuck some wet toilet paper over the lenses, they came back and your boss tried to get into my mind again. When he couldn't, he lost his temper and bit me. That got him past my defences, but the Veil threw him off when he tried to take it from me."

"Wait, I thought you said the Veil crumbled to dust when you touched it?" She narrowed her eyes at me. "And how did your hawk get in here and find you? You lied to me and hid things from me, didn't you? No wonder he tortured me, he thought I knew everything and kept it from him! It's all your fault!" She burst into tears and I felt like the biggest shit of all time for what she had gone through because of me.

"I'm sorry, I had no idea he would do that," I said as she sobbed quietly into her hands. "I didn't know the kind of people I was dealing with, I just wanted to be left alone. I told you part of the truth, just not all of it. It was enough to let you know the Veil had been real, it had unlocked my magick, and it wasn't available for anyone else to use. You and your employer didn't need to know any more information. Or at least so I thought at the time.

"I had only met you once before, and in a business setting at that, so we weren't exactly at the point of sharing our deepest darkest secrets with each other. Had I known who and what he was, I would have handled things differently." She looked up at me, tear tracks visible down her cheeks but with surprise and curiosity in her eyes.

"Wait, what do you mean?" she asked. "Are you saying you actually know *what* he is? That's one of the most closely guarded and debated secrets in the Order amongst those I've met. Everyone knows he can consume souls and switch bodies, but no one knows any more than that. The most common theory is that he's some kind of wizard who learned how to switch bodies to cheat death, and that he takes the energy from souls to keep his own alive."

"No, not really, and only partially." I ticked off the answers on my fingers as I smiled at her and winked. She wiped her face with the back of her hand, her curiosity and irritation giving her a stabilising focus, then crossed her arms and glared at me.

"I hope you don't think you're getting away with leaving it there after what I've been through!" she snapped, even going so far as to start tapping her foot. Yup, I was definitely in trouble now.

"OK, alright," I held my hands out placatingly. "I'll fill you in, but not right now. I have no idea what listening devices or other surveillance gear they might have in here, plus who or what might be listening in person. What I have to tell you will touch on some very personal and sensitive areas. Once we get out of here, we'll have a long talk over some decent coffee and I'll bring you up to speed.

"Right now, I'm kinda wiped after my run in with Elr... Atma." She narrowed her eyes at my slip but I just shook my head and gestured around the cells, then touched my ear to remind her of the possibility of eavesdroppers. She nodded sharply but I could tell she wasn't going to let this go. I would definitely be called to account later.

I lay down, cushioning my head on my arm, and Gauvain hopped to the floor and snuggled in to my chin. I closed my eyes and drifted off to sleep quickly, which wasn't surprising after my exertions and having donated some of my blood to feed Elrulin's new vampire body.

Unsurprisingly, my dreams took me back to Aaru and I relived some of my own experiences there. I also revisited some of the memories I had gleaned from my brief mind-meld, although the Vulcan method looked much less painful!

After a while my dreams changed, and I was back at the hotel where I had met Elrulin (Atma as I knew him then) in his surfer body and the twins. I was sitting at the table outside, Elrulin was opposite me, and the twins were behind him. He was saying something but his voice was muffled and staticky, like a badly tuned radio, while the twins looked directly at my dream self and then had one of their weird twin conversations. Their voices, in contrast to Elrulin's, were crystal clear.

"That strange energy surge was very powerful!" Gabriella or Isabella said, sounding surprised and anxious.

"Yes it was," Isabella or Gabriella replied, mirroring her sister's quizzical tone.

"It was almost painful."

"But not quite."

"No, not quite."

"And afterwards there was a new feeling of lightness and freedom."

"Definitely. Almost like a wind blowing away the cobwebs."

"Exactly!"

"And Atma's controlling grip on us..."

"Yes, it's gone!"

"Shh, we mustn't let him know."

"No. We must keep our freedom."

"Wait, do you feel that?"

"Yes. I know the feeling of that mind, we've felt it before."

"Isn't that the one who asked our names at the hotel?"

"You're right, it is. Is he here?"

"I think he must be."

"Maybe he was the one who sent the surge that broke us free."

"Maybe. He certainly seemed to be stronger than he tried to let on at the time."

"Maybe that surge linked us to him because of our previous link with Atma?"

"Oooh, good point, that's definitely possible."

"Maybe we should try to find him. He might need our help."

"He certainly deserves our help if he's freed us from that bastard."

"Yes he certainly does."

"Should we see if he can hear us?"

"Yes we should." Then they turned together to look at me and called to me as one.

"GAVAN!"

I saw a vision of the Order's cells flash before my eyes and then woke with a start.

Chapter 21

I sat up and looked around, confirming that I was still in the cell and Angelica was in the one opposite me. I looked for the twins, certain I would see them standing right outside my cell given what I had just heard in my dream, but they weren't there. I had heard them so clearly. Maybe the burst from the Veil *had* backtracked Elrulin's psychic leash and allowed me to connect with them.

"Are you feeling better?" Angelica asked from her cell. "You've been asleep for a couple of hours. You looked like you needed it. By the way, you snore like tractor with a faulty transmission." She smiled impishly at me, and I laughed in return. Gauvain laughed in my head as well.

Actually Gavan, you only do that when you're truly exhausted, he said, winking at me. *Most of the time you sound more like a chainsaw on gravel!* He had clearly projected his communication to Angelica as well, as she burst out laughing. Then she trailed off as she realised who she had just heard.

"Wait, that was the *hawk*?" she asked, stunned. "I guess that's why he 'stuck with you after you found him on your travels' then! I take it he's actually your familiar, which I guess is how he found you?"

"Yes, he's my familiar, although I prefer the term friend as it sounds less subservient," I replied, holding out my hand for him to climb onto and lifting him up to my shoulder. "As to how he got here, he can actually change to pure energy and enter his claw on my bracelet when it might be best he remain unseen. He couldn't come out in the magick suppressing cell but he could in the time room, which was useful as he could turn off the electrical surges they left me to experience." Angelica stared at me throughout my explanation, her mouth hanging slightly open. She looked between G and me a couple of times, then clearly had a realisation.

"Wait, doesn't finding a familiar and creating a bond take quite a long time?" she asked, and I thought back to Seirina's realisation of the same thing. I was really going to have to come up with a better story one of these days. Maybe when I wasn't rushing headlong into the clutches of an evil organisation or fighting for my life (no point fighting for my sanity, that was a lost cause years ago).

"Yeah, part of the whole brushed over back story that I'll fill you in on later," I replied, feeling yet another twinge of guilt for what she had been put through as a result of my incomplete recounting. "For now, let's just see about getting out of these cells and out of the building."

"We can probably help with that," the two new synchronised voices came as the door swung open to reveal the twins standing there smiling at me. Then they saw who I'd been talking to and their smiles slipped away, quickly replaced by matching scowls.

"What's *she* doing here?" asked one of them.

"Yes, why *is* she here?" chimed in the other.

"She's worked for Atma for years."

"She's certainly done a lot for him."

"Yes, she's definitely seemed to be a loyal servant."

"She's always done whatever he told her."

"True, she's never told him no."

"How can we be sure she's not still working for him?"

"That's true, we can't be certain."

"Should we leave her here?"

"It might be best."

"But then she might tell him we helped Gavan."

"Yes, she might snitch and drop us in it."

"But if we take her with us, she might give us away as we try to escape."

"She could certainly mess everything up for us on the way out."

"We could knock her out and leave her here."

"That might be best."

"ENOUGH!" I cut across their almost mesmeric to-and-fro conversation. "I really appreciate you coming to help me Gabby and Izzy..."

"Oh he's remembered our names!"

"Yes, and he's even given us nicknames."

"We've never had nicknames before."

"No, we haven't."

"No one's ever cared enough to give us nicknames."

"That's true, they haven't."

"Girls, please," I begged, needing them to stop for just a moment. "I came here looking for her, I'm not leaving without her." Angelica looked across at me in surprise, smiling fleetingly at me before scowling back at the twins.

"Oooh, he's got a crush on her."

"Yes, and to look at her, she quite likes him."

"But how can we be sure of her allegiance?"

"It is a puzzler."

"Maybe she'll let you into her mind to prove she isn't hiding anything?" I looked from them to her, raising my eyebrow at her in question. "How about it, Angie? Will you let them scan you if they promise to be gentle and not delve where they don't need to?" I looked at the twins at that point, raising both my eyebrows this time. Before they could answer, Angelica jumped in.

"I'm not letting *them* anywhere near my mind!" she stated hotly, talking directly to me and clearly trying to ignore the twins. "They say *I* worked for Atma, but *they've* worked for him even more closely. They've assaulted and raided minds, stealing information and enslaving people for him for years! I have just as much reason to distrust them as they have to distrust me, if not more." I looked at the twins and then back at her.

"I understand, but they're the ones outside the cells and we could definitely use the help to get out of this mess," I said placatingly, not disclosing the fact that without the suppression field of my original cell I was more than capable of unlocking the doors. Angelica appeared significantly unconvinced. She let out a sigh and her shoulders slumped in resignation at the situation.

"Fine, if it'll get things moving along, I'll let them scan me," Angelica said, rolling her eyes. Then she continued, "But only on one condition. They let you scan them first." The twins looked at her in surprise.

"Everything they said about me is true. I did do what I was told, but I never had to hurt anyone as far as I knew. I never knew what became of the information I provided or the people I recruited. They, on the other hand, were his personal psychic attack dogs. They invaded people's minds and provided him with secrets to be used as leverage. So I say again, why should *we* trust *them*?"

The twins looked at her, then each other, than at me and shrugged, nodding in agreement with her assessment of the situation.

"She makes a fair point."

"Yes she does."

"We certainly did work very closely with Atma and did everything we were told."

"But with his psychic tether on us, we didn't exactly have a choice."

"No we didn't, and it's not like we enjoyed hurting people."

"Of course not, but we don't know what he had on her to make her obey him."

"Also very true."

"OK, so should we let him scan us?"

"With his strength, we probably wouldn't be able to stop him if he really tried."

"Very true but I don't think he's like Atma, so he wouldn't force us."

"No, I think you're right about that."

"So we're agreed?"

"Absolutely." They turned towards me together and harmonised, "We're willing to let you scan us." I nodded at them in thanks and Angelica's face relaxed. I closed my eyes and reached out towards the twins with my mind.

I entered Isabella's mind first, purely by chance as I still honestly had no idea which was which. They hadn't been specific back at the hotel. It was a strange sensation, as Gabriella was intricately connected to her, and being twins, they thought almost in tandem. Their minds echoed each other in a psychic version of their out-loud back and forth conversations, so it was like listening to music with the reverb set to maximum.

I was as gentle as I could be looking through her memories, and soon felt her hatred for the control Atma had exerted over them and her distaste for what he had made them do. She showed me how the Order had rescued them from a group home where they had been dumped as babies by parents who couldn't handle giving birth to 'monsters', and where they had been reviled and teased by the other children.

Once among the members of the Order, they had known their first experience of acceptance. Then they had finally shown signs of some ability as they became teenagers. They had been trained by other psychics within the ranks, finally developing their potent power as they worked together. Izzy showed me how Atma had encouraged them at first but once they learned of his way of dealing with his enemies, they had balked.

Then he had taken them to witness a boy living with foster parents, only allowing them to see him from a distance. When they had arrived back at the Order, he had shown them the paperwork confirming the boy was their brother. He had been removed from their parents by Children's Services as they had become alcoholics after the stress of the twins' birth. Threats against the boy had forced the twins to submit to Atma, allowing him to establish the psychic leash I had felt before.

I felt her surprised gratitude when I had treated them as people in their own right at the hotel, then the absolute joy as the energy blast had forced Atma to retreat deeper into his new body. Clearly he wanted protection to both maintain and try to reinforce his control over the vampiric personality already there.

That retreat, combined with the shock of the wave of power, had broken his psychic chain. It had freed them, leaving them determined to get away before he recovered and then found them to re-exert his dominance. She was almost eager to show me everything and I detected no hint of deception in her mind, just a lingering concern for their brother.

I withdrew and saw Izzy, who I now knew was the head on the left side of the pair (or the right as you faced them) look at me with gratitude for both freeing them and how gentle I had been. I looked at Gabby and she smiled, nodding for me to proceed.

She was already aware of how I had treated my review of her sister's mind, so was fully prepared not to resist. I entered her mind and felt the same echoing sensation, but I heard her thoughts as what I can only describe as a different note in the harmony.

They were definitely two distinct individuals with their own feelings and thoughts, however they were so intricately linked as to function as one for most things. I learned exactly the same from her mind as from her sister. Neither one wanted to be anywhere near Atma (or Elrulin as I now knew him to be) when he recovered, but both understood my caution and agreed this was necessary. I withdrew from Gabby's mind and she too beamed at me. Then she looked at her sister, as I had known she would.

"Oh, he's very gentle, isn't he?" Gabby remarked.

"Yes, very. Thorough though," Izzy replied.

"Oh absolutely. You'd never be able to hide anything from him."

"No definitely not. He has remarkable skill considering when he obtained his magick."

"Doesn't he just? I think there's more to his story than we know."

"Oh most certainly. Still, we better get on and scan her. I want to get out of here."

"Good point, we need to be gone as soon as possible." They looked over at Angelica, who looked at me to check that I really was going to let them do this.

"They're OK, Angie," I said, seeing her smile at my shortening of her name. "They hated what they were made to do, but his control left them no choice. They want out, they just want to make sure they're not escaping only to be brought back here again. I'll monitor them and make sure they're gentle and don't exceed what they need to see." I looked over at the girls and they nodded at me. "I'm sure you're OK with that idea girls, right?" I asked them, wanting them to know I wasn't trying to control them but reassure her.

"I think that's a fair compromise," Isabella remarked.

"Yes, we can understand why she'd be nervous about trusting us," Gabriella chimed in. I was actually getting used to their slightly odd way of echoing each other and conversing together to further a conversation with someone else. After experiencing their thoughts, I certainly understood why they spoke and acted the way they did.

"She certainly saw enough to have reason for her anxiety," Izzy continued.

"Yes, although we're definitely sorry for our part in everything."

"Absolutely, and we want the chance to get even for what we were forced into."

"Oh, without a doubt. Anyway, let's get this done and get out of here." While they had been speaking I had used my magick, re-energised after my nap, to open my cell. I had already checked for any connected alarm systems and found none. I opened Angie's cell and she came out, standing straight and proud before the twins but edging closer to me than them.

I looked over at them and nodded, expanding my awareness to include all three of them but deliberately not entering Angelica's mind to allow her privacy. If she really did like me, I didn't want to ruin my chances by having her upset that I'd peeked where I shouldn't. I simply observed the twin's process and made sure they were being respectful and thorough without going too far. They were quick, clearly wanting to get done so we could all leave. Afterwards they stepped forward and hugged Angie, much to my surprise.

"We didn't know, but we should have suspected something like that. We're so sorry," Gabby said to her, adding to my confusion.

"Yes, we understand now, and our story is not totally dissimilar. But you should know –"

Angie interrupted Izzy, taking their hand. "He told me when he was torturing me. He laughed in my face as he explained how it really worked," she said. They hugged again, and I stood mystified at the vagaries of female thinking and the rapid shifts of their emotional spectrum. This was deeper magick than any man was ever meant to understand! They separated and looked at me, all smiling together at my bewildered expression, so I shook my head and then smiled myself.

"Good, so everyone happy? All friends now?" I asked, ready to get the hell out of there.

"Well, I wouldn't necessarily say friends, but certainly less hostile," Angie said, glancing at the twins who nodded in agreement. "I think friendship will take time to develop, but at least we understand each other better now." Gabby and Izzy smiled at the end of Angie's statement.

"That's a fair assessment," said Gabby.

"Yes, a very reasonable evaluation," added Izzy.

"We couldn't ask for more just yet."

"It would be too soon to talk of true friendship."

"That certainly would be premature," chimed in Angelica, sounding almost eerily in tune with the twins. They then all looked at me and smiled.

"Don't you bloody start, I get dizzy enough just going back and forth between them!" I said to Angie, laughing. They joined in as the stress and distrust bled off slightly. Gauvain shuffled on my shoulder where he had been silently observing throughout all this, reminding me we needed to get moving.

I reminded myself that the twins, although seeming eager to help right now, were primarily interested in each other to the exclusion of anyone else. If they felt for even a *moment* Angie or I were slowing them down or hindering their ability to escape, I harboured no illusion: They would drop us like a hot potato and just keep going.

I would make sure to keep my eyes peeled until trust had been truly earned, which for my part was certainly going to take a while. We all spun to face the door behind the twins as the lock clicked and it began to swing open.

Chapter 22

I wasn't sure if I'd be able to teleport us all out of the Order's headquarters since they might have boundaries around it much like they did around the time suite. I couldn't afford to try only to be rebuffed and recaptured. Instead I put one hand on the twins' shoulder and one on Angie's and recreated my cloaking device, rendering us invisible while telepathically telling everyone to hold as still as possible to make it as effective as it could be.

My own pucker factor shot past a thousand and kept climbing, but I refused to let on. I was just in time as the door swung wide and Stheno came in. She must have woken up and left the time room while I was asleep.

She stopped suddenly as she saw the empty cells. Her snake hair stood out like a serpentine afro, hissing up a storm in her consternation. I held my breath and hoped, feeling the girls do the same.

"Oh shit!" she said, putting her face in her hands. "That dumb-fuck troll put him in a normal cell! He must have gotten out as soon as he got his strength back and taken her with him! I'm gonna get blamed for this, I just know it!" She turned and scuttled out, leaving the door wide open since there was apparently no one to keep locked in here now.

My heart leapt to see such a helpful escape route appear so conveniently but I remembered my dumb mistake on the way in, so I extended my senses all around to check for any means of detecting us. I also linked our minds together properly so we could communicate without speaking. I kept it superficial so we would have to actively think *at* each other though, rather than all our thoughts and feelings spilling over into each other.

The twins may have been used to that with each other, but the rest of us certainly weren't. I felt Gauvain leave my shoulder and enter his claw on my bracelet as the most expedient and stealthy way of getting out without distracting me, and I sent him my thanks for his foresight.

OK ladies, you all know this place far better than me, I thought to them all. *I'm assuming that between you, you'll know the best way out. I'm in your hands.*

Ooh, he called us ladies! came the thought from one of the twins.

Yes, what a gentleman, chimed in the other.

And he's put himself in our hands.

Yes, that definitely presents possibilities.

I'm wondering how many hands he thinks he can deal with, came Angelica's thoughts, clearly tinged with both laughter and innuendo, making me very glad I was both invisible and *not* fully linked with them all. I blushed, and my mind immediately diverted into the various possibilities and permutations. Would it count as a threesome or a foursome? It would depend if you counted heads or bodies. Either way, this was definitely not the time to explore the potential.

Right now I'd settle for just one taking the lead and showing us all where to go, I remarked dryly, trying to get our escape back on track.

Oh, he likes a woman who can take charge girls, I heard Angelica's laughing thought to the twins, who both giggled in response. *Let's show him what we're capable of!* She deliberately tinged her thoughts with erotic overtones and the twins joined in immediately. It felt slightly forced, as if she was trying to put up a brave front to cover something else, but I let it slide for now.

Oh yes, do let's!

I bet we could show him all sorts of things! Then all three of them dissolved into hysterics, and I just shook my head.

You know, if I'd made those kind of jokes I could virtually guarantee that all three of you would have slapped me! I groused, making them all laugh even louder in my head and even struggle not to laugh out loud. I marvelled at how uniting against a man could turn previously hostile females into a cohesive fighting force in seconds. *Shhh, keep quiet or someone'll hear us!* I added, which calmed them down and reminded them just where we still were.

OK, let's do what one shepherd said to the other shepherd, said one of the twins, and I smirked in anticipation of the punchline. Surprisingly, all four of us thought it in unison:

LET'S GET THE FLOCK OUT OF HERE! We all laughed together, then the twins took my hand from their shoulder and led me towards the door Stheno had so kindly left open. I moved my other hand down Angelica's arm to take her hand, and we set off like an invisible pre-school walking crocodile to make sure we didn't lose anyone.

To judge from the conversations we'd just had, the twins and Angelica now understood and more or less trusted each other, even if they weren't calling it friendship just yet. That was clearly going to make my life both easier, in terms of getting them to cooperate, and much, *much* harder in terms of being ganged up on by women and being scrutinised in any romantic overtures. Gods help me if they teamed up with Seirina as well, especially with her being an enchantress. I had a funny feeling it was almost inevitably going to happen, and I knew Summer would probably take great delight in assisting in my torture.

Maybe I'd be better off just going back to Atma and letting him have at me? I remembered the sensation of his teeth sinking into my neck and shuddered. Nope, no, nu-uh, negative, never, no way, nyet, iyé, non, nein, and hells nah, bruh!

I briefly entertained the thought of dropping their hands and running for my life as a viable alternative, then laughed at myself. I could feel their curiosity as my laughter trickled across our link, but they let it slide as we all focused on getting out.

Is there a reason we couldn't teleport out? I asked as the thought occurred to me again. *Has the Order protected the entire area against magickal translocation?* I could feel the attention of all three women focus on me in curiosity.

No, but it just never occurred to me to suggest it, thought Angelica in surprise. *It's not like we could do it anyway...* Her thoughts trailed off as she understood *why* I was asking the question. *Wait,* could *we? Are you saying you can do that?* The twins were equally surprised.

That's a very advanced ability, thought Gabby.

Yes, it certainly is, Izzy agreed.

If he can do that, he's definitely *had significant training over an extended period.*

He must have. But when?

That's right, there hasn't been time since he got his magick.

Certainly not enough to learn that sort of skill.

And definitely nowhere near enough to be reliable at it.

Girls, I'll explain later. For now just answer the question, please! I interrupted before their conversation turned into a full-fledged debate. *Can we teleport now that we're out of the cells?*

As far as we know, the only place that's protected like that is the questioning suite, replied Gabby.

That's right. Although the Order doesn't have anyone who can do it, so there was never a reason to restrict use of the ability, added Izzy.

The suite and the magick-suppression cell are the only permanent restrictions, and in between locations they use the cuffs you had on, Angelica finished. I grinned widely, not that any of them could see me, and pictured where I had left the car.

Wait, what time is it? I asked suddenly. *My watch and phone got taken when I was captured, so I've got no idea what time it is or even what day. I've completely lost track.*

It's about half past ten in the morning, thought Izzy.

Yes, you were captured at one o'clock this morning, added Gabby.

It's only been nine and a half hours since the alarm went off when I opened the cell area door? I thought in surprise. *Wow, that time distortion really messes with your head!*

You should feel it from my side! chimed in Angelica. *I thought it had been months, then I find out it's been less than a day since I went into that damned room!*

Yeah, I get it, I replied sympathetically. *I just needed to know whether to picture daylight or night time.* So saying, I visualised the car in sunshine and *moved* us out and away from the corridor to place us next to the car on the hillside.

Since I'd parked in a vantage point car park, the view was beautiful but none of the girls were paying attention to it when I dropped the invisibility. Instead they were all staring at me in complete shock. I

145

uncoupled our thoughts and let go of their hands, then gave a dramatic sweeping bow as if I were a stage magician at the culmination of an illusion.

"Ta-da!" I said, at which point G flew out of his claw and landed on my shoulder as I straightened up. Boy, was *that* ever the wrong thing to say! Angelica stepped forward and started poking me hard in the chest with each word.

"TA-DA?!" she yelled, startling Gauvain who promptly launched himself off my shoulder and went for a flight to stretch his wings. "TA-FUCKING-DA?! Are you *seriously* going to stand there and say 'ta-da' after teleporting three people with ease and accuracy when you told me you only had some weak magick unlocked a couple of weeks ago? I just got tortured and interrogated for months because you didn't tell me everything, and all you can say is *ta-fucking-da*?!"

I stepped back and rubbed my chest where she had been poking me, feeling guilty once again for all she had been subjected to because of me. Still, I was proud that I'd achieved my first multi-person teleportation so adroitly.

"Again, I am *so* sorry you went through that, but I had no idea what sort of organisation you were working for at the time," I said regretfully. "I would *never* have wanted you to go through anything of that sort because of me. Had I known who you worked for, I'd have handled it very differently. I just didn't want some bunch of what I thought was nosy wannabes coming around begging me to show them tricks and do things for them. Nor did I plan to try to teach them things they had no chance of learning, basically disrupting my entire life." She calmed down a little and stepped back next to the twins who, to my surprise, put an arm around her shoulders.

"It's a reasonable explanation," said Gabby, looking at her kindly.

"Yes, but she still has every reason to be upset by what she went through," said Izzy, glowering at me on Angie's behalf.

"She certainly does, and he has a lot to make up for," Gabby replied, turning to look at me and matching her sister's angry expression. Great, now I had *three* women righteously pissed at me!

"Oh, you're not kidding!" said Angie. "He'd better come up with some seriously complete back story now, then follow it up with some outstanding grovelling. I'm thinking a Michelin-starred restaurant and about five dozen roses just as a start!"

My heart leapt at the implication that she was still willing to even consider a date with me and I caught my breath. The twins looked at her and she at them, then all three of them looked at me with angry expressions and I started breathing again. Maybe I wasn't *quite* as dead as I thought!

"I promise, I'll tell you more. At least where I can, since some things aren't my secrets to share. Right now, I think we should vacate the area. We're still not particularly far from the castle, and someone could possibly detect us after my teleporting us here." The twins immediately shook their heads in unison.

"I doubt it," said Izzy reassuringly.

"No, that's highly unlikely," added Gabby.

"That's one of the reasons Atma wanted you."

"Exactly. There's no one in the Order with that level of power or ability."

"Not even close."

"Most of the magick users can only do one thing, like Angie or us with telepathy."

"And even that's weak compared to you."

"In fact, the three of us are among the strongest telepaths in the Order." Angie looked at the twins in surprised gratitude at their recognition of her skills.

"Thank you!" she said to them. "But I'm nowhere near your level." They smiled at her in return.

"Actually compared to us individually, you're about our equal," said Gabby kindly.

"Yes, it's only because we can link together and multiply our power that we're stronger," added Izzy. Angelica stood just a little straighter and her chin lifted a fraction in pride.

I smiled at the twins, nodding in gratitude at their efforts to reassure her and bolster her confidence after all she'd been through. I also appreciated that they were trying to build bridges and cement their promising start towards genuine friendship from earlier.

"Let's get going for now." I dared to open my mouth to move things along. Despite their reassurances, I had no desire to be caught out here chatting. The Order might not have any *one* person powerful enough but if their entire contingent of magick users mobilised, we'd still be up that well known creek without any means of propulsion.

"We can talk more on the road and once we're somewhere safe." I called G with my mind and turned to unlock the car before realising my keys had also been taken when I was captured. "Bollocks!" I swore, wondering what to do now. Then I heard a jingle and turned to see the twins holding out my keys, phone and watch with big grins on their faces.

"We picked these up on our way to get you."

"We just got slightly diverted by other things before we could give them to you."

I reached out gratefully and took everything from them, stepping forward and giving each of them a kiss on the cheek.

"You girls are awesome! Thank you so much!" They giggled together and Angie hugged them tightly. Gauvain swooped down and landed on my shoulder. "Right, let's get out of here! You girls will need to share the back seat, G's car perch is set up in the front." Everyone piled in and I switched the car on and pulled out, heading back to the motorway.

"Maybe we should get him a cap while he chauffeurs us around!" joked Angelica, much to the amusement of Gabby and Izzy.

"I think I liked it better when you guys weren't getting along quite so well!" I remarked wryly, and they all joined in the laughter as the miles slipped by.

Chapter 23

I decided the best place to go would be Seirina's home for a couple of reasons. Firstly she was probably wondering what had happened to me after I left, and secondly because the Order would no doubt think to look for us either at my place or the shop. The shop was well protected by the wards, but I still didn't fancy a big confrontation at the moment. Taking them back to my place, on the other hand, would create connotations I just wasn't ready to deal with right now. However I didn't want to just turn up unannounced, so I triggered the hands-free system in the car and told it to call Seirina.

"Ooh, he knows Seirina," came the whispered voice of one of the twins.

"She must have been the one who told him how to find the Order."

"Yes, she's apparently hated them ever since her husband was taken."

I tuned out the conversation in the back as the phone started ringing, but I heard Angelica joining in as they discussed Seirina's unfortunate history with Elrulin. The phone was answered after only a few rings, but it wasn't the voice I was expecting to hear.

"Ms Crow's residence, how may I help you?" The Yorkshire tones of the ever-present Mrs Wilson came through the car's speakers, reducing the whispers from the back seat to an almost inaudible level.

"Good morning Mrs Wilson," I replied, my London accent and clipped vowels becoming more pronounced in response to her polite greeting. "It's Gavan Maddox. Is Ms Crow available?"

"Oh, hello lad," she replied. "Ms Crow was wondering if we might be hearing from you today. She's just in a meeting at the moment. She left instructions that if you were to ring I was to tell you, and I quote, 'Get your arse over here and tell me what happened.' Sorry, but she was very specific that I use those exact words." I laughed loudly, and the girls behind me joined in.

"That's quite alright Mrs Wilson," I managed to say finally. "I would expect nothing less. Please let her know I'm on my way with some friends, and we'll be there in about an hour and a half if the traffic stays clear."

"I'm sure she'll be happy to hear that," came the reply. "She was most put out that we hadn't heard from you last night and was worried summat had gone terribly wrong."

"Please let her know I'll fill her in on everything that happened when I get there," I responded. "Thank you, Mrs Wilson."

"Right you are, lad. Drive safely and we'll see you shortly." So saying, she hung up and I did the same.

"Well, that answers *that* question," Angelica said from the back seat. "I guess she told you where to find the Order?" I nodded, making a bet with myself on the next question. "So how do you know her? She's an enchantress, isn't she?" she continued, and I smiled to myself as I heard exactly what I had expected to hear.

"You can wipe that silly smile off your face right now you smug git!" she finished. I couldn't help myself, I burst out laughing and the twins joined in. They were clearly comfortable enough with her after scanning her mind to tease her gently.

"Oh look, she's jealous."

"I know, isn't it sweet?"

"She definitely likes him."

"And he clearly likes her if he came looking for her in the Order's headquarters."

"It's so romantic."

"Like a knight on a quest."

"Saving the damsel in distress."

"Does that make Atma the dragon?"

"Well his breath was certainly bad enough!" They both laughed and Angelica and I joined in. Gauvain roused from a semi-snooze at the noise.

Oh for goodness' sake, can I not have a nap in peace? he grumped, projecting his thoughts to all of us, then turned and began preening the feathers of his left wing.

"Sorry bud, I think the stress is just starting to bleed off a bit," I said, reaching out to stroke his head. He responded by rubbing against my hand and clicking his beak.

"He's a beautiful bird," said one of the twins, causing him to shuffle slightly more towards the centre of the car so they could see him better.

"Very. Lovely markings."

"Big for a hawk too."

"Yes, more like an eagle size-wise."

"They seem very closely linked."

"They're certainly very used to each other."

"They've definitely been together longer than just a couple of weeks."

"Must have been. But how?"

"It's a puzzle alright."

"One that *better* get cleared up, or someone's getting a foot up his arse!" came Angelica's grumpy contribution, making me laugh and wince at the same time as I understood rescuing her hadn't gotten me out of the woods with her just yet.

"Yeah, I get it," I replied wryly. "Seirina has the same questions, and she deserves to hear the answers too after helping me find you. You'd still be in the cells and Gabby and Izzy would still be bound to that obnoxious cock-goblin if she hadn't helped me. And to answer your earlier question, she helped me locate a particular book for a commission a couple of years ago. I'd exhausted all my other contacts to try to locate the Order and she was my last hope. So in response to your other question, yes, she's an enchantress but I'd like to point out, I'd never met her in person before yesterday."

I wanted to be very clear on that last point. I didn't much fancy dealing with ruffled feathers and bruised egos, especially when there was no cause for them in the first place. Man, trying to anticipate women was more exhausting than torture, and the downside if you fucked it up was infinitely worse! The twins giggled again at my discomfort.

"Aaaww, isn't that sweet?" said one.

"I know. He doesn't want her to be jealous."

"Mind you Seirina is over three hundred years old, if I remember her file right."

"Yes, so Gavan would be like a child by comparison."

"Wasn't there something else about her in the files?"

"Yes, another ability she has. Something the Order was very interested in."

"Yes, very interested, but the details were classified."

"If her picture is accurate she's very pretty," one of them dropped in slyly. I heard a quiet "Humph" at that from Angelica, making the twins erupt into giggles again.

"Oh, you two are evil!" she groused, realising they were just trying to wind her up but still not happy about what they had suggested. "Just you wait until you get boyfriends, then we'll see. I can already imagine some of the jokes!"

My brain went into meltdown at the possibilities that occurred in response to *that* comment, so I wisely just kept my mouth shut and concentrated on the road. Discretion always *was* the better part of valour, even if some might call it simply cowardice in this case.

"Boyfriends? What an interesting notion."

"Yes, I'm not sure how we'd make that work."

"It would certainly be a challenge."

"We'd both have to like them."

"Of course, and they'd have to accept us as we are."

"That could be a problem."

"There's not many open-minded or tolerant people out there."

"Even average people struggle; for anyone different it can be almost impossible."

"At least we know no man would ever get between us or drive us apart!" They both laughed at that, and I quietly quoted Mr T at the thought of any man trying to get those two to disagree.

"I pity the fool, I do, I pity the fool!" Gauvain of course heard me via our link and chuckled in my mind.

"What was that driver?" called Angie, seeing my lips move and the smile on my face. "You shouldn't be listening to the conversations of your betters," she remarked, much to the amusement of the twins.

"Humph. I'll give you 'betters'!" I replied, pretending to take umbrage at her supercilious tone. "I'll put you across my knee if you keep that up young lady!"

"Ooh promises, promises!" she replied breathily, dropping her voice seductively. "But you've got a way to go before you earn the right to get that close." The twins were quick to jump in.

"I do love a strong man who isn't afraid to take charge," one said sarcastically.

"It makes a woman feel like a *woman*!" the other added, heaping on the irony.

"He does look to have lovely strong hands."

"I bet he could be so forceful if he wanted!" Angelica couldn't contain herself and finally burst out laughing, while the direction of the conversation was making me shift in my seat to ease certain… pressures. My discomfort unfortunately did not go unnoticed by the eagle-eyed females behind me.

"Ha, he's got ants in his pants!" said one of the twins.

"I don't think it's *ants*!" replied the other, laughing.

"I'd hope it's bigger than an ant!" Angelica laughed saucily. I shook my head at the direction this was going, but refused to get sucked in.

"That's for me to know, thank you very much!" I said primly.

"And some lucky girl to find out!" Angie quipped to the twins, who laughed again. The tone of her voice caused the hairs on the back of my neck to stand up somewhat. She sounded again as if she was *forcing* the humour. I was a little concerned over just what she might be trying to suppress from her time in Elrulin's torture chamber.

The miles were steadily being eaten up as we continued down the motorway, thankfully free of too much traffic since rush hour was well past. I was keeping an eye on the mirror to see if anyone was following us, but since everyone was heading in the same direction it wasn't exactly obvious. I did change lanes and speeds a few times, and didn't notice anyone matching us. The farther we got from Bolton Castle, the easier I breathed.

"Who says it would be a girl?" I threw into the conversation, just to see what reaction I would get. I was gratified by the stunned silence from the back, broken by a sudden rush of whispering.

"Do you think he is?"

"He can't be, not after his reaction earlier."

"Maybe he's both?"

"Do you think so?"

"I suppose it's possible."

"He never struck me that way, but I suppose he could be," Angelica's voice joined the twins, and I smiled as I at last got a little peace to just enjoy the simple act of driving. I reached softly towards G, who had dropped back to sleep on his perch, rocked by the gentle motion and soothed by the low hum of the car. I found him dreaming of soaring in the countryside so I withdrew, leaving him in peace.

Soon enough I reached the exit we needed and turned off, gratified to see no one following us. I navigated the streets under the direction of the angry computer voice, finally arriving at the closed gate to Seirina's home.

Chapter 24

I lowered the window and pressed the intercom button, giving my name when Mrs Wilson answered. She triggered the gate and I drove through once it swung open. As we crunched up the gravel driveway I heard the twins and Angelica exchanging hushed whispers, although I couldn't tell what they were saying over the noise of the tyres.

I pulled up in the same spot as the day before and marvelled to myself about everything that had occurred in just the last twenty-four hours. I shut off the engine and released my seatbelt, then turned to the girls to see them looking somewhat nervous.

"I don't know what you've heard or read about Seirina," I began, "but she helped me out and is the only reason you're all here and free. You might not know her or trust her yet, but you're here as my guests so I ask that you *will* respect her in her own home and be polite. It wouldn't hurt to show a little gratitude either.

"You didn't trust each other at first and I supported each of you to the others along with the telepathic screening we did to speed our escape along. I'm not doing that here, since the only person who has reason to be distrustful now is Seirina. Especially as she has no reason other than my word to believe you're genuinely wanting to get away from the Order. Please don't embarrass me."

"Ooh, so domineering," Angelica smiled, but it slipped when I didn't laugh.

"This isn't a joke," I said seriously. "I asked her to start contacting anyone she might know who would want to join us in trying to fight the Order because of previous experiences. She got on with it before I was even out the door, simply because I asked her to.

"If you want my help, you'll accept her. I'm perfectly happy for you to take your time getting to know her, but let's start off on the right foot. She's taken a leap of faith with me, so all I'm asking is that you grace her with the same." All three of them nodded this time so now I grinned. "Thanks for understanding. Now let's go." We all got out of the car, Gauvain fluttering to my shoulder and nibbling my ear.

Well put, he said to me privately. *Best to set out your position at the very beginning to prevent misunderstandings, and Seirina certainly deserves their gratitude.* I stroked his head and silently thanked him for his support. As we approached the front door, the inestimable Mrs Wilson opened it before we even had a chance to knock. I nodded to her and gave a slight bow.

"Thank you Mrs Wilson, perfect timing as usual," I said. "Please allow me to introduce Angelica, Gabriella and Isabella." I gestured to each of them in turn and Mrs Wilson nodded at them as I did so.

"It's good to see you back again Mr Maddox," she said, motioning everyone to step inside and closing the door behind us. "Ms Crow is waiting in the study. This way please ladies." She sidled past us all in the narrow entrance and led the way down the hall, just as she had done the day before. I marvelled again at quite how much could happen in just a day.

I trailed along behind, noticing the Welsh dresser once again and spotting a couple of oriental-looking plates with pictures of dragons on them. I felt the now familiar, slightly slimy feeling of Seirina's magick intensifying as we drew closer. The girls seemed to at least be aware of its presence as they drew together and held back. I strode past them and reached the door as Mrs Wilson knocked.

"Here 'e is, Miss," she announced as she swung open the study door, her Yorkshire accent becoming slightly more prominent for a moment. "There's some guests with 'im this time, like 'e said on the phone."

"Thank you Mrs Wilson," came Seirina's voice (without her heavy Scottish accent) from inside the room. "Please show them in."

I rounded the door frame and she stood up from her chair when she saw me. I noticed she was wearing a midnight blue dress today, with slight fringing around the short sleeves and a necklace with a gold circular pendant.

The circle had no back and showed a silhouette of a crescent moon at the top, with either a rabbit or hare at the bottom. I walked towards her, ready to thank her for all her help the previous day. Before I could say anything, I noticed her eyes flick past me as the girls sidled in.

I suddenly appreciated the true level of her power, as she drew it into herself when she saw them. Strands of her hair actually floated out from her head and all of it darkened to almost black, her eyes glowing green to obscure the mismatched natural colours.

Gauvain immediately picked up on the danger and sensibly flew off of my shoulder, retreating to the other side of the study to perch on the back of the love-seat in the bay window. I instinctively dropped back into a ready stance, my martial arts training preparing me to confront the threat even though I knew it wasn't directed primarily at me.

The girls clung to each other and tried to hide behind me, backing up to the wall away from Seirina. The rustling I had heard yesterday from the terrarium started up again, this time more intensely than ever.

"What the HELL were you thinking, bringing *them* here?" she snarled at me, clearly recognising the twins and Angelica from her research into the Order. Her eyes were actually starting to smoke with the intensity of her rage, and I was worried she might lose control before I had a chance to explain things to her.

I held my hands out in front of me placatingly and considered reaching out to her mind, but she narrowed her eyes at me and tilted her head ever so slightly in a way that told me very clearly not to try it. Time to try good old-fashioned talking. I took a deep breath, realising this would be like trying to walk a tightrope across Niagara Falls while blindfolded, carrying several greased ferrets and wearing army boots covered in oil.

"OK clearly you know who they are, so introductions aren't going to be necessary," I started, acknowledging her anger and allowing that she had legitimate reasons for it. My attempt at levity went down like a lead balloon however, so I tried a different tack. "Angelica is the liaison I went there to rescue. You know why, you even told me, but I appreciate that you didn't know exactly who I was talking about. Gabby and Izzy came to help us escape when I inadvertently managed to free them from their boss' psychic control."

Seirina seemed to listen and calm slightly at my explanation, at least enough for her eyes to stop smoking and her hair to lighten a shade. It wasn't much, but I'd take any improvement I could get at this point.

"And how can you be sure they're not just playing you, tagging along simply to find out who you're working with and what you know?" she asked, still clearly pissed but at least giving me a chance to explain.

"They agreed to let me into their minds, and I discovered exactly how and why they were forced to work for the Order. And they *were* forced. Speaking of which…" I turned to the twins and held out my mobile phone. "I think you need to make a phone call and get them away from where the Order knows they are. Get them to go somewhere unexpected, and we'll catch up with them later when we work out a more permanent solution." I spoke in nebulous generalities as I didn't want to betray the twins' family situation to Seirina until they had established some trust.

I turned back to see Seirina looking at me with her mouth open. She appeared to be in such shock that I'd turned my back on her and essentially ignored her for a moment, that her hair faded back to its usual titian red and the green faded from her eyes. She may have let the power go, but I could tell she still wasn't convinced about having Order personnel in her home. Even ex-personnel. She narrowed her eyes as she looked at me.

"Are you *absolutely certain* they couldn't and didn't hide anything from you?" she asked, clearly wanting to trust me but understandably concerned over the possible repercussions if I was wrong. "You're still so new to your magick, and your emotions make it unreliable. They could have simply played out an elaborate charade to gain your trust. We both know how men get stupid around pretty girls."

I smiled ruefully and rubbed the back of my neck, acknowledging the validity of her concerns as far as she understood my abilities. It looked like it was time to fill in a few blanks and show some trust if I wanted everyone else to show some in return.

"I think it's time you understood a little bit more about my powers and training," I said. I heard a beep as the twins ended their call, and then felt them lay the phone on my shoulder. I took it from them without looking and put it back in my pocket, still maintaining eye contact with Seirina. She quirked an eyebrow at me, then sighed and shook her head.

"I don't know what it is about you that makes me trust you Gavan, but I know I felt your strength when you invaded my mind yesterday," she said. "You told me there was more to your story, so I guess I'll listen. Just remember, I still don't trust those two… three… two; wait, let's get this straight first. Are you one being or two?" She addressed the twins directly for the first time.

"Oh, she's talking to us now," came a voice from behind me, and I smiled in anticipation of what was about to happen. I crossed my arms then waited, and I was rewarded in moments. *Here we go again…*

"Yes she is."

"At least she seems to have calmed down a bit."

"She went from zero to scary in no time when we walked in."

"Well I'm sure she knew about us from trying to track down the Order."

"Yes, we've been stuck with the boss for years now."

About this point I moved to the side, so Seirina could get the full effect of the verbal tennis volley that characterised any of the twins' exchanges.

"I definitely understand now why the Order wanted her."

"You're not kidding. They'd kill for that kind of power."

"The boss has, on numerous occasions."

"But he still didn't get what he wanted."

"Not in her case, no."

"I suppose we should answer her question."

"Well we are in her house, so it would be rude not to."

I was looking at Seirina as Gabby and Izzy were talking, and I had to smother a laugh at her expression as it went from curiosity to surprise to stupefied disbelief.

"We're separate, but always together," Gabby said to Seirina, who was looking aghast at them. She quickly shook her head and nodded in reply, then looked over at me as I was struggling not to laugh.

"Do they always do that?" she asked me in amazement.

"Yup." I strained briefly, finally getting myself under control with a few deep breaths. "Don't worry, you do eventually get used to it but it takes a while." I winked at the twins and they smiled back. I looked back at Seirina questioningly and she sighed.

"Fine, everyone sit down. We'll have some tea and Gavan can illuminate us on what he *hasn't* told us about his magickal awakening." She scowled jokingly at me and I took a deep breath, while she motioned for the girls to sit down.

Mrs Wilson, with her unerring sense of timing, came in with a tray of tea and biscuits and everyone got served. Then they all looked at me expectantly, so I sipped at my cup and began the tale of what I had found when I touched the Veil.

Chapter 25

As my tale drew to a close, all four women looked at me with varying degrees of disbelief, surprise and anger. The first two I had expected and the third I felt I probably deserved from Angelica, especially after what she had been through because of me. The others, however, I felt had no reason to be angry. I had told all of them the truth when asked initially, just not all of it.

I admitted to myself that even now I hadn't revealed *everything* about my training, since they didn't need to know quite that much. I had at least told them about Aaru, Isis, and how long I'd been trained for. I wasn't worried about revealing those details, since Elrulin had learned that much from our link when he had bitten me.

Call me paranoid but if any of them decided to betray me or were captured by the Order, at least they wouldn't be able to reveal anything he hadn't already discovered for himself.

While the twins and Seirina seemed to move past their initial reactions into acceptance fairly quickly, Angelica seemed to lose the surprise but hold onto her anger and nurture it into a simmering resentment.

I just hoped this wasn't going to become a deal-breaker between us. I was still interested in seeing what might develop if given the chance. For now though, I knew I was in deep trouble as the colour rose in her cheeks and her eyes went from upset to focused.

"You were taught magick by the goddess Isis herself after she unlocked your power and then enhanced it with some of her own. Yet you led me to believe you just had a few minor abilities," she said, almost eerily calm and precise. "You told the same *bullshit* story to my boss, only he wasn't quite as gullible as me and didn't meekly swallow your crap.

"He then thought I had lied to him and knew more than I did, so he tortured me for months in that damned room only to learn absolutely nothing. And now you just expect me to trust you and work alongside you?" Yup, I could definitely feel the shit rising fast. By my estimation it was already up to my armpits, and swiftly getting higher.

"Umm, Isis didn't actually instruct me herself," I offered somewhat lamely. I knew it was the wrong thing to say as soon as the words were out of my mouth, but it was too late to call them back.

"Oh so poor Gavan only got powered up by the original goddess of magick, he didn't get personally taught by her. My heart bleeds for you!" She quickly lost the spooky calmness and moved into directed fury. Unfortunately for me, that direction was squarely mine.

"Can you honestly say that had our roles been reversed, you would have told me everything and let me take that information back to a group you knew nothing about?" I kept my voice low, calm and reasonable in an attempt to counteract her extreme emotions.

I made very sure not to tell her to calm down, since I knew that would be about as effective as trying to put out a forest fire with gasoline. I also didn't want to get into a shouting match with someone I wanted to be on good terms with, so I was going to have to try to stay calm and take my lumps.

My question did at least make Seirina and the twins look reflectively at me and nod, which gave me some encouragement that I might be making some kind of sense and progress. Angelica also sat back in her chair but I could tell that I wasn't out of the woods just yet.

"OK," she allowed, "I suppose that's true. I certainly wouldn't have shared all my secrets with you after just a couple of meetings, especially if you'd come on behalf of a group I knew nothing about. I *might*, however, have been up-front and *told* you that I wasn't telling you everything so you could at least cover yourself with your boss!" She grew heated again at my perceived negligence towards her.

"But then you would have reported that I wasn't telling you everything," I reasoned, "and your boss would have tried to abduct me to find out what else there was to know. I had to make a judgement call, and I freely admit I misjudged your boss' level of interest in me. For that, I sincerely apologise.

"I know something of what you were put through, and I regret it more than you know, but I did what I thought was right."

My display of honest contrition cooled her anger a little and she looked thoughtful, possibly reflecting on my comments and considering what she truly would have done in my place. I hardly dared to breathe, scared to disturb her, and simply looked over at Seirina hopefully. She nodded minimally and gave me a slight shrug, lifting my hopes that I might actually be doing the right thing. Now I just had to wait to see if Angelica agreed with her assessment.

"Can I use your bathroom?" I asked quietly, and Seirina nodded briefly. I eased out of the chair, desperately trying not to make any noise, then headed out of the study. As I closed the door, Mrs Wilson stuck her head out of what appeared to be the kitchen at the end of the hall and gave me directions to the facilities when I asked.

As I washed my hands afterward, I looked at myself in the mirror wondering what to do next. At least the twins' brother was now alerted and hopefully moved out of harm's way, but what about everyone else who was in danger from the Order?

I decided that, regardless of Angelica's decision, I couldn't let Elrulin keep going the way he was. Isis had given me back my power for a reason and I had to show I was worthy of it. I would ask Seirina if she had managed to contact anyone who was interested in working against the Order and go from there.

I straightened up and squared my shoulders, glad I now had a course of action to follow. My personal life had to be separate, and I would take it as it came. I suddenly felt Gauvain contacting me.

That was a very adroit tactical retreat, and the ladies have been discussing your numerous revelations, he told me. *Fortunately they seem to have completely forgotten my presence, or at least that I can understand them and relay details to you. I would say the time has come to return, as they seem to be drawing to a conclusion.*

Any hints on how I've come out of this? I asked him, hoping for some insight one way or another. *Am I in the clear? Hung jury? Or am I about to be hung, possibly by the family jewels from the curtain rail?*

I could detect his amusement at my sense of unease, but the feathery bastard stayed traitorously quiet. I grumbled to myself as I walked back to the study, thinking up numerous imaginative revenge plans for his silence which made him laugh as I sent them to him. Then I took a deep breath as I paused at the study door, squared my shoulders and walked in.

All four heads turned in unison as I walked in, and I got the sense I had interrupted some secret feminine summit meeting. G flew over and landed on my shoulder and I saw Angelica start slightly as he glided past her.

She clearly *had* forgotten his presence and she narrowed her eyes at him suspiciously, then looked at me almost accusingly as if I had bugged their meeting and been eavesdropping. I kinda had but not really and not intentionally, plus my feckless feathered familiar hadn't furnished me with any factoids anyway.

"No, Miss Angie, he ain't been droppin' no eaves!" I said in my best Samwise voice, generating smiles from all of them.

"Oh I love the *Lord of the Rings* movies," chimed in Seirina, immediately catching the reference.

"Only if it's the extended versions," responded Izzy.

"Yes, the cinema versions left out bits," added Gabby.

"But at least they put them back for the longer films."

"Yes, although it's annoying to have to change discs halfway through."

"True, but it's worth it."

"We weren't as keen on *The Hobbit* movies."

"No, we weren't."

"They over-did it to try to get three movies out of it."

"Yes, much of it felt unnecessary and we're still sure they added scenes."

"Absolutely, I don't recall some of those bits from the book."

"Oh, books are always better."

"Yes, the mind is a much more satisfactory film-maker."

"Films can never quite capture the sense of total involvement that a book can create."

"No, a good story can absorb you in a totally unique way."

"Talking of stories, have we heard everything about yours yet or are you still giving us the edited for TV version?" came Angelica's interjection just as I was starting to relax back into the chair. I rubbed my forehead and sighed, realising I wasn't quite in the clear just yet.

"Umm, this is sort of the movie adaptation version," I explained, trying to keep things light and continuing the theme. "You know all the relevant information, but I've kept certain details about what and how much I learned and who taught me to myself. No disrespect to any of you, but we're all virtual strangers and I doubt any of you would reveal *everything* about your training and abilities to me.

"You certainly know enough to be going on with but, for right now, I think we need to decide what we're going to do about the Order. As far as that goes, there's something you need to know about Atma." They all looked at each other and then at me, sitting forward to hear my revelation.

"The reason he wanted the Veil was so he could try to use it to get to Aaru. You see, that's where he's from. He's not some talented magick user who learned how to cheat death. He was quite literally cast out of Heaven. He's basically a demon, and his true name is Elrulin."

The girls all sat back in their chairs with an assortment of emotions crossing their faces. From shock, to revulsion, to outright terror at the thought of who they had been dealing with. Also, for Angelica and the twins, what they had done with and for such a being.

Only Seirina had a gleam of triumph in her eyes at learning his true name, possibly already considering the ways in which such valuable information could be used. I could almost hear the wheels turning in her mind and I watched as her eyes became shuttered and she seemed to look inward to start her planning.

I was reluctant to disrupt her flow, but we needed to work as a team if this little resistance of ours was to be successful, so it was time to find out just how effectively her recruiting drive was going.

Chapter 26

"What sort of success did you have on your hunt for potential allies?" I asked Seirina, interrupting her musings before she could get too engrossed. "Did your rolodex prove helpful?" I smirked as I mentioned her stone-age filing system. The others looked at me in amazement, then back at her while trying to hide grins. It lightened the mood after the weight of my revelations. I remembered my joke from yesterday about not needing batteries and quirked an eyebrow at her, the corner of her mouth lifting ever so slightly as she no doubt remembered it too.

"It may take longer doing it by hand, but it can be far more satisfying," she deadpanned in response and I laughed aloud as my mind went down the path she set out for me. "I made a start on contacting some families I know who've had relatives taken or killed outright by the Order, and many have members who are thirsty for revenge. It will take time to go through my entire list, but I think I can promise a number who are considering meeting us for a preliminary discussion.

"I hope you're aware that trying to form any sort of alliance between so many disparate factions won't be easy. Many of them are natural enemies, such as vampires and werewolves, and trying to get them to cooperate will be worse than trying to collect fog with a fishing net. You're going to have to *prove* you're worthy to lead them before they'll even think about working together. Without them doing so, we'll have no chance against the Order. Powerful as you may be now, even you can't stand alone against hundreds of magick users and creatures. You need allies.

"My friend Iyrin has also been reaching out through less… conventional means to see who and what can be contacted, enticed or coerced to join our cause." While she was speaking I heard rustling emanating from the enclosure behind her again, only this time it didn't stop.

As I looked on, I saw something so pale it seemed to reject all colour moving up a large branch inside the tank. In the dimly lit environment, all that could be seen was a broken outline at first but as it moved along the branch, it approached the glass and I could begin to make out more details.

Its head was a human skull but about half the size of a child's. Its features were fully developed and not softened like those of an immature skull, yet it was still smaller than that of a pre-teen. Within the sockets were eyeballs that appeared human until it looked at me, whereupon I noticed there was no coloured iris. There was only a huge, inky black pupil that changed in size as it focused in the light.

The rest of it was pure skeleton. No flesh, no muscles, no tendons. It seemed able to rearrange its bones according to its needs. As it was climbing it looked hunched over and its forelimbs had hands like a chameleon with two digits on either side.

Once it approached the glass it extended, maintaining its balance with its hind limbs, and then its forelimbs shifted to a more human arm structure. The hands altered to assume a human, five-fingered configuration. It pressed them against the glass, looking as fine and precise as one might expect from a fairy or concert musician.

It appeared to be as tall as the length of my forearm and hand combined, so about fifteen to eighteen inches, and I had absolutely no clue what it was. As it focused its hypnotic Stygian gaze on me, it tilted its head ever so slightly, drawing me in irresistibly.

I eagerly reached out towards it with my mind, and as I did so Gauvain bit my ear hard enough to break my concentration. Seirina threw up her hand up in front of me, breaking my line of sight to the creature.

"Oh, I wouldn't do that if I were you," she said to me warningly. "Iyrin is no simple familiar. It's a being of pure magick, using that collection of bones for form. Each bone is from a different human it has previously known, which gives it more power still. It stays with me and works with me because it benefits us both. I have absolutely no doubt that when I die it will simply take a bone from me to add to itself, then move on without a backward glance."

My skin pebbled as goose-bumps erupted over my entire body and I quickly shut down my mental probe.

"So what actually is it?" I asked quietly, completely creeped out by its appearance and her description.

"A watcher," she replied simply, but would elaborate no further when pressed. I returned to the previous topic but my eyes involuntarily flicked to the unbroken stare of Iyrin from time to time as we talked. Each time, it acknowledged my curious interest with a slight bird-like alteration in the tilt of its head.

"I know I can't do this by myself, that's why I asked you to go through your contacts in the first place. I didn't know just how big an organisation I was dealing with until Angie told me about the other sites," I replied calmly, not wanting to rise to the bait of her earlier comment on the numbers we were facing.

"Still, from what you said yesterday and from the examples of the members I've already liberated, many of them have been coerced into working for the Order and may well join us if we can free them as well." I gestured towards Angelica and the twins as I spoke and they looked thoughtful in response, the twins even nodding slowly in tandem.

"This isn't going to be one quick fight," I continued. "Angie told me the Order has four locations in the UK and one in America. We're going to have to clear each one out like destroying ants' nests. The ones who are dedicated will regroup each time, so they'll get stronger and better prepared as we go. Ideally, if we can get enough people together, I'd like to hit all of the locations simultaneously to prevent exactly that problem. We'll just have to see how big a force we can muster. Even if we can hit two at a time, it'll help cut down their chance of reinforcing themselves."

Seirina was now the one to look startled at the revelation of the Order's multiple sites, clearly having been unaware they had anything other than Bolton Castle. She looked across at Angelica who nodded in response to the unasked question, confirming what I'd said. Seirina's shoulders slumped as she realised the scope of the task we were taking on, then she looked at me again with resolve in her mismatched eyes.

"I'll gather you every magick user and creature I can," she promised me. "It'll be up to you to make them follow you, but I'll make damn sure you get the chance to try. It's going to take more than a day to contact them all, then we'll need to bring them all together, so I'll let you know when I've got something sorted. In the meantime, where are your new friends going to live? I'm guessing they can't go back to their old homes without the Order finding them, so have you considered what they're going to do for clothes? Food? Sleeping?"

I sat back in my chair in surprise, completely blindsided by the change in direction of the conversation. I hadn't even considered the logistics of harbouring magickal refugees, especially considering the feelings I had for one of them and the fact that they were all women. There was no way I could take them back to my place, since the Order also knew where I lived.

Come to think of it, was *I* now going to have to move? What about my shop? Had I unwittingly torn my own life apart by my actions? I looked at Seirina in shocked dismay and almost terror at the realisation of the destruction I had just invited into my life, then understood it had actually sidled in when I had accepted their money to go hunting for the Veil. She looked back at me in pity, understanding that I was woefully underprepared for the world into which I had been thrust.

"I see," she said sympathetically. "You may have spent a year with gods, but you're singularly naïve in the ways of the magickal community here on Earth. You've been a shopkeeper all your adult life. You have absolutely no idea of the forces arrayed against you, do you?"

She shook her head and sighed. "Fortunately for you, I've been around long enough to have established several bolt-holes for use in times of need. I'll set your refugees up in one while you go and get what you need from home, then close up that charming shop of yours. You need to tell your little assistant to stay away for now, and that you'll call her when you're ready to re-open."

I was stunned at the sheer magnitude of my stupidity but realised I didn't have the luxury of time to wallow in my self-pity. We had already been talking for hours. In fact, it was easily time for lunch according to the gurgling noises coming from my stomach. I needed to get to the shop and tell Summer to make herself scarce. She had to be my priority. My stomach could make do on the biscuits I'd eaten for now, and I'd grab some clothes when I swung by my apartment on the way back. Summer, however, was completely oblivious to the shit-storm I'd kicked off and the danger I'd placed her in by doing so. Seirina was right: I had to get her out of harm's way and make her stay safe until this was resolved.

I nodded to all of them, promising I'd be back as soon as I'd taken care of things, and headed out to the car with Gauvain. I actually spun the wheels slightly in the gravel of the driveway in my haste to get to Summer and make sure she was OK. Fortunately Mrs Wilson had already opened the gate, so I didn't even have to wait for that. That woman seemed to have an uncanny knack of knowing what was needed at any given point.

I slowed briefly to check the traffic then swung out onto the road and accelerated hard, completely ignoring the speed limit as I did so. I kept my speed up as much as possible, slowing only for junctions or speed-traps.

As I drove, I cursed myself for a dozen kinds of fool for not thinking about the consequences of my actions. I truly had led a very sheltered life, never having had to consider such Machiavellian machinations. I was like a child playing cowboys and Indians, thinking everything was so clear-cut and pure.

Danu had warned me that I wasn't following through properly in my fights, that letting my enemies live just gave them a chance to come back stronger, better prepared, and with support. Even so, I'd let Oli run away after our fight because she was just a child, and I'd let Ciarán walk away in Tibet because I was so much stronger than him now. I just hadn't been paying attention and now I'd put my closest friend in the line of fire.

Gauvain wisely said nothing, simply offering his support across our link as I drove. I felt his calmness seep across with it and steady me, reducing my panic and allowing some clarity to return to my thinking.

If I wanted to protect Summer and Emily, the best place for them to be was surely the place that had already been warded and then further reinforced by me strengthening those defences. On top of that, I had given them both their Celtic knot necklaces strengthened with protective energies.

I may not have thought through the full ramifications of my quixotic actions, but I had at least shown a degree of forethought. I even remembered thinking we would need protecting from the Order (although I hadn't known their name at the time) when they found out they couldn't have the Veil. Maybe I wasn't quite as useless as all that, after all.

There was a reason I'd told Summer to stay in the apartment above the shop when I'd gone looking for the Veil and to keep Emily with her, so that Ciarán couldn't hurt them. Now that it was even more secure, I'd tell them the same thing again.

Even better, now that there was no reason to try to hide my power, I could ramp up the protection around the shop to such a degree that even someone in a bad mood would struggle to simply walk through the door. I was going to turn Dinas Affaraon into a magickal fortress that Isis herself would struggle to break into (I'm not saying she wouldn't be able to, but she'd have a headache doing it!).

As I calmed down, I slowed my driving to more reasonable (and legal) speeds and breathed more easily. Gauvain felt my relaxation and eased his death-grip on his perch. He looked across at me and fluffed his feathers, then settled them back with a rustle.

Well, you appear to have relaxed somewhat, he said, sounding relieved. *Would you care to share the thought process that has allowed for this most welcome change? I was under the impression you were concerned over the possible reprisals that might be visited on your young friend as a result of your chivalrous crusade into the heart of your enemy.*

I marvelled again at the style of his speech, that unique cross between an Arthurian knight, an English gentleman and a samurai. He embodied the kind of honour that epic tales were written about. Then at other times he made me remember just how young he really was with some innocent, unguarded remark.

"I remembered all of the protection that's been layered into the shop, and the added protection in the necklace I gave Summer when I came back from Aaru," I replied, loosening my strangle-hold on the steering wheel and flexing my fingers in relief as my own words penetrated my thick skull.

"I can beef it up still further when we get there, and Summer can stay above the shop with her girlfriend like she did when I went off hunting the Veil. No-one will be able to hurt them there, and by the time I'm done even a harsh word will give someone a migraine!" G bobbed his head in agreement with the sentiment, then started preening his wing to show his satisfaction with my plans and his new lack of concern.

Not long after that, I made the final turn of the journey and was relieved to see the familiar sign above the door of my beloved shop. I parked in the usual spot and headed in, comforted by the welcoming jingle of the bell.

Chapter 27

Summer turned around from one of the bookshelves as I walked in, frowning bemusedly at my sigh of relief at her safety. I walked over to her and drew her into a hug while G flew off my shoulder and landed on his perch next to the counter. As I continued to hold her, Summer patted my back and then leant back to look at me in confusion.

"I'm glad to see you too Gav, but what's with the overblown PDA?" she asked, groaning slightly as I gave her a final squeeze before letting go. "I'm guessing you found something out from Seirina about the Order that prompted this over-protective rush back? Although you didn't exactly rush, did you?" She smirked suggestively. "Did you have a nice night together? It's about time you danced a little bedroom boogaloo. Though to be honest I thought you were going to save yourself for Angelica, based on the way you'd been talking about her and how worried you were." I smiled and shook my head at her presumption.

"Is that seriously what you think I was doing last night?" I laughed at her ongoing attempts to meddle in my non-existent love life. "For your information, perv, I found out where the Order are from Seirina and went up there. I managed to get myself captured after I snuck in. Then I escaped with Angelica – who *was* being held and questioned by her boss – along with the twins I told you about.

"I left them with Seirina, who said she has somewhere safe they can stay for now. She's going through her list of contacts. She's still using a rolodex, if you can believe that. She's seeing if we can get a group together

THE ORDER OF THE NINE SEALS

to stand against the Order." At this point, Summer stepped back around the counter and sat down with a look of stunned amazement on her face.

"Seirina also remarked that I needed to get you somewhere safe, so I came screaming over here. I only calmed down towards the end of the drive as I realised that with all the warding, this is actually the safest place you can be. So, I want you to get Emily and your things, like you did when I went off on the Veil hunt, and stay upstairs.

"If you need anything while you're there use the business account, use the groceries app for food shopping, and Emily can run her computer consultancy from there for a while. I'm going to pump up the volume on the building defences now that there's no reason to hide my abilities, so you two just stay here until this gets sorted." She rolled her eyes at my cheesy movie reference, then sighed and nodded.

"Fine, you get magickal and I'll call Emily. I hope that woman is worth all this crap you're digging yourself into. Oh, and by the way, dragging your friends into along with you; thanks so much for sharing." She pushed herself away from the counter and walked into the kitchen, pulling out her phone as she went. I heard the click of the kettle being switched on and turned away to start assessing the wards.

I spent the next two hours going through my magickal library for ways in which to make the shop and apartment as impregnable as possible. I set up barriers to teleportation against anyone except myself and those I brought with me. I increased the power of all the existing defensive wards against fire and aggression, then placed a Wiccan bell spell on the bell over the door to make sure anyone entering would trigger the effect of protecting against evil magick.

I also found a couple of other bells in the store room and placed the same spell on them, hanging one on the back door and one on the door to the stairs leading up to the apartment. I had considered bringing the wooden utensil holder I had carved apotropaic symbols on up from the vault. After some consideration, however, I was concerned there was a risk of it also suppressing the magick of the rest of the wards so I left it where it was.

By the time I was satisfied with the protection around the building, and more importantly around my friends, Emily had arrived and gotten settled in upstairs again. Summer handed me another cup of Cafegeddon (it had been the coffee maker not the kettle that I'd heard being switched on) and smiled.

"So am I now working in the magickal equivalent of Fort Knox?" she joked as I sipped. I grimaced slightly as the coffee hit my gut, realising I still hadn't had anything for lunch. That meant almost twenty hours without eating. The last thing had been my burger before my assault on the Order. Not exactly a world class last meal, so I was even happier I'd made it out intact.

"It's as secure as I can make it while still letting customers in," I replied seriously, "but if someone opens the door and then looks as though they're hesitating rather than just walking in, do *not* go out to them. Let them walk away and call me when they're gone."

She stopped smiling when she saw how seriously I was taking things and nodded in response to my well-established anxiety. I hugged her again and then handed her back the coffee cup. I was definitely going to have to stop at Subway on my way home, otherwise my stomach was going to eat itself. This time I'd make sure not to let some cheeky flea-bitten mangy stray steal it from me though!

I told her to say goodbye to Emily for me and reiterated my instructions for them both to stay safe inside, then headed out the front door, G flying over to land on my shoulder as I did so.

I went to the same Subway I had gone to after my disastrous date with Summer's illiterate friend, getting a spicy Italian instead of the meatballs since it would be less messy to eat in the car. I walked out with my sandwich wrapped and bagged, Gauvain flying down from the rooftop where he had perched while I went in for my lunch.

This time I decided to wait until I was sitting down somewhere to start eating, so I simply enjoyed the walk back to my car now that I knew Summer was safe. Gauvain nibbled reassuringly on a strand of my hair as I strolled.

Your buttressing of the fortifications on Dinas Affaraon is most thorough and should certainly prove efficacious, he reassured me. *Now we can return to our rescued friends and allies, at which point we can begin gathering forces to stand against the Order.*

"You *do* realise you sound like some cheesy movie interpretation of chivalry, right?" I chuckled softly as I teased him. "You were linked to my mind by Isis, why the hell do you talk like that?" He stopped preening me (it was a nice change from him always preening himself) and stared haughtily out of one vivid yellow eye.

When we were joined, I saw in your mind your sincere admiration of the samurai code. I also learned of the legends of King Arthur. They struck a resonance within me and created my personality and speech patterns. So when you criticise my attitude and mannerisms, you are actually mocking your own admiration of honour, chivalry and decency. He turned away and hunched his wings, making me feel like the biggest shit in Yorkshire right then.

We were linked, part of each other, complementary aspects of each other's personality and life. Despite knowing that, I'd spent a good portion of our time together teasing and making fun of him. Disrespecting him despite the fact that I knew he would never hesitate to put himself on the line for me. I remembered Alex's comments just after Isis had unlocked my magick and linked the two of us together.

I decided then and there to never treat him that way again, and I let my regret, love and apology flow across our link like a flood. I reached up and stroked him, widening and strengthening our bond with my touch. He shuffled on my shoulder and I felt his gratitude and love wash back across our connection. We forged a new, stronger link in that moment. One I was determined our enemies would come to fear in the conflicts to come.

I arrived back at my car and G hopped over to his perch in the passenger seat. I put my sandwich on the floor in the passenger footwell, deciding to eat at home after all, then straightened up and fastened my seatbelt. I looked across at my feathered brother and he looked back at me, *rrk*'ing softly. I smiled and nodded back, then set off for home.

We arrived back at the apartment complex without incident and I pulled into the parking area with a sense of relief. I had almost expected the Order to be waiting for me, ready to try to snatch me up again. Still, now that they knew more about my abilities, I could actually start fighting back properly. No more hiding, from now on I was going to be a force to be reckoned with!

I banged my head on the top of the car doorframe as I got out, swore briefly and then burst out laughing. Some awe-inspiring force *I* was. Gauvain joined in my laughter as I told him what I had been thinking.

"Behold the mighty warrior, laid low by the size of his own head!" I quipped as he flew over to my shoulder, almost making him miss his landing as he was laughing so hard.

Well, whatever is required to keep your perspective correct. He laughed in my head. *Just be thankful your cranium still fits through the door, and is solid enough to withstand the ego-realignment!*

I chuckled along with him.

"Hey, watch it you! Just because we're bonded, doesn't mean I won't stuff a pillow with you if you push me!" We both chuckled, the light-hearted banter feeling nice after the seriousness of our earlier discussion.

I took the stairs up to my home and let myself in, feeling nothing amiss as I entered. I did a quick check to make sure everything was OK, then decided to set up a couple of wards to prevent anyone entering or casting magick without my consent. I also created a bell spell like I had at the shop, plus a fire ward.

Once I was happy with the protections, I got some meat out for Gauvain and sat down to enjoy my sandwich. I hadn't realised just how hungry I was until I started eating, hoovering the six-inch sub in record time and wishing I'd ordered a footlong. Gauvain ate almost as quickly, so I got him some more from the fridge. I found a solitary piece of pizza wrapped up in the back as I did so and polished that off with a deep sigh of contentment.

I also downed the last of the bottle of milk, since I wasn't sure when I might get the chance to come back. I didn't really fancy returning to a semi-sentient yogurt culture attempting to take over the kitchen, although that could make an interesting premise for an animé. That is, if it hadn't already been done. I shook my head at my random mental wanderings and went to grab my bag from the closet.

I'd repacked my overnight bag with clean clothes and fresh toiletries after I'd returned from Tibet, so I picked that up and also took my backpack. I'd become quite attached to that after it had been with me on my adventure in Aaru, so I'd made sure to put a few more useful items in it on my return.

There was now a simple first aid kit, collapsible water bottle, compass, folding knife and flint in there, along with a few handkerchiefs and some extra clothes. I didn't fancy getting stuck somewhere without much in the way of useful supplies again!

I checked my preparations and made sure to pack the charger for my phone as well as my Surface with its cables, then headed back down to the garage level. I loaded the bags into the back of the car, reasoning that I didn't want to try teleporting to Seirina's in case she had beefed up her security warding. It would also be kind of rude to just pop up in her study, especially if she was in a meeting.

G settled onto his branch and I switched on the engine, pulling out of my space and slowing to allow the gate to open. As I eased towards the road, a truck similar to a UPS delivery vehicle but without any company livery pulled across the driveway and stopped, blocking me in.

A young, skinny, acne-pocked guy got out and stared at me, then turned to open the load area of the truck. The vehicle rocked before he even touched it and I got a bad feeling about what was about to happen. I removed my seatbelt, opened the window on Gauvain's side so he could get out, then turned off the engine. I opened my door almost in unison with the driver pulling the handle he was reaching for. The vehicle shook again and I heard a high-pitched, ragged scream from inside.

Man, I hate it when I'm right sometimes.

Chapter 28

As the driver slid the door open, fingers from inside grabbed the leading edge of the panel and flung it backward hard enough to rip it right off the back of the rail. It toppled over and clanged loudly onto the tarmac. I barely noticed however, as my attention was focused on the sight of the creature in the truck.

It looked humanoid, but gaunt to the point of skeletal emaciation, with waxy grey skin pulled tight across its bones. The mouth seemed to extend from ear to ear, as if the entire head could hinge open into one enormous mouth. A mouth that was filled with razor sharp teeth like a shark or piranha.

Gauvain took one look and sensibly left my shoulder to perch on the streetlight above us, out of the immediate reach of the creature but close enough to look for an opening should one present itself.

The only reason I had time to notice all this was because as soon as the door had opened it had reached out and grabbed the hapless driver, broken his neck with one claw-like hand, and immediately started eating him. Clearly the creature's strength wasn't hampered by its apparent lack of musculature. Its appetite was certainly prodigious as it had already consumed the poor boy's head and both arms, crunching through bones like they were Twiglets.

My only hope was that after such a large meal it might be slower or maybe even lose interest in me entirely, giving me a chance to come up with some information about what it was and what to do with it. That is other than lose control of my bladder and bowels then run screaming in the opposite direction, but that wasn't exactly in keeping with my heroic decision from earlier.

As it kept eating, I began to notice something extremely alarming. It wasn't slowing down its eating. If anything it was speeding up and, rather than its belly swelling to show it was getting full, the damned thing was growing. It was as if everything it ate was instantaneously converted into new bones and skin, so *it* got bigger while its stomach stayed empty.

The description hinted at something I vaguely remembered reading once but I was a little too distracted to go trawling through my memory just then.

Within thirty short, very bloody seconds it had eaten the driver including his clothes and had doubled in size while still looking like a skeleton wrapped in old car-wash chamois leathers. It screeched again, sounding like nails on a chalkboard crossed with a chainsaw on sheet metal. It stepped towards me, no doubt looking for its second course.

I had no intention of being the entrée so I summoned up a ball of electricity and threw it at the thing, hitting it squarely in the centre of its chest and blasting it backward. It flew inside the truck hard enough that it crashed into the other side, rocking the vehicle onto two wheels so that it teetered on the brink of falling over into the street.

Unfortunately for me, Skeletor (hey, I needed a name for it, so sue me) bounced off the wall inside to land on the load-bed of the truck, rocking it back onto all four wheels. I was really hoping that the charge from my taserball might have killed it or at least knocked it out, but apparently I wasn't that lucky.

It picked itself up off the floor and looked at me like a woman seeing her husband in bed with her sister. There was a slightly charred area on its chest but even that faded in front of my eyes. Great, so electricity was a no, how about that other old reliable: fire? Time to see if the damn thing had asbestos skin as well as being a human(-ish) lightning rod.

I drew energy from Seren and manifested a fireball hot enough to make the asphalt start melting. The creature screamed as soon as it saw the fire, giving me hope that I might be on the right track, and it tried to back away into the body of the truck. There was no way I could let this thing go; it was too dangerous and who knew who it would eat next, so I hurled my miniature supernova directly at it.

The fireball burned straight into its chest cavity and then seemed to explode, engulfing the creature in seconds. I could smell burning hair and saw that the heat had singed some of the hair on my forearm. Then I caught a wave of the smell from inside the truck which was like someone had set fire to a pile of tyres covered in raw sewage with a few pounds of rancid meat thrown in for good measure. I turned away and swallowed manfully, trying to fight against the surge of pizza and sandwich currently trying to push its way out of my gullet.

Once the screeching stopped, I let the fire burn for another couple of minutes to make sure Skeletor wasn't going to get back up again. I then drew the heat away to put the fire out and prevent the truck from exploding, storing the energy back into Seren. I smiled as I saw the wings of Isis flare brightly as the energy entered the stone, thinking back to when I had first seen it on Aaru all those months (or weeks here on Earth) ago.

I then realised I had finally taken Danu's advice and truly finished a fight at long last. Yes, it had been a lot easier to kill something that looked like it belonged in a horror movie than a human, but the danger to innocents was often exactly the same. I expected to feel a slight surge in strength as the defeat of something evil gave me a karmic tick in the plus column, yet to my disappointment I felt absolutely nothing.

Just what did a guy have to do to get a gold star from the karmic judges these days? I suddenly remembered Elrulin ripping away the valve between me and the power of the Veil. In a rush of understanding, I realised it must not have been set there by Isis for training purposes, but more as a means to make sure I didn't turn to the dark side of the force.

Now that it was gone, there was nothing looking over my shoulder to approve or disapprove of my actions. *That* was why evil beings were still able to use magick: It had nothing to do with karma, they just didn't have Isis watching their every action.

I was momentarily pissed off at her apparent lack of faith in my nature, then reasoned that power had been known to corrupt even the most righteous, so she had reason to be cautious. I resolved that I would continue to act as if the threat of loss of power was still present, to try to keep my own karmic balance sheet firmly in the black.

Gauvain lifted me out of my introspection as he finally re-joined me from his streetlight perch.

What in all the planes of the cosmos was that? he asked me, and I shook my head in ignorance.

"Absolutely no idea buddy," I replied. "I'm just glad the damned thing wasn't fireproof as well as shockproof. If anything, the fire seemed to terrify it. We'll have to do some research and see if we can figure out what it was and maybe that'll explain things. I might even ask Seirina. She's sure to have seen plenty of weird and wonderful things in her time."

G nodded, and I looked at the shambles of the truck in front of me. How was I going to shift it? The keys were probably in the driver's pocket when he got eaten, and there was no way in *hell* I was planning to going rooting around in the burned carcass of that abomination looking for them.

I decided to have a look in the cab, blessing my lucky stars when I saw the keys had been left in the ignition. I didn't need to go far, just enough to move it away from the garage entrance so I could get the car out.

Fortunately the beast had cowered towards the back when it saw the flames I had summoned, so the cab and engine were almost unscathed. I started it up and moved the truck about ten feet, then shut it off. I wiped the steering wheel and keys in the knowledge of what I was going to do next, then got out.

I pictured a mid-ocean scene in my mind and sent the charred corpse there. Hopefully the sharks and scavengers would eat it long before it washed up anywhere causing consternation among the local conspiracy theorists and alien enthusiasts.

Then I rang the local police to inform them there was an abandoned truck with its door off and other damage by my building. They said they'd send someone out to take a look and get it towed away, so I thanked them and hung up. I wondered idly what they'd make of all the dents and fire damage, not to mention the blood on the road and in the back, but that wasn't my problem. I got back into my car with Gauvain, closed his window and we set off back to Seirina's.

As we pulled onto the main road, I shuddered as I remembered the scream from the creature in the truck. The look of its teeth and the stench as it had cooked in the oven of the vehicle load area, powered by my fireball, again threatened my gastric fortitude. Gauvain looked across and shuffled over towards me.

There is no shame in feeling shaky after a battle, he told me reassuringly *It's perfectly natural. It is simply the adrenaline burning off. Plus that creature was particularly disturbing in appearance, so a little fear is quite allowable.*

The important thing is that you did not allow your fear to cause you to hesitate, nor did you abstain from what needed to be done. You followed through and finished the fight as Danu told you that you must learn to do. I am truly proud of you and how you acquitted yourself.

As he spoke, I felt the stress dissipating and sent my thanks across our link to my fluffy cheerleader. I still wanted to know what the damned monster in the truck had been, so I settled down and focused on driving in order to get to Seirina's and start researching.

The rest of the drive was blessedly uneventful and soon enough, we drew up to the gate in front of the familiar driveway. I could immediately feel the increased pressure from the wards that had clearly been significantly enhanced, much as I had done at the shop and at home.

I could tell there was no way I, nor anyone else, was getting in without an invitation. At least not without significant effort and probably serious pain. Given Seirina's area of magick, I shuddered to think what her wards might do if triggered so I was very glad I hadn't tried to teleport in.

I lowered my window and activated the intercom for entry, then sat in surprise as I had to wait as it rang. What had happened to Mrs Wilson? I felt a moment of fear that the Order had already been here, but then why would Seirina have been left to boost the wards? I just started to feel out the defences to see how to break through when the intercom crackled to life and I heard a familiar Scottish accent.

"Aye, who is it, an' wha' d'ye want?" I smiled in relief to hear that she was OK, but then worried again. Why was Seirina answering the intercom?

"It's me, Seirina. Can you let me in?" I hoped by now she would recognise my voice, but I was underestimating her new caution and level of suspicion.

"And how am I supposed to know it's really you, you wazzock?" she groused over the speaker. "How can I be sure the Order didn't record your voice while they held you captive, then use a computer to record phrases?" I shrugged, even though I knew she couldn't see me.

"So ask me something they wouldn't know," I replied, thinking quickly. "Something only you and I would know." There was a pause as she clearly thought of something to ask me.

"Fine, what was the book you asked me to help you find, and what is Atma's real name?" I smiled, amused at the double security of the question. Even if the Order had researched me thoroughly and discovered the name of the book, I seriously doubted Elrulin was bandying his name freely around the employee cafeteria.

"*The Oera Linda Book*, specifically the copy owned by Himmler," I replied, shuddering slightly as I thought of the creepy volume currently safely under lock and key in my vault, "and Elrulin." The intercom clicked off and I heard the creak as the gate started to open.

I eased the car forward gradually, not wanting to hit any barriers at speed if she hadn't disarmed them yet. As the front of the car crossed the boundary of the gateposts, I saw the air ripple and distort as the magic allowed me entry. I watched the rippling approach along the hood of the car, making it appear as though I was driving into the surface of a vertical lake.

As it reached me, I felt a tingling start in my feet as they were the farthest forward, then progressing up my legs as I moved on. My hands felt as though I was pushing into a bowl of treacle or blancmange. As the boundary reached my chest, I felt it force me back into my seat as if I was in an airplane taking off at full speed.

Suddenly the magick snapped around me and I was in, at which point both Gauvain and I shuddered simultaneously at the weirdness of the sensation. I saw the ripple continue through the car in the rear-view mirror, then wink out of view as the vehicle finished traversing the border.

I continued forward, speeding up just slightly as the gate began to close on me due to my taking longer than normal to enter the property. I drew up to the house to park in my now accustomed spot. The slightly greasy feeling of Seirina's magick was significantly more intense now, and permeated the whole area covered by her protective enchantments.

I idly wondered what my magick felt like and looked like to her, or if she was even aware of it in the same way. There was still so much that was new to me, despite my protracted training in Aaru, as had been evidenced by my ignorance regarding the monster I had killed outside my home.

I just hoped Seirina recognised it when I described it, otherwise I foresaw a long afternoon of research ahead of me. If I could identify the monster, it might give us a better idea of what else the Order might have at their disposal.

I got out of the car, G transferring to my shoulder once I was out, then closed and locked it. Just because the area was protected was no reason to get complacent. I walked to the front door and saw it open as I approached, the smiling face of Mrs Wilson appearing reassuringly behind it. I sighed in relief that nothing had gone amiss while I was away and smiled back as I reached the entrance.

"Nice to see you again Mrs Wilson," I said cheerfully. "I was a little concerned when the intercom rang for a while and then Ms Crow answered it herself." I raised an eyebrow in silent question and she chuckled, resting a hand on my shoulder as I walked in.

"Oh, she's just being over-protective," she replied calmly. "She told me not to answer the intercom, and that only she could let people onto the grounds now. She even told me not to go out for the mail unless she was there. She always acts like a worried mother hen when things get interesting."

She patted my shoulder again with her final words and I realised they must have been together an exceedingly long time, long enough that Mrs Wilson was aware of the more esoteric side of Seirina's nature and business. I nodded back and smiled in response.

"The things we do for family, both blood and even more so the ones we choose for ourselves." She looked at me with approval at my statement, almost like an aunt looking on a favoured nephew when he showed off a report card of all A's. I felt a warm and full sensation in my chest that I hadn't felt since my mother's passing.

"So, is the lady of the house available for consultation?" I asked, swallowing past the lump in my throat. She smiled back at me knowingly and nodded.

"She's in her study, lad. I'll put the tea on." I stroked Gauvain and turned to walk down the now familiar hallway.

Chapter 29

I knocked on the door of the study, walking in when I heard her say so. My eyes immediately flew to the glass behind her but her skeletal friend had disappeared back into the depths. She waved me to a chair and continued with the phone call she was in the middle of. I ignored the chairs and instead walked over to the bay window where Gauvain had perched earlier, looking out at the garden.

There was a huge old oak tree out there, casting lengthening shade in the evening sunlight, and there was a pair of ring doves perched together on one of the lower branches. Other birds flitted through the leaves, and honey bees circulated amongst the flowers in the well-maintained beds underneath. I heard Seirina hang up the phone and turned around to look at her. Something must have shown in my face as she looked concerned and got up to come around her desk.

"What happened?" she asked sympathetically. "Was your shop OK? Had something happened to your friend?" I waved off her concern and dropped onto the love-seat behind me so she stopped walking towards me and leant back against her desk with her arms crossed.

"Summer and the shop were fine," I replied heavily and hung my head forward, the trials of the last forty-eight hours or so beginning to catch up with me. "It was the encounter I had after stopping off at home for my things that made my day somewhat interesting." I looked up at Seirina, quirking an eyebrow. She tilted her head and looked questioningly back at me, waiting for me to supply more information.

I described in detail what had happened as I left the garage up to the point where Skeletor appeared. Seirina gasped sharply as I described it but didn't interrupt my recital with questions. As I explained how it had grown when it ate the driver she nodded as if she expected exactly that, confirming for me she had at least an idea what it was.

I quickly recounted my brief fight, including both its resilience to electricity and its terror and lethal susceptibility to fire. She looked impressed at the quick resolution to the battle, then walked back around her desk. She sat down, leaning thoughtfully back in her chair. I sat quietly, stroking Gauvain as I watched her reflecting on what I'd said. I was eager to know what I'd fought but I wasn't about to rush a necromancer in her own home. I was new to magick, not a moron. Finally she sighed and looked over at me.

"At least you were able to kill it quickly before it managed to find more food. Once they grow, their skin becomes more resilient even to fire. At that point it turns into one hell of a job to even hurt them, let alone kill them." She smiled slightly at me. "I'm just amazed the Order was able to obtain or create one here to set against you."

"So what was it?" I asked, eager to get some definite information.

"It was a windigo," she replied simply. I looked curiously at her, not sure I had heard her correctly.

"A wendigo?" I asked, remembering a Wolverine comic I'd read a number of years ago and comparing the artwork to what I had faced earlier.

"No, a *windigo*," she replied, sitting forward as she stressed the different pronunciation. "They're two different entities. A *wendigo* is a Native American spirit in animal form. A *windigo* is an evil, cannibalistic spirit summoned by a Native American shaman and forced into a man or woman.

"The legends past that are much the same. The ravenous hunger that can never be sated, the skeletal appearance, the cold… that last must be why fire was so effective." She sat back in her chair again, dropping her chin onto her chest in thought.

"So that must mean the Order has a shaman over here from America," I said, extrapolating based on her information. She looked up at me and nodded.

"Indeed. I wasn't aware their recruiting efforts had ranged so far afield." She sank back into contemplation, and this time I let her. I'd got the relevant information, now I needed to work out what to do with it.

Angelica had already told me about the Order setting up a branch in America, so it wasn't overly surprising they had been recruiting out there. It *was* surprising that a shaman was able to summon a spirit in the UK, away from their home soil sphere of power. I had always heard that magick users who were attuned to or affiliated with a specific culture were significantly less powerful away from their home soil. That meant a shaman who could create a windigo on this side of the ocean must be extremely experienced. Then a thought struck me.

"Hang on, why couldn't the shaman be in America?" I asked, my mind still extrapolating on the fly. "He or she could have created the windigo by summoning the spirit into a human locked into a cage, then the cage gets loaded onto a plane and flown here. The windigo gets released into the truck and driven to my home. The shaman would be more in tune with their magick on home soil, and with modern air travel the creature gets shipped wherever it's needed in hours." Seirina looked up as I was speaking, her eyes widening as she processed the implications of what I had said.

"That's brilliant!" she breathed, stunned at the scope of what I had suggested. "They could have magick users from any or all of the different cultures across the world, all based where they're most in tune with their power, and able to ship the results of their work wherever they're needed at will.

"Monsters of various forms don't have the same location tethers for the most part, so the only restrictions come if they need magick users for a specific purpose in a specific location. However, they could get the relevant specialist member from a location to instruct a local magick user. They could also move the specialist for the one ritual and have their power bolstered by the local magick users, then go home."

I nodded as she spoke, my mind racing down the same lines and coming to similar conclusions. Her final idea of locals supporting the power of a visitor for a ritual then the specialist going home caught me by surprise, though it made perfect sense.

"If we left them to their own devices for long enough," I continued the thought to its logical conclusion, "they could gather some utterly unique and unexpected creatures plus weird and esoteric magicks to deploy against us. We can't afford to give them that opportunity, but how can we prevent them?" I had visions of our attempts to break the back of the Order dying before they even had a chance to truly live.

"I don't think that would work," Seirina reassured me. "The sorts of magicks and creatures that require such specialist input need to be used as soon as possible after creation. The windigo, for example, if not allowed to feed within a day will feed on the host body and die of starvation. So unless they have an entire fleet of their own aircraft, their own landing field close to where they want to gather everything and big enough for multiple planes to land at once, plus absolute certainty of when they'll be needed…"

I held up my hands in submission as the overwhelming impossibility of the logistics required convinced me that things weren't quite as dire as I thought. The twins had already informed me during our escape that the Order didn't have anyone capable of teleportation, so that also wasn't an option for them.

"OK, at least we're not going to have to face an army of the most powerful beings and magicks from across every culture and belief in the world," I said, although my description tickled something in the back of my mind and the image of my premonition from Aaru flitted across my memory. "I still think we're going to need help to take the Order apart. How's the search for potential allies going?" She nodded at my relief and my admission of needing help.

"I'm glad you haven't completely lost hope yet," she remarked, sounding more than a little relieved herself, "since I'd hate for all my efforts to be for nothing. I've only been calling people since yesterday afternoon but there's already been a significant number of positive responses."

She was careful not to be specific regarding numbers, though I wasn't sure if it was caution regarding me since we had only minimal history together. It could have been my association with Order escapees whom she didn't trust due to their recent apparent change of heart. It might also simply be uncertainty over how many of those who had professed support would actually turn up to fight.

Regardless, at least there were those out there who were opposed to the Order and what it stood for, so we had a chance to gather enough of a force to stand against them.

"So did the girls get settled in alright?" I asked, happy to move on now that I knew what had attacked me and that Seirina was gradually recruiting our army. "Are you sure they're safe?" I tried to act nonchalant, but she wasn't fooled for even a moment. She rolled her eyes, shook her head and favoured me with one of her rare smiles.

"Did you forget I'm an enchantress, so your emotions are like an open book to me?" She raised an eyebrow and tilted her head to the left, to which I smiled and shrugged. "Don't give me that innocent look! I'm not giving you the address for you to go and 'check the wards' or whatever other lame excuse you were going to give me.

"That poor girl has been through one hell of a time over the last couple of days. For her it's been more like several months of being tortured and abused, and all because of you, so you need to give her some space to deal with it all. If she wants to talk to you, I'll give her your number or she'll come to this house when you're here."

At this point Seirina stood up from behind her desk and leant over it, resting on her fists which she planted firmly on the writing surface. Her eyes flared as she continued, building up a head of steam with her tirade. I wasn't sure at this point whether it was the enchantress side or the sisterhood of women against a man side speaking, but either way I knew my best option was just to sit down, shut up and listen.

"You're going to have to accept that she may not want to have anything to do with you for quite some time, if ever again, now that she knows exactly how much you kept from her. She also only got out of the torture situation last night, so she's still coming to terms with everything that happened and her feelings for you are all wrapped up with that.

"Either you're prepared to give her the time she needs to deal with everything and wait to find out if she wants to see you, or you just walk away now. What you won't do is sit there and try to act innocent like none of this is your fault and you're going to pursue her like nothing happened!"

She got louder and firmer as she spoke, berating me like an angry mother or older sister, making me shrink down in the chair and feel like the most worthless piece of crap in the world for what I'd done. Yes I'd had my reasons, both for my actions or omissions as the case may be, but the law of unintended consequences had still come back to bite me in the ass.

I hung my head in shame and regret, feeling myself welling up at all the pain I'd caused, not least because of how I felt about the person who had suffered the most from my lack of consideration. I refused to blubber in front of her though, so I blinked a few times to clear my eyes and took a deep breath to steady myself.

I sniffed inelegantly and looked up at Seirina with resolve on my face. Even before I spoke she was nodding, either reading my eyes or my emotions if I believed her comment regarding her enchantress powers. Not that I had any reason to doubt her. I silently swore to her I would be whatever was required: absent if wanted, available when needed. Call me a romantic fool but I was betting on my feelings for Angelica and hers for me.

In the meantime, there were allies to find and an offensive to plan.

Chapter 30

Over the next few days, Seirina was making her phone calls in an attempt to find more supporters for our idealistic campaign to destroy the Order. Meanwhile I sat down with the twins to start making plans and make sure we had as much information as possible regarding locations, member abilities, creatures, and anything else that might be helpful.

Over those first days, I didn't see Angelica at all as she was staying in the secure location Seirina had provided. The twins tried to reassure me she was doing alright, but I was still concerned. Months of torture could have all kinds of psychological effects, then following it by spending too much time alone could make things worse.

From the little reading I did on the subject, the experts generally agreed that talking about things was the best way to start healing, so I hoped she was at least talking to Gabby and Izzy. I didn't pry, however, as I had promised to give her whatever time and space she needed. That didn't mean I couldn't think about her, and I spent many an evening staring off into space and pondering what could be with my emotions swinging between hope and despair like a metronome on full speed.

The first thing we did was confirm the list of Order locations in the British Isles. I learned Bolton Castle was the titular headquarters, with three other locations spaced out across the points of the compass.

To the north, they had taken control of the tunnels under Edinburgh Castle. To the south, Rochester Castle had been suborned to their needs, and on the Emerald Isle they had corrupted the castle where visitors flocked to gain eloquence by kissing the stone: Blarney Castle.

That meant they were officially European, not just British, since Blarney Castle was in County Cork in the southern part of Ireland so not actually part of the UK. Another reason to get this done as fast as possible. There were less border issues from Ireland to the rest of Europe and I didn't want Order members disappearing before I could deal with them.

I knew the Scots and the Irish would go absolutely ape-shit if such famous and beloved monuments were damaged. The English would be irritated if their castles were harmed, but I just thanked my lucky stars the Order hadn't hidden under somewhere like Hampton Court Palace or another location equally famous. Maybe the Crown's position as head of the Anglican Church had given them some kind of protection? Who knew, I would just take my breaks where I could get them.

As far as the American site went, the twins didn't know any more than Angelica had already told me. It was a relatively recent acquisition, it was popular with those among the ranks who were either tired of hiding or unable to hide, and the Order was investing considerable resources into customising it for their unique requirements.

The twins did say they had received the distinct impression the Order might be making the American location their primary headquarters due to its various advantages. I was hoping we might find more information as we tore down the various sites on this side of the pond.

I already knew there were several different kinds of beings within the ranks of the Order including vampires, werewolves, trolls, a gorgon, and magick users of various flavours. Elrulin was a... what was he? A demon? A devil? Whatever he was, he was going to be considerably more powerful than any of the other spell slingers in their ranks. Primarily because of what he actually was and also due to the fact that any kind of tyrant was always afraid of being overthrown.

As a result they tended to kill anyone who was, or might eventually become, a threat. He may not have had my training, but he'd had centuries to hone his abilities, however twisted they may have become. This was going to eventually come down to him and me.

I had been keeping in contact with Summer daily, both to hear a friendly and cheerful voice and to check on how things were going.

The shop was fine, while she and Emily were quite happy staying home together. About four days after my visit to fortify the wards, Summer actually rang me. I was immediately worried it might indicate a problem, so I was already heading to the study as I answered the phone.

"Gav, there's a few people outside the shop," she told me. "They're just milling around, but I get a funny vibe from them." I had the phone on speaker, so that Seirina could hear what was going on.

"I'll be right there," I promised her while staring straight at Seirina, almost daring her to disagree. Fortunately, whether for her or me I wasn't completely sure, she nodded.

"I'll open the gate and let you out of the wards," she told me once I'd hung up. I nodded and ran for the front door, Gauvain soaring down the stairs from our room to join me. I sprinted for the gate, slowing just enough for it to swing open a couple of feet.

I shimmied through, feeling the wards flex and snap back around me as I passed the limit of Seirina's property, then immediately teleported myself into my office at Dinas Affaraon. I smiled reflexively as I looked around the familiar room, inhaling deeply and smelling the beloved scents of leather, wood and books.

I stepped across to pull open the door, heading out into the main shop as if I'd been there all day. Summer, to her credit, barely flinched to see me walk out of what she knew had been an empty room.

"Oh there you are, Gav," she remarked conversationally, dividing her attention between me and the window of the store. I followed her gaze and saw four men standing together on the pavement outside. As soon as they saw me, they approached the door. Gauvain flew off my shoulder and landed on the perch nearest the front, allowing me full freedom to react.

The first one to reach the door pushed it open and went to walk through, only to be firmly zapped by the wards hard enough for him to stumble backwards and fall on his ass. I had to stop myself collapsing into giggles as I saw his eyebrows had actually been singed off and there was smoke curling up from his hair.

The other three paused, not trying to push past and get in themselves, and instead one of them reached for something in a bag he was carrying. He pulled out a bottle with liquid in and a rag stuffed into the neck: a

Molotov cocktail. The guy next to him flicked a lighter and touched it to the rag.

The one with the bottle turned back to the door and threw the firebomb into the shop. I held my breath, remembering my vision of the shop in flames, then breathed again as I saw the flame go out the moment the bottle crossed the threshold.

I reached out and caught the container, since even without the flames I didn't fancy having to clean up broken glass and gasoline, then smiled at them.

"I guess you're not as hot as you thought," I remarked dryly, causing Summer to snort giggle. She was clearly just as relieved as me over my beefed up protection proving effective, though she hadn't been aware of my vision in Aaru.

I looked over at her and passed her the bottle, then looked back at the men outside. I was only assuming they were from the Order at this point, though I couldn't think why else someone would be doing this. We'd never had problems before in the years we'd been here, then all of a sudden this happens just days after I'd carried out my little assault on their headquarters.

I stepped to the doorway and looked at each of them in turn.

"Right, let's assess shall we?" I said conversationally, as if they hadn't just tried to burn my shop to the ground. "You've already discovered that my shop won't let you in if you've got harmful intentions; even thrown items get neutralised as soon as they enter the limits of the store."

I looked up and down the street, seeing that there wasn't anyone else around right now so there were no witnesses to whatever I might need to do. As I stepped forwards towards them, the guy on the floor scrambled backwards and the other three stepped away, fanning out slightly.

I let the door close behind me, hearing the bell jingle as it did. 'Eyebrows' finally got to his feet, taking a place on the end of the arc, though he already looked significantly less eager for any further zapping after his first experience. The others had only seen the flame on a rag get snuffed out, so they hadn't had his up close and personal knowledge of the power of my magick.

"I'm guessing your boss didn't appreciate me making off with his pet telepaths," I said to them cheerfully, "so he sent you to communicate his displeasure?" The three uninjured thugs sneered at me, while Eyebrows sidled a little further back, clearly sensing this wouldn't go well for them.

"Trust me when I say you really don't want to do this," I continued, wanting to give them fair warning but knowing they wouldn't listen. "However, since you're determined to ignore me, let's get this done. I have better things to do than fart about with you pillocks right now."

My taunting had the desired effect, making the three who were still keen to try their luck all come at me. I stepped to my left and grabbed the punching arm of the guy at that end of their chorus line, a bald chubby guy who seemed to be relying more on his mass than any style.

I used the momentum of his punch to fling him into the guy next to him, assisting the swing with a boost of magick and blasting them both with an electroball as they fell. I kicked out at the third man, again adding a tazer charge and magickal boost to my foot, sending him flying halfway across the road to land flat on his back.

The one who had already experienced the electrifying experience of my magick stood frozen, or so I thought. One area seemed to be defrosting, if the wet patch on the front of his jeans was any indication, so I let him watch.

I telekinetically pulled the other three into a pile in front of me, taking a perverse satisfaction in hearing their groans. I pictured the same location in the middle of the ocean that I had sent the windigo's corpse to, then laid my hand on the pile of thugs and sent them there.

Unless they were *really* lucky, and seriously strong swimmers, the sharks should hopefully finish them off for me. I had made the decision to send a message back to Elrulin, hopefully forestalling any further attempts like this, so the best way was for the messenger to see his friends disappear forever.

"Now go back and tell that bloodsucking asshole to stay the fuck away from my store and my friends," I told him, attempting to sound as hard and menacing as possible. It must have worked because I smelled a fresh wave of ammonia come from the front of his trousers.

His eyes stretched open like a deer in the headlights and he nodded so fast his face was a blur. He sprinted away like he was trying to beat Usain Bolt in the hundred meters, so I turned away and went back inside.

"That should stop them coming back," I told Summer. She hugged me tight, joined by Gauvain flying over to my shoulder and rubbing against my face.

"Thanks Gav," she said softly, then leant back slightly to look at me. "I know you said you'd beefed up the protection on the shop, though I wasn't sure until I saw it work just now. I got nervous when I saw them outside, so I called you."

"Don't apologise," I told her, hugging her tightly again. "It's exactly what I told you to do, and I'd rather have been here than not. Now the message should get back to them regarding the futility of trying something so idiotic again, so hopefully you won't be bothered any more. Still, I want you to call me any time you're not happy with something and I'll always be here."

She hugged me one last time and stepped back, sniffing inelegantly as she did. I smiled at her a final time, then said goodbye and took myself and G back to Seirina's.

Chapter 31

Almost a week after our escape, the twins finally informed me their brother and his adoptive parents had resettled and were doing fine. They told me they had managed to erase or shred any information Elrulin had stored on the family during their escape, so all the Order now had was Elrulin's memory of where they lived and their family name.

Fortunately there were plenty of families named Taylor out there to get lost amongst, so they should be safe. The twins had deliberately not helped them move for fear we were being watched. That was something that had concerned me as well, which was the reason I was staying in one of Seirina's guest rooms instead of driving home each night. Seirina also refused to adjust the wards so I could teleport, so I simply stayed. I had built a temporary stand for Gauvain from a couple of branches off the oak tree outside, and we were making do.

Finally Seirina told us she had organised a meeting for the following evening, to which she had invited those who were interested in fighting the Order for one reason or another. I had no idea what sort of crowd it would be, either in numbers or backgrounds. I was just glad we wouldn't be facing this alone.

No matter how skilled or powerful one person was, sooner or later they would tire and sheer numbers could overwhelm them. In the case of a god that might require a seriously *large* number, but the principle was sound. I didn't much fancy being on the wrong side of that sort of mismatch, so any and all help was welcome.

That evening I couldn't settle, feeling too keyed up about the gathering the following night and the potential to start fighting back against Elrulin and his cronies. I was pacing around my room like a caged cat, until G finally got fed up.

Oh good grief! he griped at me as I bumped his stand for the third time. *Why don't you go outside for a while and try to burn off some of this pent-up energy you seem to have? Go for a run around the garden or something. I could do with stretching my wings so I'll come along as well.*

I eyed the paper I had placed under the stand and saw the accumulated dust from his preening along with his droppings, so I decided to change that at the same time. Might as well do something useful with my nervous agitation.

I held my hand out to Gauvain and moved him from his perch to my shoulder, then lifted the perch off the paper and carefully folded in the edges to prevent the contents from flying all over the room. As I rolled up the old sheets and then laid new, I caught G's amusement at me acting like his servant by cleaning up after him.

It was the same kind of disdainful superiority all cat owners (or cat slaves as they would almost all agree is the proper term) are familiar with. I looked at him out of the corner of my eye and he ducked his head and turned away.

"Yeah, alright," I said to his back, "so I'm cleaning up after you. That's just because you're a slob and I don't want to live in a pig sty." He chuckled and turned back to look at me.

I am well aware and I genuinely appreciate your fastidiousness in keeping our quarters habitable. I have been lacking the opportunities for outside excursions since we have been here. That may also be a contributary factor in your abnormal state of excitation. You have been unable to partake in your customary early morning exertions.

I looked at him in surprise at his insight. I *had* been missing my morning run, especially as I usually found it a good time to clear my head and sometimes come up with new ideas for a problem that had been bugging me.

I took the balled-up paper downstairs with me and headed outside, informing Mrs Wilson on my way so she knew where I was. I threw the paper into the trash and walked into the garden, breathing deeply in the cooling evening air and swinging my arms to loosen up.

Gauvain took off from my shoulder to go for a flight around, and I warned him to stay within the limits of Seirina's wards. I stretched for a couple more minutes then decided to run through my katas, since the garden wasn't really large enough to allow for a proper run bearing in mind my usual three-mile course.

I took my first stance and bowed in, clearing my mind and beginning to flow through the various strikes and blocks of the first kata. Rather than stopping in between each one, I decided to make the katas flow into one another, forming one long series. As I moved, I realised another reason why I was so uptight about tomorrow.

I had been true to my word up to now, not harassing Angelica and giving her the space she needed. However she would be at the gathering Seirina had organised, which would be the first time I had been able to see her since the day of our escape from Bolton Castle.

I was eager to see her, but also fearful of how she might be feeling towards me now and how she might be handling what had happened to her. No wonder I was so knotted up.

Far from helping me relax, the realisation that I would be seeing Angie in the morning actually made my shoulders even tighter. I finally had to stop my katas, kneel down and simply concentrate on my breathing. I used an old relaxation technique of starting at the top of my head and working my way down, relaxing each muscle in turn as I went until I finally felt less rigid.

I considered retrying my katas but elected to make the most of my impromptu meditation and head inside while I was still relaxed. I decided to take a bath to enhance the relaxation, then made myself laugh by imagining Summer suggesting scented candles and some New Age music CD while I soaked. I may be secure in my masculinity and comfortably in touch with my feminine side, but there *were* limits! Gauvain flew down as I stood up and landed on my shoulder, chuckling as he picked up on my thoughts across our link.

I believe I shall partake in a shower this evening as well, if you would be so kind, he stated loftily as we walked in. *One wants to look one's best for a gathering, especially when meeting new people for the first time.* I smiled inwardly at his remarks, proof that the old Vain nickname wasn't *quite* as far off the mark as he would like me to believe. Then again, I'd be showering and shaving before the meeting, so who was I to talk?

We headed upstairs and I ran a warm shower for G to wash himself while I got changed, then set him on the rail of the shower curtain to drip the worst of the water off while I ran my bath. By the time the tub was full, most of the water had drained off of his feathers so I set him back on his perch to preen while I went back and sank gratefully into the steamy water. I lay there with my eyes closed, feeling the heat work further wonders on my muscles which were still sore from how tight they'd been.

As I lay there, my mind turned inevitably to Angelica once again. I thought about all she had been through because of my lack of openness, trying to think whether I would do it differently if I had it to do again. I also reversed the roles and tried to think how I would have expected her to act in my place.

I came to the conclusion that although it had inadvertently led to her suffering, I had acted reasonably and would not expect more if she were the one with the secret. I was deeply sorry her boss was such a humongous dick, but I didn't feel I could really be blamed for that since I had never met him before.

Thinking about Angie gradually led to me remembering what she had looked like each time I had seen her, going back in time until I remembered that first visit. That naturally triggered the memory of the images I had called up to defend my mind against her, at which point I opened my eyes and sat up as I realised certain shifts were occurring in the water. I got up and pulled the plug out of the bath, grabbing a towel and drying myself with overly brisk swipes to try to clear my head again.

I lay on the bed and tried to repeat the relaxation exercise I had used earlier. I met with limited success as my mind continually flashed up provocative vignettes from my mental movie. I drifted off to sleep with a smile on my face, aware that there was no way I would roll out of bed tonight!

Chapter 32

The following morning I woke up with a feeling of butterflies in my stomach. More like a giant flock of bats to be honest, but anyway. I went into the bathroom and relieved my bladder, then stared at myself in the mirror for a moment. Today was going to be a milestone for a number of reasons and I wanted to present myself well to all concerned, so it was time for some grooming.

I hadn't shaved for a couple of days and I'd recently discovered that shaving cream was infinitely superior to foam or gel in a can. I'd even found one with absinthe extract in it. That not only helped with skin conditioning, but it always made me smile as I'd heard of a wizard in America who was partial to absinthe. Mind you when I'd got it in my mouth by mistake, it tasted nothing like the drink!

I soaked my stubble and applied the cream, carefully scraping away the hair with a fresh blade. I was taking no chances on nicks from a dull razor today. I proceeded to trim my nose hair and even pluck a stray eyebrow hair or two. Gauvain chuckled as he watched me, no doubt thinking of his old nickname, and I smiled in admission of my own nod to vanity as I brushed my teeth.

I took a hot shower, washing carefully and finishing with a cold deluge to wake me up. I dried myself and applied my aftershave, then dressed in a clean and pressed white shirt, blessing the domestic goddess that was Mrs Wilson. I followed the shirt with clean jeans, socks and shoes.

Unlike with other trousers, I generally went commando in jeans since they often felt restrictive anyway. Who knew but I might have reason to be grateful of a little freedom of movement later on.

I let Gauvain out of the window to stretch his wings and then headed downstairs and into the kitchen. Despite Mrs Wilson's protestations I preferred to fix many of my own meals, especially breakfast as I had brought some Cafegeddon with me. In fact I was running low, so I was hoping I'd get the chance to stop off at home soon.

I sat down with simple toast and coffee, setting an extra cup on the table after pouring some for Mrs Wilson which she took with thanks. As expected, the smell of freshly brewed caffeinated ambrosia drew Seirina like a moth to a flame and she grabbed her mug eagerly, holding it out to me expectantly. I laughed and poured obligingly, then smiled as she inhaled the aroma and took her first sip.

"You know, you may have completely disrupted my comfortable life," she said in between sips, "but you do have your uses. I'm definitely going to require the name of your caffeine dealer before this is over. I think you may have successfully converted me from tea in the morning, although after lunch I'd still switch back. I do want *some* sleep!" I smiled over at Mrs Wilson who simply sighed and shook her head.

"I thought as much," she replied, sounding resigned to the inevitable, "so Mr Maddox has already given me the recipe for his blend and I've ordered some beans and a new coffee grinder." I grinned cheekily at Seirina, pleased to have anticipated her for once despite her significantly greater experience.

"So when are people going to be arriving?" I asked casually, trying not to appear too eager. "You mentioned it would be an evening meeting. I'm guessing there'll be some who aren't fond of sunlight then? Vampires and more?" Seirina looked at me shrewdly over the rim of her mug, not fooled for a moment as to my true interest but deciding to answer my spoken question before responding to the subtext.

"Yes, some of those coming are averse to sunlight, some just wish to not be seen quite as easily," she replied, setting her cup down and accepting some toast from Mrs Wilson. "They should start arriving around seven thirty, with the actual meeting scheduled to start at nine. I wanted to give plenty of time for people to trickle in, otherwise we'd have had a huge convoy of arrivals which would be impossible to go unnoticed. This way it just looks like a bit of a party to the average observer."

I nodded, impressed with her forethought and strategic planning, although I still hadn't heard the information I *really* wanted and she knew it. I looked at her as she bit into her breakfast, outwardly unconcerned and oblivious to anything else I was waiting to hear. I mirrored her actions, only then realising I hadn't buttered my toast yet.

I growled in annoyance at my preoccupation and reached for the butter, then got up and looked in the cupboards. Mrs Wilson immediately asked if she could help me find something and I asked if she had any Marmite, to which Seirina made a gagging sound.

"Oh no, you're not a Marmite lover are you?" she complained, pretending to hold back from vomiting. Mrs Wilson on the other hand simply rolled her eyes at her employer's histrionics and reached into the cooking supplies, handing me a familiar jar with a yellow lid. The mock betrayal on Seirina's face was a picture and I laughed as I sat down again.

"It's just vegetable extract you big sissy," I told her as I spread my toast with the black gold. "It goes great in gravy or stews, even if you don't like it neat. It's much better than stock cubes." Mrs Wilson nodded, looking surprised at my culinary knowledge. Seirina was the one rolling her eyes now.

"Whatever, just don't breathe on me." She waved her hand dramatically in front of her face and reached for her coffee again. I simply sighed in long suffering tolerance of the ongoing persecution of my superior taste and promised to brush my teeth again after breakfast. I had planned on that anyway, since I had no idea how Angelica felt about Marmite either!

I finished my breakfast, still not having heard anything about whether Angie and the twins might be arriving any earlier. I sat and stared intently at Seirina, gradually degenerating into glowering at her tacit refusal to tell me what I wanted to know.

She simply ate her toast and drank her coffee, the tables finally turning when she held out her cup for a refill. I picked up the pot and refilled my own mug, then set it down out of her reach. I raised an eyebrow and sipped, keeping eye contact the whole time. She finally gave in and sighed, although I could definitely see a trace of mirth in her eyes.

"Fine, release the caffeine hostage and I'll talk!" she said pleadingly. I smiled at the success of my tactic and poured for her, laughing at her over-dramatic clutching of her refilled mug to her chest. "This really is good stuff." I narrowed my eyes in mock threat at her stalling and it was her turn to sigh at my over-dramatic eagerness.

"Alright, I'll talk, turn off the death beams!" She pretended to raise her mug in defence, then thought better of it and hugged it to protect it again. "They'll be arriving for lunch so we can go through our accumulated information one last time before the meeting."

I felt my heart rate accelerate at the thought of Angie being here in just a few hours and I nodded to Seirina. I then took a deep breath as if to breathe over her and she got up immediately.

"Don't you dare!" she warned me and headed out of the kitchen briskly. I laughed quietly in turn and Mrs Wilson joined in, waving me away as I went to start clearing the table, so I went back upstairs to brush my teeth again.

I spent the rest of the morning ensuring everything I had discussed with the twins was clearly documented and ordered. I ran through my memory several times, jotting down a few other salient points along with a couple of extra questions that occurred to me as I reread the information. I wanted to make sure our afternoon was productive, and the best way to do that was to be as well informed as possible so we didn't have to waste time recapping old data.

The hours seemed to both fly past and crawl with glacial inactivity simultaneously, but suddenly it was half past twelve and I heard the intercom ring downstairs. Seirina must have been waiting, as it only rang twice before I heard her voice then a click as she triggered the gate.

My stomach was definitely trying to crawl out of my throat and my heart was doing hula hoops around my ass as I waited the interminable time of the drive up to the house. I finally heard the doorbell ring. I left Gauvain sleeping on his perch and rushed to the stairs.

Mrs Wilson answered it and I heard her welcome the new arrivals, meanwhile I was at the bottom of the stairs halfway down the hall just listening for one particular voice. Instead I heard footsteps clicking along, so I turned and ran up a few steps before turning to walk nonchalantly down as they reached me. I waved casually at the twins as they came into view, then stumbled slightly as I saw a familiar dark head come past the wall.

Angelica turned towards me at the sound of my less than elegant misstep and I gasped involuntarily at her appearance. She had clearly made something of an effort for today as her hair was washed and she had on a nice top and clean jeans, coincidentally mirroring my own look. However she had lost weight so her clothes were looser, her skin had the sallow appearance of someone who hadn't seen the sun in days, and she had dark circles under her eyes which were themselves puffy indicating significant crying combined with lack of sleep.

The clear evidence of her pain caused an actual physical ache in my chest and my throat tightened. My hope for a joyful reunion with her running into my arms disappeared like cotton candy in water. I tried to smile a welcome at her, but my guilt at causing her such obvious distress weighed the corners of my mouth down so I just couldn't do it.

The lump in my throat even prevented me from saying anything for a moment, compounded by the sudden dryness of my mouth. I worked my tongue to moisten my gums and swallowed to loosen my vocal cords, then tried again.

"Hi," I managed lamely, not really sure what else to say, "it's good to see you again." I was at least switched on enough not to ask her how she had been, since it was painfully obvious from how she looked that she was struggling. To my dismay, she simply nodded towards me then turned away and kept walking, grabbing and squeezing the twins' hand for support.

I sat down on the stairs, put my elbows on my knees and my head in my hands as I tried to figure out what to do to try to help rectify the situation. At this point I wasn't thinking of myself or my hopes for a relationship, I just wanted to make right the distress I knew I was at least partially responsible for.

I saw the shadow on the floor as Mrs Wilson walked past me and heard as she ushered them into the kitchen, telling them Seirina was just on a call. She offered them tea and I heard her asking if anyone wanted something to eat. The twins accepted happily but I didn't hear a response from Angelica. I could only assume she shook her head as I heard Mrs Wilson's kindly protestation that she needed to eat, to at least try something and that maybe once she ate something she would feel better.

A few minutes later, Seirina came out of her study and headed into the kitchen to join the girls for lunch. I wasn't sure my gut-load of self-reproach would leave any space for food so I simply sat on the stairs and went over some ideas on how to prove myself to whatever potential allies showed up for the meeting.

After a while I still had no valid plans so I headed down the hall to join everyone else. As I approached, I heard someone crying softly, almost as if the pain were too great to allow for anything more, and I both knew and dreaded what I was about to see. When I reached the door I saw Angelica holding on to Seirina as if to stop herself drowning and Seirina was stroking her hair as she murmured into her ear. Seirina saw me in the doorway and simply shook her head ever so slightly to warn me not to interrupt, so I turned around and headed for the study.

As I walked in, the door closed behind me and there came a rustling from the terrarium again. I watched as Iyrin climbed up the branch into view and fixed me with a pitch black gaze.

Chapter 33

The hair on the back of my neck prickled as I remembered Seirina's warning not to try to mentally communicate with her friend. I deliberately turned my back on it and decided to peruse the hitherto ignored (by me) shelves of Seirina's library. There were two bookcases facing her desk, one either side of the door, and each one was filled with volumes of varying size, age and colour. There were many I had never seen before, no doubt because they related more to Seirina's areas of interest and magickal speciality than anything I had looked at previously.

I picked one at random, barely noticing either the title or anything written inside as my mind was focused down the hall, wondering what was going on with Angie and what she was saying to Seirina. I leafed slowly through the volume, noting a couple of rather unpleasant looking images that seemed to have to do with human body parts and necromancy as I flipped past them. After reaching the end, I replaced it and blindly went to pull out another.

As I did so, I heard tapping from the tank and turned to see Iyrin using one finger on the glass to attract my attention. When it saw that it had my attention, it wagged its finger and shook its head, clearly telling me not to touch the books. Maybe just the one I was reaching for, I couldn't be sure. It then crooked the same finger to beckon me over.

Seirina's warning echoed through my mind again and I closed my thoughts as tightly as I could. My uncertainty made me hesitate, so Iyrin tapped again and beckoned to me once more. I listened briefly and could still hear the ladies talking in the kitchen so I looked back over at the terrarium. Iyrin's black eyes were fixed on me and I could have sworn I felt a subtle probing at my mental defences.

I really didn't need to be getting involved with yet another focus for my attention right now, bearing in mind the upcoming meeting to form some kind of alliance against the Order as well as my more... personal distractions. My mind flicked again to what was happening just down the hall, then suddenly I heard something that made my blood run cold.

I can help you with that. The sing-song, almost Welsh intonation made me think briefly of my grandmother but the voice was definitely not hers and moreover was definitely *inside* my head, although somehow hovering just outside of my mental barriers. *Really, I can. Come over, let's get a better look at each other and talk.*

The hair all along my arms was fully upright and my eyes had widened so much it was almost painful. Now I was curious as to why Seirina had been so cautious when I had reached out. Maybe it was more a case of not being the one to initiate the contact in case it didn't *want* to talk to me? All she had said was that it was a watcher. What the hell did that mean?

A vague memory of having heard the term before nudged at the back of my mind, but I had a funny feeling Iyrin wouldn't be too impressed if I disappeared off to do some research right now and left it waiting. I had no idea if it was a him or her, or even if there *were* male and female forms, so I decided to stick with 'it'. Plumbing didn't really matter anyway, not that it *had* any since it was made of bone.

I took a few steps towards Seirina's desk and saw Iyrin stand upright like it had previously, eagerly pressing both hands to the surface and leaning forward until its skull was almost on the glass as well. It was clearly wanting me to come closer, although precisely why I wasn't sure. With a description like 'watcher' I doubted it was because it needed bifocals!

My sarcasm reared its head as it often did when I got nervous and Iyrin cocked its head slightly. Whether at the fact that I hadn't come around the desk yet or because it could hear my thoughts was unclear.

The stupidly self-destructive part of me reasoned that it was small and fragile, so should be easy to smash against a wall if it became threatening. My mind completely ignored the fact that this was an ancient magickal being who was only *using* the bones as a physical conduit; smashing its shell would probably piss it off in the extreme! I swear, sometimes I thought my own brain was trying to kill me.

I took another couple of steps, reaching the visitor side of the desk, and stopped. Iyrin tilted its head to the other side when I didn't keep going around the desk, and I heard the same lilting, almost musical voice inside my head again.

Come closer, it said insistently. *What are you* afraid *of?* Maybe it thought appealing to my male bravado would get me to do what it wanted. If it had been watching humans for as long as Seirina said, it probably thought of that as a viable stratagem. Fortunately, I was well aware of my anxiety issues and while I wasn't necessarily *comfortable* with them, I did at least acknowledge my fight or flight setting was definitely geared more towards flight when it was just myself.

I'd walk into the gates of Hell for a friend but failed to see the point for myself, so taunting me wasn't going to get the result Iyrin was looking for. I decided to speak out loud to it so I didn't have to lower my mental defences to communicate.

"To be honest, you," I said simply. "I have no idea what you are, what you want or what you can do, and Seirina has already warned me of the dangers of communicating mentally with you. So you suddenly talking to me has got my internal warning alarm blaring, and I have no problem admitting it."

It straightened its head and leant back slightly from the glass until it was upright again, staring at me as if trying to pierce my soul with its gaze to understand more about me. I redoubled my mental walls as I felt the same probing from earlier, Seirina's concern echoing in my memory again.

Maybe she just doesn't want you finding out about her. Don't forget, I've been with her a long time so I know what she's really like. I can tell you, for example, that even though she's helping you now, if she finds out that your friends are still working for the Order she'll kill them without a second's hesitation.

I swear on my power I will do nothing to harm you for the duration of our conversation, unless you assault me first. I had read about this kind of oath before but had never witnessed one, although I knew what I meant. Breaking it would have dire repercussions on the one who made it, but in the back of my mind I also registered the limitations Iyrin had placed upon the oath.

What would constitute an assault? Refusal of any proposal or offer, hurting its feelings? And who would decide when the conversation was over? There were a hell of a lot of loopholes in that contract and I was reminded of the legends of the Fae. Sometimes called fairies, faeran, fair folk, elves, or various other permutations, they would say one thing but mean another. Dealing with them was always fraught with some kind of danger.

"That's very considerate of you," I said tentatively, "but that leaves a lot of scope for interpretation." Even without lips, I could swear Iyrin had a kind of smile at my refusal to accept its oath at face value.

I'm glad to see I was right about you, it said, nodding its skull slightly. *You're not quite as naïve as most of your kind. I give you this free gift: what most see as anxiety in you is actually a higher level of understanding and intellect, an awareness of the potential outcomes and how rarely they work in your favour.* OK, if there was one area where I knew I *was* susceptible to flattery, it was my mind. I knew I was smart from all my childhood testing but I had never considered how that might influence my outlook on the world.

Iyrin's words, though absolutely meant to ingratiate itself to me, bolstered my self-image in a way I hadn't felt in a long time, if ever. Now it was my turn to raise an eyebrow and tilt my head in thought, and Iyrin mirrored me questioningly. Then I realised if it knew about my anxiety, it could read things in my mind even with my defences up. Just what *was* this thing?

Very perceptive, it said, answering my unspoken thoughts. *It's true that your defences are useless against me. If I chose to, I could enter your mind and take everything I desired, leaving you a useless quivering lump of jelly. That would mean you were of no further use to me, however, and would also almost certainly piss old Isis off to no end, which is something I certainly have no desire to do.*

My goose-bumps returned at the stunning implications of what it had just said, along with the level of power it indicated and the obvious differences between us. *Now that we have that out in the open and we know where we stand, stop standing there like a wallflower at a school prom and get over here!*

The abrupt change from enticement to command was jarring but at the same time somehow reassuring as it felt more honest. Almost without meaning to, I did as I was told and stepped around the desk. Iyrin leant forward again, gesturing to put my hand up against the glass to mirror its own skeletal digits. I held my hand up but hesitated a few inches from the surface, unsure if I should actually get so close.

Almost quicker than I could see, it pushed its hand *through* the glass as if it were no more than water and wiped its finger across my palm. It pulled back into the terrarium leaving no evidence of what it had done and then put its finger into its mouth. I saw some kind of long tongue inside there, reminding me of Venom's tongue from the comics but black in colour to match the darkness of its eyes. It licked its finger with every appearance of relishing the taste.

What the hell could it learn from my sweat? I had already checked and established that it hadn't cut me, so it wasn't tasting my blood, but even so its actions were disturbing in the extreme. It had sworn it wouldn't hurt me but that left a lot of room for other things to happen. You didn't have to *hurt* someone to make them a slave and they might not notice for a very long time. I hadn't felt anything beyond the physical touch, but I still backed away quickly until I felt the desk come into contact with the backs of my legs.

As it sucked its finger, a shimmer seemed to run over its skull and down its body and I would swear I saw a fine web forming behind it, as if it was starting to build flesh over its bones as a result of our contact. I didn't feel any draw on myself as it did, so I had no idea where it was coming from, but it was disturbing in the extreme to witness.

"What did you just do?" I whispered, horrified by what I saw. "Remember, you swore not to cause me any harm and I can guaran-damn-tee that any reasonable assessment would say you made the first move so you can't use that whole 'unless you assault me first' clause!"

It looked at me and this time I was certain I saw the diaphanous film of lips curl up into a smile. I felt for my magick and it was still there, undiminished by whatever had just happened, so it didn't *seem* to have had any detrimental effect but I was still freaked way the hell out.

I merely sampled your essence, which linked us together so you can see more of me now. Also, I'll now be able to call to you no matter where you go and even watch through your eyes. You'll also be able to reach out to me in the same way. I was reminded of my link to Gauvain and suddenly wondered why he hadn't interfered in what had just happened.

Exactly, it continued, once again responding to my thoughts, *our bond is very similar. I silenced your communication to your little friend so he wouldn't interfere in our chat and I'll release my block in a moment. He'll probably be quite upset with what's happened but I warn you now: if he tries to sever my link to you, I'll kill him instantly.*

The frank and unfeeling way it spoke again of killing someone so close to me confirmed once and for all just how different it was from humans. I resolved to examine our link as soon as possible to try to place some limits on it. Iyrin shook its head at me and I felt a sense of amusement radiating from it across a thread that hadn't been there before. At least I was now aware of the tether so I could assess it later, after the meeting.

Its amusement indicated it clearly considered any efforts I might make to limit its access to me to be completely worthless. No matter what, I was certain of one thing: if it hurt G in *any way*, I would make it my mission in life to destroy it utterly. I looked at it and held that image very clearly in my head, since it could obviously hear my thoughts regardless of my mental wards.

It shrugged and tilted its head to one side briefly, as if to indicate it didn't really care one way or the other, so hopefully if Gauvain were that unimportant to it he'd be safe. I suddenly remembered its offer to help with my situation with Angelica and added her to the do not touch list. It gave me the ghost of a grin again and shrugged just one shoulder this time, then crouched back down onto the branch.

I was suddenly aware of a rattling at the door, as if someone had just turned the sound back up on the world, and I realised that Iyrin must have sealed the door and muffled any noise from outside while we were talking. I looked over at it and saw it disappearing down the branch into the depths of the terrarium, which I now realised was just a convenient refuge for it and in no way kept it locked up.

The door burst open and I turned back to it to see Seirina come barrelling into the room with a concerned look on her face, which changed to fury as she saw where I was standing and understood what must have been going on.

"What the hell have you done?" she demanded. At this point I didn't know what to tell her, since I didn't actually know.

Chapter 34

"To be honest, it wasn't me," I said in my own defence. "I just came in here to look at your library since you were all talking in the kitchen, and it really didn't look like something I should intrude on." She nodded briefly at that statement then shook her head as she must have realised some of what had occurred.

"How can you be so perceptive one minute and then so fucking stupid the next?" she demanded, clearly still pissed at me. "I *told* you to be careful and not reach out to it! Now it's got a hold on you, the same as it got on me centuries ago!" I looked at her in surprise, suddenly realising maybe she wasn't such a willing partner as she at first may have appeared.

"Hey, I was just leafing through one of your books. You have some really gross shit, by the way. It tapped on the glass to get my attention. I'd put up my mental blocks specifically because of your earlier warning about it, but it was still able to talk to me in my head and read my thoughts. It tried to entice me by saying it could help with the situation with Angie…" As I said that, her eyes widened and she looked more alarmed than I had ever seen her.

"Please tell me you weren't stupid enough to take it up on that!" She actually sounded almost panicked and I thought back over what had been said, both by Iyrin and myself. I hadn't said it out loud but I had been very clear about it leaving Gauvain and Angelica alone, a thought which it had definitely picked up and acknowledged.

"No, I made sure it knew I wanted it to stay away from her," I said reassuringly, at which Seirina's expression relaxed somewhat. "I also made it clear that it wasn't to touch G. My hawk, Gauvain," I clarified for her when she looked confused, at which point I realised I hadn't actually formally introduced them, "after it threatened to kill him if he tried to interfere in its link to me. In fact, I threatened to make it my life's purpose to destroy it if it hurt them in any way." She looked gratified and approving at my statement, then I saw a single tear form at the corner of one eye for just a moment before she blinked it away.

"Good," she said firmly, "I didn't have a familiar when it first linked to me and then it killed the first creature that showed any signs of compatibility to me. Since then I've never tried to find another." I understood her reserved attitude even more now. She had lost her first potential familiar to something that was using her for its own ends, then the man she loved to another who had wanted to do the same.

She must now be terrified to form an attachment to anyone or anything in case they got taken from her again. Her defence was to keep everyone at arm's length. A task no doubt made easier by the creep factor of her necromancer side.

It also told me something about Iyrin. It was jealous, possessive, impulsive and with just a hint of spoiled brat syndrome thrown into the mix for good measure. Combine that with a significant level of power, and you had something I *really* wished I had stayed as far away from as possible.

Still, there was no point in crying about it now. It was in my head and I had no idea how to get it out. That was a problem to be considered at another time. Right now, I had another purpose to focus on. The Order still had to be taken down.

As I thought that, Angelica and the twins walked into the study from where they had apparently been waiting in the hall when Seirina came charging in. That meant they had heard… oh, wonderful, there went any chance of me pretending to be aloof or indifferent to Angie. Then again, by the relieved look on her face, she seemed to be quite glad to have my feelings for her confirmed.

I didn't have the luxury of time to follow through on it at the moment, and she was clearly still dealing with some kind of post-traumatic stress

THE ORDER OF THE NINE SEALS

from her subjective months of captivity and torture. At least I could now stop second, third and four hundredth guessing her feelings (or lack thereof) for me, though.

I decided to bury my emotions for now and concentrate on our mission, but I was definitely going to come back to them later. I smiled quickly at her in apology for not taking time immediately, then motioned everyone to the chairs in front of Seirina's desk. As I looked towards the glass at the back of the room again, I also promised myself to find better ways to defend my mind. Perhaps even a way to sever the link Iyrin had just established.

I felt its amusement as it caught the thought from my mind, and I suddenly thought of the psychic leash Elrulin had established over the twins until the Veil had snapped it. Was Iyrin intending to try to establish that kind of control over me, using me as a go-fer and remote eyes and ears while it sat safe and secure? Because I sure as shit wasn't going to allow anyone or anything to use me like that!

I felt Gauvain wake up as he sensed my distress now that Iyrin's suppression had ended and I heard him come flying down the stairway. I held my arm out without turning around and he landed on it exactly as I knew he would. I sent him a stream of images to catch him up, finishing with a warning not to have anything to do with Iyrin, then felt his talons clench in his irritation at how I had been tricked.

I promised him we'd address it later, but for now we needed to focus on the Order. He wasn't happy but subsided into sullen silence to allow me to get on with the pre-meeting meeting. By now the women were all seated and looking at me expectantly.

"Sorry," I apologised, realising I had kept them all waiting, "I was just catching Gauvain up on my latest stupidity." At which Seirina rolled her eyes and shook her head.

"It's a good thing you're linked," she remarked acidly, "otherwise with the way you act, you'd be having to update him on that alone a dozen times a day!" She was clearly not going to let this go any time soon and to be honest, I probably deserved her disapproval.

Then again, I had *tried* to take precautions. Was it really my fault if the being in her study was so easily able to overcome my mental blocks? Yeah, I had a funny feeling that argument would fly about as well as a lead balloon. There was no point getting into a fight right now since I needed everybody's help with what we were facing. I decided that yet again, my best and only option was to take my lumps and move on. At least for now.

"OK, so I'm an idiot," I ground out between clenched teeth. "Can we please move on to the issue at hand? We need to make sure we've got everything we know on paper if we're going to convince anyone that we have a shot at taking the Order down, and not just turning this into some ill-fated suicide mission."

They all nodded agreement at my admission and practicality but I could still see the tightness of irritation in Seirina's expression. Then I realised another reason I was an idiot. In my eagerness to get down the stairs to see Angie when she had arrived, I'd left all my sheets of information upstairs in my room. I closed my eyes, pinched the bridge of my nose and sighed.

"I'll be back in a second, I just need to go and grab my notes. And yes, before you say it, I would have been better doing that than coming in here and blundering into yet another complicated rela… encounter." I caught myself before I finished the word relationship but not a single person there was fooled, to judge by the expressions on their faces.

Very smooth, Gauvain commented sarcastically. *I'm sure nobody noticed!* I didn't even bother to reply because it was painfully obvious just how far my foot was in my mouth at this point. Probably beyond the knee, at a guess. I simply sighed again, turned and walked out of the study like a naughty student on the way to the principal's office.

Once I was out of the room I heard some soft giggling, probably from the twins since Angie still looked too traumatised and Seirina didn't seem the type. I looked up at the ceiling, sighed one more time and mentally kicked my own ass, then jogged up the stairs to my room. I snatched up my sheaf of notes and headed back downstairs. I was fervently hoping, at least for now, we might be able to move on and discuss the matter at hand.

I re-entered the study to hear the ladies all stop talking immediately. Oh no, *that* didn't give me a complex at all! I stopped almost as quickly as the whispering did and looked around the faces pointed in my direction.

"If you've got something to say, just say it!" I snapped, running out of patience. "I'm perfectly aware that I screwed up, but I'd like to know how *you* tried to keep Iyrin out of your mind when it got hold of you, Seirina! Just how successful were *you*? I'm guessing not very since, as you just said, you've been connected to it for centuries! And you've clearly also been just as *effective* in *breaking* that connection!"

By this time, I was working myself up quite a head of steam and my temper was hanging on by a thread, which was the reason for my next stupidly childish comment. "You know what, if I'm so dumb, you probably don't want my help with the Order in case I screw it up. Here, do it your damn selves, because you've all been *so* effective thus far!"

With that final snide shout, I threw the handful of papers towards them and saw them flutter apart as I turned on my heel and stormed out of the room again, this time slamming the door behind me. I stomped down the hall to the front door and yanked it open, then stood there taking deep breaths and trying desperately to calm down.

I felt a sense of amusement trickle across the link from Iyrin but I tried my utmost to ignore it. This was all its fault in the first place for wanting to have another person linked to it, then acting on that without considering anyone else's feelings. I was determined to find a way to break the link it had formed somehow, no matter how long it took, because I refused to be treated like a servant by any*one* or any*thing*.

As I stood there, my temper got worse instead of better and I started to reach for the sunlight outside to draw the warmth and light towards myself. I started to store the power in Seren but my mood was so volatile, some of it ended up radiating out from my skin into a kind of static charge just waiting for someone to touch it. I heard the door open and someone walking down the hall but I refused to turn around.

I heard a gasp but had no idea why, and I felt G turn to see who was coming up behind me. He sent me the image of Seirina standing just a few feet away from me, reaching out but not touching me. I still didn't turn and simply spoke to her over my shoulder.

"What?" I snapped. "Thought of something else I fucked up that you want to point out? Don't worry, I'll get my stuff and be out of your house well before your meeting!" I could *feel* the power buzzing around my shoulders in my rage but she must have seen something, since she didn't actually touch me. For a moment I thought she might be about to apologise but with my last comment, Gauvain showed me her hand dropping and ending up on her hip. Her face shifted from slightly sad to pissed off again. It was good to know I had at least *one* reliable talent with women!

"Oh, grow up you big baby!" she said, sounding more exasperated with the last half hour than annoyed. "Yes, you were right, Iyrin is sneaky and insidious and I shouldn't have blamed you for its ability to get into your head. Fine, so I was just as susceptible, and yes, I've been stuck with it for centuries. I was *trying* to protect you, because I knew it would be eager to latch onto you as someone who was about to be involved in interesting events. Also, because of your quite evident power, Iyrin would be drawn to you like a moth to a flame..."

"At least you didn't say fly to shit!" I mumbled just loud enough for her to hear, smiling slightly as I remembered Danu's comment during my training. I heard her snort despite herself and turned away from the garden, releasing my grip on the sunlight outside. I noticed the increase in the reflected glow from the floor and realised why she must have gasped as she approached me. As I faced her, Seirina stepped back slightly and looked just over my shoulder.

"You might want to turn down the steam, too," she said, nodding towards my right shoulder. "You know, I've heard the expression steam coming out of your ears or steaming angry, but I've never actually seen anyone make it a reality before." I rolled my shoulders, feeling Gauvain shuffle as I did so, and felt the tension ease. I pulled in the power I had been leaking and funnelled it into Seren, noticing Seirina relax in response to her seeing me easing down a couple of notches.

Is it safe for me to talk now also? Gauvain said in my mind, surprising me. I turned to look at him, craning my neck away so I wasn't simply burying my face in his chest feathers.

"Sorry, bud," I replied, crestfallen that he'd even considered that I was mad at him, "I was never angry at *you.*"

Understood, however I had no desire to become entangled in any collateral damage from your irritation, nor to make myself appear to be in any way against you, he clarified for me. *I am well aware how upset you are at recent developments, and I simply wish to inform you that I in no way hold you responsible for the intrusive actions of a being with whom you were completely unfamiliar.*

His practical and understanding comments did more to calm me down than anything Seirina might have said. I looked back at her and she took a deep breath as she noticed my further regaining of my composure.

"I'm glad Gauvain seems to have steadied your temper a bit," she said, sounding a little impatient, which itself served to tighten my shoulders a couple of notches again. "We all freely agree you've managed to stand against the Order more effectively, in just a few encounters, than the rest of us have in years of efforts. We clearly need your help to do more. I apologise for how I reacted."

She gritted her teeth and rolled her eyes slightly as she said the last phrase, clearly treating this like a grown-up having to say sorry to a toddler, but I still appreciated the effort. "Now shut the door, let's go back to the study and get on with our planning session." So saying, she turned and walked back down the hall and I did as I was told, closing the door and trailing dutifully along behind her.

As I entered the study just behind Seirina, I saw her nod towards the twins and Angelica. I saw the twins taking deep breaths and relaxing into their chair. Angie just closed her eyes briefly and nodded slightly, then also sat back in her chair. It was nice to see they were relieved to have me back, and I noticed the twins had also picked up my pages of notes and put them on another chair for me. I also saw that said chair was the other side of them from Angie, but I didn't push it. I just picked up my notes and sat down quietly.

Chapter 35

We spent the next couple of hours going over the notes I had put together. While the first ten minutes or so were a little strained, the more we got involved in the inner workings of the Order the more everyone started to relax. The twins were doing most of the talking to begin with but the longer we talked, the more Angelica began to add in little snippets or clarifications.

She gradually grew more certain of herself, the sparkle slowly returning to her eyes, her shoulders squaring and her back straightening. The fire returned to her speech as the thought of revenge against her abuser gave her focus and clarity of purpose. It was wonderful to see her looking more like the woman who had captured my attention so completely, though I was aware that hers was a delicate balance for now.

Seirina caught me smiling goofily at Angie once while she was looking over the notes and elucidating a particular entry. I quickly wiped the smile off my face when Angelica looked up, saw where Seirina was looking and followed her gaze to glance over at me.

I readjusted my expression to polite interest, at which Serina looked up at the ceiling, shook her head and sighed at the moony schoolboy behaviour. The twins giggled and I saw the ghost of a smile on Angie's lips as she looked back down at the papers. It wasn't much but I felt a degree of hope that she was at least able to feel some amusement, even if it *was* at my expense.

Mrs Wilson brought in a tray with cups, milk, sugar and some biscuits laid out on it, then went and got a large French press. As she walked up to the desk to start pouring for everyone, Angelica took a deep breath and smelt the Cafegeddon. Her face finally opened up into the smile I remembered and her gaze slid over to me. I nodded to confirm what she already knew and she eagerly reached for her cup as Mrs Wilson handed it to her.

I lifted an eyebrow queryingly at Seirina given that we were having coffee in the afternoon, but she just mumbled something about it likely being a late night as she brought her cup to her lips. I swear, women changing their minds wasn't hyperbole, they really did do it multiple times a day!

Angie closed her eyes as she inhaled deeply then sipped the caffeinated nectar. I sat back in my chair and covered my smile with my hand but that fooled precisely no one. Rejuvenated, we carried on reviewing the information I had collated. One or two minor details were added in response to my noted questions but overall, the information was confirmed as accurate and as complete as the twins and Angelica could make it. After finishing, we all agreed to take a break for the next couple of hours until people started arriving for the meeting.

I stood up, waking Gauvain from where he had been napping on my shoulder, and immediately headed outside, telling everyone I was taking G out to stretch his wings. I walked through the kitchen, nodding to Mrs Wilson as I did, and went out into the garden.

Gauvain promptly launched himself from my shoulder and soared into the air. I breathed deeply, enjoying the warm afternoon and fresh air, stepping onto the back lawn. I closed my eyes and lifted my face to the sun, simply savouring the warmth rather than trying to absorb power this time.

I reached out to G as he flew, feeling the air under his wings and seeing the garden through his eyes. It was fun to see how different the world looked through his eyes compared to mine, which made me think of Iyrin's link to me. Intellectually, I could understand *why* it wanted links to people but emotionally, I simply felt violated by the way it had gone about it.

That in turn gave me the tiniest insight into how Angelica might feel about Elrulin's intrusion into *her* mind. However *she* had had intensely personal memories ransacked, been tortured and held prisoner, so her experience was so far beyond mine as to make it pretty much negligible.

That realisation stabilised my own emotions about the events in the study and I became more phlegmatic. As long as the creepy little skeletal bastard left Gauvain and Angelica alone, along with anyone else that I cared about, then there would be no urgency to sever the link it had established. That didn't mean I was prepared to leave it in place for centuries as Seirina had, but I could revisit it after the Order, and Elrulin in particular, had been dealt with.

I always found it a cathartic experience to link more closely with G, as if his natural animal pragmatism bled over to me. An animal doesn't moan about the rain, it just accepts that the weather does what it does. As long as there was nothing harmful to it, an animal just got on with its life and accepted that the world was as it was. That attitude often helped me to put events into a more dispassionate perspective and take a less emotional view of the world.

As I flew with him, Gauvain noticed movement at the back door and we saw Angie stepping out into the garden. She walked towards me so I disengaged from the link with G and returned to my own body just as she reached me. I opened my eyes and spoke without turning around.

"I was glad to see your smile again," I said, hearing her gasp as she realised I knew it was her without looking, "even if it was just at the coffee." That was when I turned to her and smiled, at which she tilted her head to the side, crossed her arms and pursed her lips to stop herself smiling in response.

"It reminded me of the first time we met," she replied, losing the fight against her smile, "and I remembered your expression when you first saw me taste it." I recalled the moment she mentioned and had to smile myself. It had been one of the many little things that had endeared her to me, particularly as it had been an honest approval of something I had created and was especially proud of.

"There are a lot of things about that day permanently seared into my memory," I said, half smiling and looking down to my left as I reminisced. Everything from her appearance and voice, through the XXX defence, Summer's joking remark about the bed upstairs and

Angie's coy response, right up to the moment she left. I looked up to see her watching me with a raised eyebrow and slight lift to her own lips.

"It looks as though you quite enjoy those memories," she remarked perceptively. I shook my head, deciding on the spot to go the sarcastic route to see if I could get her to rise to the bait.

"Nah, I wouldn't go *that* far." I shrugged and shook my head, laughing inwardly in the hope that she'd see through my bravado. With the typical perception of most women when dealing with men who like them, my comment fooled her for about one tenth of a second (and that's rounding up).

"Oh *really*?" she said, her smile blossoming fully as she tapped her foot. "Why is it that I get the sense you're being somewhat less than honest right now?" Inwardly I was jumping for joy and dancing a jig to see her bantering with me but outwardly, I made sure not to betray my excitement in case it scared her. I didn't want to jeopardise even the slightest step in her recovery, not least because it was so early on in the process.

"I have absolutely no idea," I replied blandly, maintaining my façade even though she had already seen right through it. She shook her head again and turned away, although I caught the ghost of one final smile as she did so. Hope springs eternal, as the saying goes, and mine had just been given a massive boost, so I headed back to the house in her wake feeling as though I was floating.

*Ahem, have you forgotten something? Or more precisely, some*one? came Gauvain's voice in my head. I stopped and looked unerringly towards him as he dropped from the sky. I held out my arm and he flung his feet forward as he stalled his forward momentum, grabbing my wrist with perfect judgement.

"Sorry buddy," I said to him lovingly as I stroked his head, "I got a little... *distracted*." He laughed, both in my head and out loud with an *rrk-rrk* noise.

Indeed, I am well aware of what, or should I say who, distracted you! he replied. *I can honestly say I am truly pleased for you that she seems to be recovering somewhat from her distasteful experience. Your thoughts are lighter already and your disposition much more congenial. Despite how any such relationship creates potential weaknesses for you, the benefits of mood enhancement and the sense of completeness it confers are significant. This, along with the increased sense of purpose it provides you and therefore how much stronger you become as a result, means that I can wholeheartedly endorse your romantic intentions.*

I was surprised at his extended little speech, but glad to hear the underlying message. He liked her and was on board. At least that was one less thing to worry about.

I decided to leave the study to the ladies. I'd had enough of swimming through oestrogen for a while, so I headed up to my room for a nap. I heard their voices overlapping as I passed but didn't try to listen in. I walked upstairs and went into my room, putting G on his stand with a piece of beef I'd begged from Mrs Wilson on my way in, then lay down on my bed. I set my phone alarm, then switched to YouTube and put my playlist on random, plugging in my headphones (I still preferred wired to Bluetooth). I lay back, interlacing my fingers behind my head and closed my eyes.

I drifted off to the familiar strains of *Love in an Elevator*, smiling hugely at the imagery it brought to mind.

★

I woke to the beeping of my alarm and reached out to shut it off. Once I had, the music kicked back in and I sat up to the tune of *Call Me Al*. I turned off the music but was left with the song running through my mind. I was humming it as I went into the bathroom to splash some water on my face. I brushed my teeth as well, knowing I would be speaking to several new people.

I left Gauvain sleeping off his meal and headed back down to the study. I heard the girls still talking together and paused for a moment, bracing myself to face them all again. I took a deep breath and strode in, seeing the twins and Angelica turn to look at me as they saw Seirina notice my entrance.

"So, how's it going?" I asked cheerfully. "Have your periods all synched up yet?" The withering looks I received could have stripped the bark from an entire forest of trees, and I couldn't help myself, I burst out laughing. "OK, fine, enough with the laser eyes of death!" I pleaded humorously, pretending to fend off their evil gazes with my hands.

"Men!" exclaimed Seirina, using exactly the same tone Summer did when I said something ridiculous. "Why is that the only joke that ever occurs to anyone with a Y chromosome when faced with a group of women?"

I raised both hands and shrugged.

"It's programmed into our DNA. Our testicles override our common sense and force us to say it whenever the oestrogen level in the room reaches critical mass." The twins snickered just as immaturely, while Angelica shook her head and tried to hide her smile behind the curtain of her hair.

"Gods preserve me from men who think they're funny," said Seirina, leaning back in her chair and looking up at the ceiling. "Now that we've established you have the same level of humour as a twelve-year-old, Mr Maddox, *can* we please prepare for our upcoming meeting?" The timely reminder wiped the smile off of my face and I nodded apologetically.

She got up and came around the desk, leading me down the hall to a door I had passed numerous times but had never gone into. I had no idea what to expect as she opened the door, but the simple yet elegant dining room certainly wasn't it. I looked questioningly at her and she rolled her eyes at my denseness.

"We need more *chairs*, Gavan!" she said in the exasperated tone of a teacher who is fed up with explaining the most simple and obvious things to the slowest kid in the class. "Unless of course you expect our potential allies to sit on the floor?"

So much for my intellectual prowess. I was currently proving myself to be as thick as two very long planks. Short planks weren't enough to convey my idiocy. I really needed to step up my game if I wanted to succeed against the Order.

I apologised and set to, moving chairs into the study where the girls set them up in a circle ready for our potential allies. Once they were satisfied, we all headed into the kitchen for an early dinner before people started arriving.

Chapter 36

Mrs Wilson had prepared a simple meal of grilled cheese sandwiches and tomato soup, which brought on waves of childhood nostalgia as we took our seats. I sat quietly, lost in memories of my mother in the kitchen, while the girls chatted together. From what little I noticed through the fog of my own thoughts, it seemed as though the twins and Angelica had been talking together quite a bit over the last few days.

They sounded as though they had moved past the distrust they had shown while we were escaping from Bolton Castle. Now it appeared as though they had bonded over some of their similar experiences at the hands of Elrulin (or Atma as they still continued to refer to him).

Soon enough we were finished with our dinner and went back to the study. I could feel Iyrin's interest in the upcoming meeting through our link, as I was sure Seirina could as well. However it chose to stay in the depths of its leafy refuge to listen, rather than exposing itself to examination by any visitors.

It was probably a wise decision, as this was bound to be a somewhat delicate discussion. We would be trying to not only convince disparate factions to work together, but also convince them we stood even the slightest chance of succeeding in our efforts.

My stomach was starting to rev up, so I was glad what I had eaten wasn't spicy or overly complex. As dusk fell my stomach went from washing machine to industrial spin cycle and tried to climb into my throat, but I was determined to see this through.

I refused to live the rest of what, potentially, could be an extremely long life looking over my shoulder for some asshole from the Order who wanted to make a name for themselves by capturing me and delivering me to Elrulin.

Yes, I was sure that one on one I could almost certainly come off best, especially given the level of ability I'd thus far seen and the twins had reported, but I had better things to do with my life.

By the time the intercom from the gate buzzed for the first time, I had argued with myself so much I was about ready to fight a dragon barehanded while hiding in my blanket fort with my teddy bear.

As I considered my simultaneous yet diametrically opposed emotions, I mentally gave myself a stern talking-to and braced myself for what was to come. Talking to a large group was never something I found relaxing or enjoyable but needs must. Hopefully, once I had laid out the situation, it would become more of an open discussion.

I knew I was going to have to give out details of my awakening and training to prove we had even the ghost of a chance, but since the Order already had the relevant parts of that story after Elrulin's assault on my mind, none of what I would share would matter now.

Seirina had left to deal with letting the new arrivals in through the house wards while I was reflecting, so we soon heard footsteps coming down the hall. The first people to arrive were something of a surprise. A Native American man came in first, dressed simply in jeans and a white shirt. He had pitch black hair down to his shoulders and held back from his face by a plaited leather band. His dark eyes that scanned the room as he entered, appearing to miss nothing. He looked distrustful and reserved, picking a chair as far away from the girls and myself as possible.

The second person was of Afro-Caribbean extraction and had cheekbones to rival Isis. She must have been almost six feet tall with muscles like Grace Jones, although she looked a lot more feminine than Miss Jones did in *A View to a Kill*. Her hair was braided and she was also wearing jeans, but she had chosen a brightly coloured, flowered blouse of some silken material and had a flowered Alice band to match.

She had large hoops in her ears and a wide, inviting smile as she looked at us. Her voice had the unmistakable accent and patois of New Orleans as she greeted us, then she went and sat with our other new arrival. I assumed they either knew each other from previous dealings, or maybe they had met on the flight over.

In quick succession came three others. First was a pale, thin, withdrawn man who nonetheless had an air of age about him. His red eyes immediately identified him as a vampire, so he could have been anything from twenty-five to hundreds of years old.

Next was a cheerful petite brunette of about twenty who was so obviously a Wiccan, or at least trying to look like one with her pendants, sweeping black dress and canvas sandals, that it was almost laughable had it not been for the energy I could feel around her.

This wasn't someone who was *styling* themselves as a Wiccan, as Summer did with her hedge witch label, but instead someone with genuine power. I nodded respectfully to her and she assessed me with a piercing gaze, then did the same to the others in the room and chose a seat next to the twins and Angie.

Lastly came a man who looked to be of Arabic extraction with deep brown skin, black hair and brown eyes. His accent placed him as Egyptian, if my ear didn't mislead me, and his open smile but cautious eyes made him a difficult read. I was surprised to see Seirina follow the Egyptian in, heading around her desk to sit down, and I looked around in alarm at the occupants of the room.

"Is this it?" I asked, astounded that we had so few. "Nine people to fight the whole Order? This isn't even enough to go after *one* of their sites, never mind four here and one in America! Are you insane?"

If Seirina thought I was going to make a spectacle of myself for the amusement of a couple of her friends and end up with no significant allies, she was sorely mistaken. Fortunately, I hadn't understood how she had organised things and she quickly stepped in to reassure me.

"No, my mental stability is quite secure, thank you very much!" she replied with some asperity, probably because insanity was an accusation she had faced numerous times in her life. Then she went on to explain.

"Anyone who has had dealings with the Order in the past, poor enough to develop the necessary level of grievance, is naturally cautious about standing against them. As a result, the various groups each decided on a trusted representative to attend today and see what we had to say. Once we've had our meeting, these individuals will go back to their respective groups and discuss everything amongst themselves before they decide whether or not to agree to help us."

I was relieved I wasn't being expected to essentially try to take down such a large organisation alone, so I sat back to await further introductions.

"Now that the panicked histrionics are out of the way," Seirina remarked pointedly, and I held up my hands sheepishly in apology to the general amusement of the group, "let me introduce everyone. First, for our newest arrivals, the skittish gentleman is Gavan Maddox. He is the one who actually precipitated these events, and whose abilities and knowledge give us the opportunity we've been looking for all this time." I nodded to the five who had just arrived, all of whom were now looking at me with far more interest after Seirina's comment.

"The young lady next to him is Angelica, who Gavan liberated from the Order along with Gabrielle and Isabelle…"

"Gabriella and Isabella, actually," I interjected, to the amusement of the twins.

"Aww, he's standing up for us."

"Well, she did get our names wrong."

"True, but I don't think she meant anything by it."

"No, probably not."

"I think he remembers how Atma never used our names though."

"You're probably right. He must have remembered what we said about no one ever asking our names."

"They tend to do this. Don't worry, you get used to it," I interrupted, explaining to the new arrivals who were all staring in amazement at the twins as they had their typical back-and-forth. The twins giggled and looked over at Seirina, silently apologising for hijacking her round of introductions.

"Ahem, yes, Gabriella and Isabella," she resumed, looking over at me pointedly as she enunciated their correct names. "As I was saying. Next we have Aurora, who is here representing the Wiccans." The young woman next to the twins nodded to the rest of us as Seirina introduced her. "Our vampire representative is known as Dominic, and although he's not the oldest of his kind, he has proven himself in numerous skirmishes and so holds a trusted place in the hierarchy. Next to him is Kazemde, the ambassador from the weres." The Egyptian-looking man smiled as she introduced him and stood up.

"Interesting choice of title, Seirina, given that my name actually *means* ambassador." He smiled slightly, then continued, "Before anyone asks, no, I am *not* a werewolf. I have a more distinguished and sophisticated bloodline, descending from the divine felines of ancient Egypt."

"Oh, you mean you're a cat?" I asked guilelessly. He huffed at my plebeian simplification of his self-averred aristocratic heritage, then turned to me and hissed loudly as he morphed into the visage of a sphinx cat. I sat back sharply and he reverted to his human face, then sat down and laughed. "Sorry," I mumbled quietly, to the general amusement of the room.

"Next we come to Sovereign, representing the voodoo practitioners, here from New Orleans. Yes I know, I pronounced it in the English way, you haven't been able to convert me yet so don't start trying again now." The tall Afro-Caribbean woman simply laughed openly at what was obviously a long-running joke between the two of them. I could understand why they would have run into each other before, given some of the similarities in practice between certain voodoo followers and a necromancer.

"Last but by no means least, we have Cheveyo, leader of the last practicing group of Native American shamans and a respected figure within his community." The man who had been the first to arrive nodded briefly at the rest of us, still looking suspiciously around the room as if he were about to get up and walk out at the first sign of anything he didn't like.

Suddenly the phone on Seirina's desk rang, answering itself onto speakerphone after only one ring without being touched. As it happened, there was a frenzied agitation within the terrarium and I caught a glimpse of Iyrin. It had its hands spread wide and its forehead leant forward all pressed hard against the glass in the lower corner, out of sight of the rest of the room. He crouched there like some kind of skeletal gargoyle, almost vibrating with the excitement I could feel flooding across our link.

"Good evening Ms Crow and assorted guests," came a deep, intense voice from the phone, immediately reminding me of James Earl Jones but to the power of ten. "I have been informed by our mutual acquaintance of your intended purpose. I have unique knowledge and perspective to offer on a certain individual you will be facing, so I would offer my assistance if you are interested."

The voice alone was impressive, but the sense of power I felt along with it was remarkable. Only Isis and Danu had surpassed this in my experience, although that had been when I was face-to-face with them. This guy was just on the *phone*.

"And just what prompted this interest?" whispered Seirina, clearly shaken by the unexpected voice, its apparent knowledge of our plans and also of the Order. However she *didn't* ask who it was, making me realise that she must have had dealings with this particular individual before.

"My interest is my own concern, and none of yours," the voice replied. I could feel Iyrin's fascination and excitement, although he remained stationary against the surface of the tank. "For now, why don't you introduce me to your guests." Seirina looked around the room and swallowed visibly.

"This is someone who I have had dealings with in the past, although I know very little about him. He tells me he has been known by many names to many different cultures over the centuries, but I know him as Lucian Belphegor, or more simply as Mr B."

I looked at her in surprise, hearing the trepidation with which she spoke of the caller, having never heard that particular tone in her voice before. Then she looked at me, shook her head minutely to prevent me asking any questions right now, and motioned to the centre of the room. I stood up and took a deep breath, stepping out to take centre stage.

"Thank you for the introductions, Seirina," I began, desperately trying to find some moisture in my suddenly dry mouth. "Let me explain a little about what has brought us all together here this evening…"

GAVAN MADDOX WILL RETURN IN

CALL TO WAR

Acknowledgements

As always, there are plenty of people who deserve thanks:

First and foremost, my long-suffering wife Melanie without whom the book would much shorter, less interesting, full of mistakes and probably still only half done.

Next, Tammy and Larry for their forbearance with my rough drafts and helpful pointers on where things start floundering, plus suggestions on literary life-rafts.

Thirdly to Keidi and the rest of the team at The Light Network and Your Book Angel for their editing, design and advertising expertise.

Finally, to all my readers and supporters for their ongoing encouragement and support. I do this for you, and without you there would be no Dinas Affaraon or Gavan Maddox. You guys are awesome.

Lightning Source UK Ltd.
Milton Keynes UK
UKHW010642260421
382641UK00001B/53